DISPLAYS OF INNOCENTS

'Show me yours again. Sit up here on the bath and let me see.'

'Please, Patti, I think that's enough. You helped me shave and now I've done you. I really must get dressed and, besides, the boys will finish their golf and be back soon.'

'Helen, I'm not asking you; I'm telling you. Just do as I say. After all,' she continued innocently, 'I haven't yet decided whether I really ought to tell Geoff that I caught you masturbating.'

There was steely cold in her eyes as she stared at me, and no doubt that she intended to get just what she wanted by whatever means she needed to use. When I didn't move immediately she casually leant forward and took hold of my nipple tight between her thumb and forefinger and simply pulled, twisting viciously as she did so. I tried to brush her off but she wouldn't let go, so I had no choice but to scramble up and sit in front of her. Only then did she release my nipple, but she immediately grabbed hold of my knees and angrily yanked my legs wide open.

'That's better. Now I can see you properly,' she said.

DISPLAYS OF INNOCENTS

Lucy Golden

This book is a work of fiction.
In real life, make sure you practise safe sex.

First published in 1999 by
Nexus
Thames Wharf Studios
Rainville Road
London W6 9HT

Typeset by TW Typesetting, Plymouth, Devon

Printed and bound by
Cox & Wyman Ltd, Reading, Berks

ISBN 0 352 33342 1

Contents

1

Emma's Tale – The Birthday Present

The police inspector placed his black leather gloves inside his cap and carefully laid it on the table at his side.

'Come along, Mrs Harris. Don't keep us all waiting.'

He leant forward again and peered at me, his dismay at my utterly ineffective excuses almost turning to pity. But he had heard them all before, better ones no doubt than mine, and his kindness had long since evaporated. I did not know what more I could say.

Mark had come home early, I suppose it was a little after four, and he'd been edgy, so I assumed the game had not gone well; I didn't press him, nothing at least beyond polite enquiry. We had supper and then settled down to watch television. There was nothing much on: the end of the sports programmes before the crop of Saturday pap, starting with *Baywatch*. That programme had become something of a joke with us, each saying that we only watched because the other wanted to. I always maintained Mark just wanted to ogle the tall big-breasted girls and he teased me because he knew I had a fantasy of being seen walking around without much on. However, other than some English to mark for my third years, neither of us had much to do, and I hoped that watching some of this might get him into the mood for an early and romantic night. I toyed with suggesting going out for a drink; it would have been fun but really too expensive and we couldn't afford it, not with this being the month in which fell five family birthdays including both of ours. Mine had just passed the previous weekend, and Mark's was yet to come. He'd given me a cookery book and some frillies and, although he had initially promised me something more, a surprise of some sort, in the end nothing had come of it and now, a week past the date, it was clear nothing would. So we settled down to mugs of instant coffee and comfortable escapism.

Having allowed myself to be carried away to a golden sunny Californian beach, the sudden ring on the doorbell was a harsh intrusion. I glanced across at Mark, with a vague thought that it was probably some friend of his. He looked over at me, then pushed himself out of his chair and went to the door. I could hear the voices.

'Good evening, sir. Are you Mark Harris?'

'Er, yes.'

'And is Emma Harris at home?'

'Well, yes.'

Then the voice dropped; not just the pitch but also the tone, as if it were a little less confident. 'I think you know what this is about, sir, don't you? Shall we come in?'

'Er, well, yes, come in.'

'Thank you, sir. Through in here, are we?'

The living-room door was pushed open sharply and two policemen came in, Mark following. The two were both in uniform, such a deep dark blue it was almost black, with caps like American policemen wear; and gleaming leather gloves. Mark lingered at the door behind them but they strode right into the centre of the floor, almost filling our tiny space, and entirely ignored him. They looked at me a moment and then one, taller, older and clearly the senior, spoke.

2

'Emma Harris? My name is Rawlins and this is Sergeant Westley. Would you turn that off, please?' He nodded at the television. When I was sitting down again, he continued, still standing in the centre of the room.

'We are investigating the theft of a number of items of clothing from a shop in the High Street, Martine's Ladies-wear. Do you know the place?'

'Yes, I've been there.'

'Yes, Mrs Harris; we know you've been there. You were there on the, let me see, on the fourth of this month and again on the eighth.'

'Well, yes. First I bought a sweater for my mother-in-law for her birthday and then I went again last Saturday with my husband. He bought me some clothes for my birthday.' I could hear myself babbling.

At last Mark jumped in to help me. 'Yes, that's right. It was Emma's birthday and I . . .'

The policeman turned on him. 'Would you mind waiting in the kitchen please, Mr Harris? This shouldn't take very long.'

Mark looked at each policeman and at me. 'But I . . .'

'The kitchen, sir, if you please.'

We all watched him as he turned to go and the door swung shut behind him. I was left alone with the two men and the senior one resumed his questions.

'On this last visit, that is to say last Saturday, what sort of clothes did you acquire?'

'All sorts.'

'All sorts, Mrs Harris?'

'Well, underwear mainly.'

'Mainly?'

'Just underwear.'

'I see. Really, you might just as well have admitted that at the start, Mrs Harris, rather than wasting time. Did you pay for this underwear?'

'Well, no, my husband did. Ask him.'

3

'I am asking you, Mrs Harris.' He paused briefly. 'But you admit you did not pay for it.'

'Well, look, Sergeant, I . . .'

His head snatched up at me in black fury. 'Inspector!' he roared, spitting the word out at me, drawing out its length so as to emphasise not just the rank but the full extent of meaning: someone appointed to scrutinise, to 'inspect' things, to 'inspect' people. He glared at me until I could no longer hold his gaze and had to look away.

'Now then. I suppose you do not have the receipt?' It was barely a question, more a comment on my culpability, but I shook my head in any case.

He sighed, with resignation and weariness at being confronted by so petty a crime, so weak a criminal. In many ways it was not so much the words that I found so unsettling as his tone, or rather his lack of tone. He was just repeating a formula, mechanically going through a set of motions, but the machine in which I had become enmeshed, one which to him was utterly familiar, was all new to me, new and frightening, and his voice was so utterly unemotional, unexcited, uninterested. How could I hope for any sympathy or compassion in so arid a ground?

'Where are these items?'

'Upstairs. In my room.'

'Hmm. You had better fetch them down. In fact, fetch all your underclothes. Sergeant, go with her.'

I led the way, acutely conscious of the huge mass of a man tracking me, treading so close behind my steps. As he followed me upstairs, I was calculating the relative heights of his line of vision and my bottom.

In our bedroom I started to take the clothes out of the dressing-table drawer and lay them on the bed, but the sergeant just pushed me aside, pulled the entire drawer out and tucked it under his arm, stuffing back the two or three things that I had already taken out.

4

'Where else?'

'That is all.'

'All right. Follow me,' he said, but just outside the bedroom he paused.

'What about in there?' He nodded at the open bathroom door.

'Just a few things waiting for the wash.'

'You mean *dirty* things?' The expression put into the adjective displayed his disgust at the moral as well as physical condition.

'Yes.'

'Fetch them.'

In the laundry basket, sheltering under one of Mark's shirts, were two pairs of knickers and a bra. I picked them out and followed him carefully down the stairs back to the living room.

The inspector was now sitting in the middle of the sofa and looked up at us as we came back in. The centre of the room had been cleared, the coffee table pushed right into the corner, and the other armchair was back against the wall. I didn't want to meet the man's gaze and slipped into the small armchair, still clutching the three items from the laundry but managing to stuff them out of sight behind the cushion as I sat. All other eyes were on the sergeant, who had paused in the centre of the room, paused just too long for us to ignore him, and finally upturned the drawer, tipping the whole contents unceremoniously on to the floor. They sprawled in a heap of pastel nylon and fragile lace, of inadequate straps and transparent gauze; a jumbled accusation of wickedness. Yet muddled in among them, like dande-lions in a rose bed, were my old faithfuls, the faded, sagging victims of too many washings, once so glamorous and now so withered, scrubbed through to nothing. They lay there no less an indictment of decadence than the fresh ones; a whore is no less a whore because her youth is past.

5

Grouped around the pile, we all silently read the history of some and the promise of others, before the inspector finally broke the silence.

'And how much of this haul did you obtain from the shop in question?'

'I really can't remember now. I get quite a lot of things there.'

'I see.' He made it sound like an accusation, or even an acknowledgement of a confession. I wished I had said 'buy' instead of 'get' but it was too late. He prodded at the heap with the toecap of his heavy black shoe, smearing my things across the carpet, and then leant forward and used the very tips of his fingers to pick up a pretty pair of cream silk bikini pants, one of my newest and best, which he dangled carelessly in the air with a look of utter disdain on his wrinkled mouth. They looked so fragile, swinging gently in the grip of his black leather gloves, before he let them drop back down into the heap.

'I believe you obtained five items on your last visit.' He pulled a little notebook out of his pocket and read, clearly with little understanding, the descriptions given to him. 'Two brassieres, white nylon lace and elastone – size 34A. One set comprising three pairs of high-leg mini briefs; cotton; assorted prints; size – medium. Correct?'

'Yes.'

'Where are they now?'

'Well, they are there, mostly.'

'Mostly?'

'I think they are here. I'm not sure.'

'I see. Please show me which are the ones you acquired recently.'

I knelt down in front of them both and started to hunt through the pile. I knew I wouldn't find them all because I was wearing one of the bras and one of the pairs of knickers, while another pair had been in the pile from the wash and was now stuffed securely down the back of my chair. I fumbled through the heap a few times, trying not to look too closely, trying to look as if I really was searching.

'Come on, Mrs Harris. Quickly, please. There is no point in wasting our time. We will wait here until they are found, even if you look through the same pile another ten times.'

I pulled out the tiny gauze bra and the one pair of knickers that were there and the sergeant immediately leant forward and took them out of my hand. He looked them over.

'They have the right labels, sir, but no security tag. She must have removed that.'

'I see. Thank you.' He turned back to me. 'The rest?'

So I turned round to my chair cushion and pulled out the little clutch of clothing. I could feel myself blushing as I offered up the incriminating handful, my cheeks blazing like warning beacons betraying me. Although my brain knew I had no cause for shame, my heart would not be convinced.

'Why were you hiding these?' He lined them up across his upturned palm.

'I don't know,' I whispered.

'And this is all of them, is it?'

'One of the pairs of knick . . . of panti . . . of knickers I got then. The others are older.'

'Which pair?'

'The white ones with flowers.'

The sergeant pulled them up and passed them across to his boss, the inspector, who held them out in both hands, opened them out and finally turned them inside out. I could see, they could see, a mark – a small dark streak along the inside. He glanced across at me and then laid them down with the others.

'And these other ones?'

'No, not them.'

7

'Where are the rest, then? Have you disposed of them?'

'I have them on.'

'I see. We will need to see them.'

I felt the flood of shame tingling up my neck and flaring out across my cheeks again, the prickling under my arms and the deeper throbbing in my chest. I stood up to go and change out of them but he stopped me.

'Don't leave the room please, Mrs Harris.'

'But I will have to change.'

'No, that will not be necessary. Just remove the outer garments.'

'Here?'

'Yes, Mrs Harris, here.'

I sat back down again, my head whirling. How do you react to that kind of situation? I was practically sure that he did not have the right to make me do that; there should have been a woman police constable present or something, but his tone was so sure, so adamant. My cheeks were burning hotter, and I knew that I must be appearing utterly guilty, and that was not fair. I was innocent. I was almost positive that Mark had paid for them. I would have known if he hadn't.

The sergeant leant back against the wall and, as he did so, the handcuffs hanging from his belt clattered. The inspector sniffed.

'I suggest, Mrs Harris, that it would be better to get this over with now rather than my having to treat it more formally, which will inevitably get into the local newspapers. What will your friends and colleagues make of that? Not to mention the parents of your pupils; what will they think when they read all this about you?'

Put like that, I had no choice. He was right. The consequences of publicity were unthinkable. I hesitantly slid each arm in turn back inside the sleeve of my sweater and then pulled it up over my head and laid it over the arm of my chair. I had nothing else on underneath except the bra which they wanted to see; a bra identical to the one I had already surrendered to their examination. It was quite sheer, because my breasts are not very big and I do not really need the support. I did not dare to look down, but I knew that it was hiding nothing, that my nipples were completely erect and pushing out the front of the thin lace. Neither of the men made any secret of staring.

Having kicked off my shoes and unzipped my jeans, that was as far as I could get without leaving the security of the chair. I glanced across at the two men but their expressions told clearly that they were not going to allow any leeway. I stood up and pulled my jeans down. They are quite tight and dragged my knickers down a little way as well, but I quickly pulled them back up again and, as soon as I had laid the jeans over the top of the sweater, I sat back down in my chair. The inspector leant back to get a better look at me before speaking again.

'Stand up, Mrs Harris. Check them please, sergeant.'

'Yes, sir,' he said with too much enthusiasm and stood up, carefully peeling his gloves off, the fingers of one hand methodically stretching one by one at each black leather finger of the other, before neatly laying them down. He came round behind me and I felt the strap of my bra being brutally pulled out and twisted over, almost pushing me off balance.

'It's the same, sir. Same make, same size – 34A.'

He let the strap go, then I felt his fingers dig into the top of my bottom and he pulled the waistband out.

'Same, sir. Just like the other two pairs.'

Then he came round in front of me again and looked into my eyes just for a moment and I assumed he was finished. I was wrong. With one hand he suddenly pulled out the cup of my bra at the front and shoved his thick stubby fingers inside, delicate as lumps of wood, pushing my nipple out of the way of his search. He

9

didn't even bother to grope me; my femininity was no more than a nuisance to him, an annoyance impeding his examination. After searching around the sides and underneath of my breast, he moved across to the other one and repeated the action, again callously and disdainfully rolling his fingers across my nipple, catching it between his fingers and glaring disgust at the erect desire it betrayed. He grunted, shook his head and withdrew.

He still hadn't finished, for next he plucked out the front of my knickers and peered in suspiciously before again pushing his hand well down inside them. It was the back of his hand against my skin, against my hair, but he searched right down and then, finding nothing, pushed in again through the leg opening and felt along the material right between my legs. I knew it was moist, I could feel myself seeping as well as sweating, but he just carried on. The backs of his harsh knuckles pushed up against me, almost separating my lips, without any concern for me at all, oblivious; whether I was panting with desire or sick with disgust, it mattered nothing to him. He fumbled over my skin, his fingers shoving their way right into my crease and then back round my swollen clitoris. When he was finished, he stepped back and made a great play of pulling a handkerchief out of his pocket and carefully wiping his hand and fingers. Then he sat down, although I was not invited to, and it was only then that I realised I had been left with my knickers pulled halfway down my bottom. The instant I started to adjust them, the inspector ordered me to stay still.

'Now then, these other items, here,' he said, as he disdainfully jabbed his foot at the pile in front of him. 'Which of these were obtained at the same shop on other occasions?'

I looked down and tried to think. 'Well, quite a lot of them.'

'Sort them out, please.'

I don't know what came over me. I obeyed, of course I obeyed, but I could have knelt down. Instead I squatted. Even squatting, I could have tucked my legs to one side. Instead I spread my knees apart and reached down between them. I felt myself blushing to the roots of my hair as I did so, but that was not enough to prevent my making a spectacle of myself. My view was more oblique than theirs, but where the material had been pulled away at the top of my thigh, a small tuft of hair was escaping past the elastic. And there was a gap between the elastic and my skin, which from their angle . . .

I sorted out the things that I knew I had bought at that shop, the newer ones at least, and carefully laid them separately from the rest. When I was done, I looked again at the two men staring down at me and waited for the next command. The inspector held out his hand for the pile and I meekly passed it over. Then, as I remained on the floor in front of them, the inspector scrutinised each item in turn and called out a description for the sergeant to write down. Twice he called out 'G-string', although they weren't really that, just quite skimpy, and several times he said they were 'stained' or 'soiled'. Finally he dropped them all back on the carpet and leant towards me.

'We will need to take for identification the five items you stole on the last occasion.'

'I didn't steal them.'

'So you say. We will have to take them anyway until our enquiries are complete. The sergeant will give you a receipt.'

I swallowed. 'I will go upstairs and take them off.'

'Here will do.'

I just couldn't believe his insolence! 'What? I can't do it here! You cannot make me do that!'

'Please, Mrs Harris, don't make things any more

11

difficult than they are. You can take them off here or we can go back to the station and you can do it there. It makes no difference to me, but you are not going out of my sight until I have the evidence I require.'

Then he added, as an afterthought, 'It is certainly more private here.'

So they waited. They just sat there, watching me, waiting for me to move. They were so composed and their eyes so expressionless, like wolves patiently encircling their prey, knowing their strength and that I was growing weaker by the second. Finally I reached round and unhooked the bra, slipping the straps off my shoulders and crossing my arms in front of me. Keeping my arms tucked in, and with one hand covering my other breast, I offered the garment forward tentatively. At least this way I could keep my nipples covered, hiding the shame of their visible arousal.

'Give it to the sergeant, please.'

I hobbled across to him and passed it into his hand before quickly retreating to my place. He looked at it superficially, turning it over in his hand before dropping it on to the pile on the sofa. Then he returned to his place and looked over at me in mine. Again they remained impassive and watched and waited. Finally the inspector spoke again.

'Take off your knickers, Mrs Harris.'

They were such clear words, so unmistakable, so simple a command and yet he was just as aware as I was of the meaning in the words, of the burden they carried and how much was conveyed in his being able to give that order and in my having to obey. My mouth was unbearably dry and I was again aware of the pulse of my heart against my forearm. I slowly dropped my hands down to my waist and slid the tiny garment down over my hips, my thighs, my knees, my calves, and finally stepped out of it. I crossed again to the sergeant, then again scuttled back.

The sergeant examined them and again passed them across to his superior. He too turned them over and over, looked carefully inside, and not only at the place where the label would have been, but also at the dark wet stain that now covered so much of the material. He dropped them down beside him and, looking up at me, spoke to his colleague.

'Give the young lady a receipt, sergeant.' Now that I was stripped naked, defenceless, even my name had been taken away.

'Please check the items we are taking and ensure they are correctly recorded, then sign the receipt.'

I almost croaked out the words. 'I'm sure they're right.'

'Count them, please.'

I was sure he just wanted to force me to move from my place, to lift my arms away from giving the tiny covering they offered, but I had no option but to obey. I carefully counted the five items, conscious of the staring eyes as I squatted on the floor. When that was done, I looked round to see the sergeant sitting in the chair I had used and he indicated the receipt which lay on the coffee table beside him. This too seemed to have been arranged so that I would have to stand right next to him and then to bend over to sign it, to expose myself further to their eyes, feeling the sway of my breasts as I leant forward.

He passed me the piece of paper but did not offer me a pen, and I had to ask if I could borrow one. When I was done, I straightened up again and tried to be sarcastic when I returned the pen, but it is hard to be superior when you are the only person in the room who is naked.

'Sergeant, would you ask Mr Harris to come back in, please.'

This was another shock. To my shame, I had almost forgotten Mark. Now I was to be further humiliated by

13

his being brought back in to see the level to which I had sunk. I felt as if I had not opposed their impositions as much as I could have done, or as much as Mark would have expected from me.

While we waited for them to return, the inspector continued looking at me as I stood in front of him, trying to be defiant in spite of my vulnerability. I scraped a little modesty by clasping my hands in front of me and squeezing my arms together across my breasts but, just as we heard the footsteps returning to the door, the inspector spoke again.

'Keep your hands behind your back, please.'

Just then Mark walked in and glanced over at me, first at my face and then down my body. I could follow the movement of his eyes tracing over me, hovering at my breasts, then down farther at my immodestly trimmed triangle, trying to probe within before returning to my breasts again. The eyes paused there, noticed my prominent nipples, and he knew immediately it was not from cold.

It was almost more, no, not almost, it *was* more humiliating having to stand like that in front of Mark than if he hadn't been there. Without him, the two men were just doing a job and I had to do what was needed. With him there, real life suddenly returned; a life of jeans and dresses, of putting clothes on to go out of the house, to go shopping or to meet friends. Not a world where you stand naked in front of strangers; stand with your hands behind you, not even trying to cover yourself.

The inspector spoke again. 'Well, sir, I'm afraid that we are not satisfied by the information given to us by your wife. We have examined several items of clothing which we believe did come from the premises in question and your wife has been unable to provide any proof that they have been paid for. In the circumstances, we will have to take them with us until we have completed our enquiries. Your wife has kindly agreed to this. Do you have any further questions?'

He looked across at me then slowly shook his head. 'No.'

'Fine, then we will leave you. Thank you for your co-operation, sir, madam.'

He stood up and, with a last glance over at me, turned to the door.

Mark suddenly stirred. 'Oh, yes. I will show you out,' and he led them both into the hall. I heard the steps retreat and the sound of the front door opening, then a few more goodbyes and thank yous before it closed again.

Mark returned, slowly, it seemed almost reluctantly, but maybe I was just too sensitive. He stood by the door and tossed the handful of underclothes on to the sofa, almost exactly where they had been assembled over the last hour. He looked around the room, at the furniture shoved up into the corners, at the piles of clothing, debris like so many discarded desires, and at me sitting hunched naked on the hard chair.

Finally I caught his eye. His flickered free, then back; he swallowed.

'Well?' he asked.

I finally let out the breath that seemed to have been held in my lungs since the men had arrived. I smiled, and tried to draw him in.

'Perfect. Just right.'

'Good.' He seemed relieved, but not to have understood enough.

'No, Mark, not "good". Perfect. I honestly didn't think you understood so completely. There is nothing, not the tiniest little detail, that I would have wanted different. It was even better than I had pictured. Just fantastic! Thank you, Mark.'

'Yes, well, you're welcome. Happy birthday! My pleasure.' He paused, then grinned. 'It *was* my pleasure too, actually, more than I expected.'

'Where did you find them?' I asked. 'They were brilliant!'

He chuckled. 'You will never know.' He held out his hand and glanced upward, through the ceiling. 'Shall we . . .?'

2

Nadine's Tale – Paying the Price

I am not shy, OK? I mean, some girls just are shy, and I'm not. I've got a good body, the sort that boyfriends have always admired and girlfriends have been jealous of. Don't get me wrong; I don't mean I'm some kind of weird exhibitionist who prances around half naked or anything like that, but neither do I get embarrassed if I realise that some bloke is giving me the once over. I feel pretty certain that he's going to like what he sees and I find that quite flattering.

So when Mike came home and told me how he had got into a mess at work, that the sales director, Mr Winter, was threatening to fire him, I kind of thought it shouldn't be too difficult to persuade the old man to think again. I have generally been successful at persuading men to think about whatever it is I want them to think about, even men that I don't really know. I had only met Mr Winter once at the office Christmas party, when he had tried to kiss me under the mistletoe, but I didn't take that personally; he had wanted to kiss all the girls.

Mike is in sales, and so he gets paid by results. This means that there is always a temptation for all the reps to try to secure extra orders by giving extra credit. The firm knew it went on from time to time and had been tightening up on it, but Mike was still doing it, deliberately keeping the invoice back until a month or even two after the delivery notice was passed. It meant the customers got a month's free credit at the firm's expense and, as long as all the paperwork was balanced out before the end of each quarter, nobody was any the wiser. Nobody should have been any the wiser this time, but Mr Winter had done a spot check and Mike had been found out. Warnings had already been issued several weeks ago that if any more cases were found, the rep responsible would be sacked.

Mike was pretty worried as he told me the whole story, because we had just bought our first house and we wanted to start doing it up; we wanted to try for a baby; we wanted to be getting established, and we certainly didn't want to be trying to live on just my pay, which was a pittance in any case. Eventually I decided to go and see Mr Winter for myself. Mike is not the overly jealous sort; I mean he was attracted to me in the first place because I showed him more of myself than a girl normally does, so he understands what kind of girl I am. Even so, I decided it would be better if he didn't know about me seeing Winter because, right from the beginning, I kind of thought this was going to mean more than flashing a bit of underwear at him, and I wasn't sure how Mike would take that.

So I went over during my lunch hour on the Thursday, when I knew Mike and most of the reps would be out on their rounds and there would be little danger of meeting anyone who knew me. I was shown into Mr Winter's office. It was a huge room at the end of the modern office block which stuck out at the end of the factory, with a big square window looking out on to the car park so he could keep an eye on the time everyone arrived and left. He had a vast heavy desk and a pair of straight and quite uncomfortable chairs neatly arranged in front of it. He had clearly done the management training courses. At his invitation, I took a seat, and hitched my skirt up a couple of inches.

He looked over at me, doing little to hide his annoyance at being interrupted by the wife of one of his junior staff, and I did my blushing routine.

'Mr Winter, I'm sorry about the problem that Mike has caused and I know he is too. The thing is we really need this job. Couldn't you give him another chance? I know he wouldn't do this again; he simply didn't realise that this is what he was supposed to be doing.'

He sighed. 'Look, my dear, I have every sympathy for you, but I am trying to run a business here and I have to impose rules and then enforce them. If I never enforced the rules, there would really be no point in having them, would there?'

'But Mike is very hard-working, and if you let him stay on he would certainly produce good results which would be very worthwhile in the long term.' I knew I was rambling, but he did not seem to be responding quite as easily as I had expected, and I did not know what else to say. I trailed off. 'Isn't there any other way we could settle this?'

'What exactly do you mean?'

So I admitted that I had heard that when one of the invoice girls had been late after a warning, he had given her a spanking. He seemed surprised that I knew about it but, after claiming that had been entirely different, he finally worked round to saying that if I was prepared to accept Mike's punishment for him, he would consider it. I had no choice but to agree. I suppose that right from the outset I had half-expected him to say he would spank me. The prospect did not frighten me, because I had been spanked once before by a man who had taken me out several times and had accused me of being a prick tease; maybe that time it had been justified. What I hadn't expected was that first Mr Winter would tell me to come back the next day for it, and second that he would want Mike to be there as well. I rather assumed he would definitely not want him there. I wasn't looking forward to having to tell Mike all about what I had done. However, it turned out that Winter saw him sometime during the afternoon and told him all about it, so that by evening he had got kind of used to the idea.

The following day, I sneaked off work early and went home to get changed. I put on a knee-length skirt and tight polo-neck sweater and, having fortified myself with a little Dutch courage, I met Mike when he finished work. We went back up to Mr Winter's office together at the time he had specified: five o'clock, a time when most of the other workers were leaving. Mr Winter's secretary, Miss Freeman, was still there, typing on the electronic typewriter that she insisted on retaining when everybody else had converted to wordprocessors. She looked up as Mike knocked on the outer door, clearly having been warned to expect us.

She took off her glasses and laid them neatly on the desk. 'I will let Mr Winter know you are here.'

She tapped on the connecting door and slid through without waiting for a response. We waited outside, listening to the last of the accounts clerks leaving the building, the last doors banging shut a floor below. Eventually, Miss Freeman emerged again.

'You can both come in.'

Mike and I filed in like naughty children, Miss Freeman bringing up the rear to ensure we didn't escape, and stood meekly. Miss Freeman scurried over beside Mr Winter, to a small chair tucked into the corner where she was almost hidden behind his huge desk. I remembered Mike saying there were rumours about the two of them.

Mr Winter remained sitting there and didn't even look at us as he shuffled together a sheaf of papers and tucked them back into a folder on his desk. He pushed this into a drawer and picked up the only remaining folder, on which I could see Mike's name stencilled in large blue letters. He started to leaf through the contents.

'Sit down, both of you. Now I can't say that I'm happy about this, not happy at all, but I understand, Mike, that it is your wish that Nadine here takes the punishment that would rightly be due to you, so that you can keep your job. Is that right?'

We both nodded, but obviously that was not enough.

'Mike, you do realise that you have broken the company rules about this? Not just once but several times, and that your contract does clearly say that in such a case your employment should be terminated immediately?'

Mike looked down into his lap and muttered an agreement.

'And you, Nadine, you realise that I am only agreeing to this arrangement, much against my better judgement I should add, because you have specifically asked me to do so? Because I would like to try to help the pair of you out of the mess into which Mike has got you? The penalty laid down by the company rules is quite unambiguous so, if I am to agree to an alternative, we all have to realise that it has to be of an equivalent severity. Do you understand that? Both of you?'

We mumbled acquiescence.

'And you are both content to accept the punishment that I will mete out in place of that laid down? I should say that you are obviously entirely at liberty now or at any time to decide to accept the company punishment, namely instant dismissal, instead.'

Again we both nodded. He was laying it on very thickly, and I suppose this was to ensure there could be no complaint that we did not know what was in store.

'Fine. Well, as you may know there have been occasions in the past, only a couple of course, when reps have tried to cut corners, and some of the young ladies have accepted a physical punishment from me instead of taking it through the normal channels. I therefore propose to give this young lady a spanking that she will not forget in a very long time and I trust that you, Mike, will also remember this next time you feel inclined to bend the rules. Is that clear?'

We both murmured agreement.

'Fine. Now then, Mike, I think you had better sit quietly and take careful note while your young lady makes amends for your transgressions. I have asked Miss Freeman to remain as an independent observer of the punishment to ensure there can be no question of any subsequent misunderstandings. Stand up, please, Nadine.'

I stood in front of him, feeling suddenly a great deal less sure of myself now than I had when I had started on this plan. Mr Winter looked down at the scatter of report sheets on his desk.

'It seems to me that Mike first allowed an unauthorised credit in April, then twice in May and twice again in June; no, I am mistaken, three times in June. All these were repeated in July, together with three new ones, although two of the earlier debts were paid off at that time. That makes a total of twelve transgressions. However, since they were each continued into a second month, if not a third, that makes at the very least twenty-four illegal debts. Not a very impressive score, and something that must clearly be taken very seriously.'

He looked up at me over the top of his glasses as I waited for him to get to the point. I was getting impatient. We all knew that in the end he would spank my bottom a few times and then we would all go home, so this elaborate ritual seemed a bit excessive. I was relieved that he had asked Miss Freeman to stay, since this made it pretty unlikely that he would try to lift up my skirt when he spanked me. All the same, his attitude was very severe and much more intimidating than I had expected.

He looked down at the wad of papers on his desk, picked them up and, while his gaze scanned down the columns, addressed me directly.

'What are you wearing under that skirt, Nadine?'

I've got to say I was pretty surprised, because I had not expected this kind of question, but I answered him because, I suppose, he had the aura of authority that I was used to respecting and answering.

'Just tights and my knickers.'

'Hmm.' It was a very derogatory snort. 'You'd better show me.'

'I'm sorry, what do you mean?' I'm sure my surprise was quite evident in my voice. I really could not see where this was all leading and could not understand why I would need to illustrate the style of tights I might be wearing. Still, maybe he got off on looking at girls in their underwear.

'Don't be coy, dear, just lift up your skirt and let me see.'

This time he did look up at me; looked me straight in the eyes most directly so that I was put in no doubt as to his seriousness, his authority and his determination. I took up the hem of my skirt, raised it to my waist and waited.

'Higher than that, girl. Come on! I need to see your knickers not your knees!'

I lifted it as high as I could, so I knew I was exposed all the way up to my waist.

'Hmm, they will not do, not at all, I'm afraid.' He sighed deeply. 'You will have to take all that off.' He actually managed to sound as if this necessity was a disappointment to him. Then he turned to Mike.

'Mike, I see that I am going to have to ask your wife to undress completely for this; you have no objection, I take it?'

During the pause that followed, I expect Mike was hoping I would respond, but I was unable to move and stayed looking forward. I expected him to object, but we both knew what the alternative was. It had already been clearly explained that we were free to give up any time and accept the dismissal that was laid down. Instead, we were given a second chance at the cost of my being required to strip completely, and this was starting to affect me. Although I had not expected it to be quite like this, the prospect was really only an extreme version of what I had been expecting. I had realised it was going to be kind of embarrassing to be put over Mike's boss's knee and then spanked, but in spite of the humiliation, there had been a strange thrill in anticipating that happening. This addition to the punishment was amplifying that, and amplifying not just the apprehension and fear but also the excitement, the exhilaration, that ran with it. I felt myself tremble at the prospect, my usual confidence pierced by a shiver of fear that prickled at my nerve endings, at all my nerve endings, but definitely at those most delicate nerves whose influence I wanted to ignore. Instead of being reluctant, I was starting to relish the prospect, and the presence of Miss Freeman was adding to my satisfaction. She was always very smart in her appearance, and I suppose attractive for her age, but she was probably a good twenty years older than me, and I found I was looking forward to showing off my figure in front of her, and of arousing her jealousy. It would be even better still if I was forced, against my will of course, to show off my figure naked.

In the long silence, Mr Winter sniffed. 'Well, Mike, do you have any objection to that, to my asking your wife to undress completely?'

The reply was barely audible. 'No, Mr Winter.'

'Sorry, lad, speak up.'

'No, Mr Winter, I have no objection.'

'Fine.' He looked back at me then glanced over at Mike again, seeming to weigh up various considerations.

'Well, we will need the skirt off in a moment, but let's just have your top off for now, dear. Sweater and bra, so as Miss Freeman and I can have a look at your little titties. Come along, girl.'

I stood up and pulled the sweater up over my head, then tossed it on to the chair behind me. I hesitated again, glancing across at Miss Freeman, who sat unmoving, watching me intently. Then I reached back, unhooked my bra strap and peeled the cups off my breasts before dropping the bra on top of my sweater. I turned to face them again and shook my hair back out of my face, knowing how the action caused my breasts – heavy, fuller than you'd think when I'm dressed – to sway. Glancing over at Miss Freeman, I saw that her thin mouth was stretched as her eyes narrowed disapprovingly, staring at my breasts, at my hardening nipples. I think she knew what I was feeling; maybe she would have liked the same thing, but I was the one who everyone was looking at, not her. I pulled my shoulders back a little further.

Mr Winter stood up and came round from behind his desk; he circled once right round behind me, and stopped in front of me again. He made no secret of his scrutiny of my breasts.

'Very nice, my dear, very nice indeed.'

I thought I detected a slight sniff from Miss Freeman, but Winter either didn't hear or chose to ignore it. He smiled at me before reaching up and first shaking and jiggling my breast in his hand and then cradling it in his palm, his thumb gently rubbing to and fro over my nipple, pushing it from side to side and encouraging it to grow even fuller, even darker.

'Yes, very delightful indeed. You're a very lucky young man, Mike, not only to have such an attractive young lady as your wife but also one who is willing, willing at considerable personal cost, to stand by you at such a time.' His mouth was smiling at Mike over my shoulder all the time he spoke, but his fingers never stopped their caress over my nipple, and there was no real warmth in his smile.

He stepped back to survey me and perched on the window ledge, folding his arms.

'Let's have the skirt off now, shall we?'

He clearly wanted to enjoy the prolonged ritual of my undressing and really I didn't mind that. Being the only one naked was strange; it made me the centre of all their attention, the focus of all their eyes, the target of all their lust, and who would not enjoy that? Miss Freeman was still hunched in the corner, looking almost as if she were waiting to pounce, and her growing disgust at Winter's growing arousal added to my pleasure that he was now concentrating on me.

I unzipped the thick skirt and dropped that down on to the chair, then kicked off my shoes and slipped down my tights and knickers all in one. When I turned to face Mr Winter and Miss Freeman again, I held my hands together behind my back. I knew what it was they were waiting to see, and it would be pointless to start acting coy, trying to cover myself up, so I let my body sway gently from side to side and pushed my belly forward a little further. I could almost feel the pressure of their gaze on me. Mr Winter shifted uneasily.

'Good. Very good.' He hauled himself up heavily and came round to me and took hold of my hand, lifting my arm to appraise me as he steadily turned me round.

'Miss Freeman, would you clear those few things off my desk, please.' As she dutifully stacked up the files on top of his bookcase and moved the telephone on to the floor, he did not watch her; his eyes were fixed on me.

'Good, my dear. Very good. Now hop up on the desk, will you, on hands and knees.'

I did as he asked, finding myself facing the window and with my bottom now pointing towards Miss Freeman and Mike. Mr Winter had not finished. His hand was running down my back and over my bottom, the fingers sinking into the delicate crease.

'Legs apart a little, my dear. That will make you a bit more steady.' His hand stayed poised over my cheeks, ready to slip further between my legs when I obeyed. I felt his short podgy fingers pushing their way between my lips and seeking out the small bud at the front.

'Well, well!' He seemed surprised. 'What have we here? Have you wet yourself, my girl?'

'No,' I whispered.

'No? No, girl? No what?'

'No, sir.' The word seemed to come naturally.

'That's better. But you certainly seem to me to have wet yourself. Miss Freeman, come and look at this and give me the benefit of your advice. What is this? Legs apart, girl,' and he slapped me on the bottom, so that I almost fell.

I heard the rustle of Miss Freeman's dress as she stood up and came over to peer at me, before her scrawny hands were pulling at my buttocks, and her thin fingers burrowed their way in, her nails scraping against me as she explored deeper and finally, inevitably, I felt one bony knuckle worm its way up inside me.

'I am afraid you're right, Mr Winter. The filthy girl must have wet herself; I cannot think what else it could be.'

Mr Winter snorted. 'Well. First she wets herself, then she lies to me. Well, Nadine, what have you to say to that?'

'Honestly, sir, I haven't wet myself.'

Miss Freeman joined in. 'When did you last go to the toilet, then?'

I tried to think. 'I think it was at lunchtime.'

'Do you need to go again?' Mr Winter asked.

All this talk, coupled with the wine I had drunk to give myself courage before I came out, was making me think that I should.

27

'Well, I wouldn't mind, sir. If I may.'

Miss Freeman took hold of my wrist and almost dragged me off the desk.

'I will take her to the senior staff toilets, Mr Winter. It will take all day if she goes down to the workers' floor.'

So, before I knew what was happening, she was dragging me across the room and out of the door and it wasn't until we were in the corridor that I realised that she meant to lead me through the building completely naked. I wanted to protest, but her determination was so clear that I didn't dare.

We passed several offices – all of them thankfully empty, although there was a light burning in one or two – and finally reached the small bathroom at the end of the building, clearly marked PRIVATE. She pushed me inside and immediately followed me, shutting the door behind us. Then she leant against the door, folded her arms and watched me.

'Come along, girl, get on with it, we haven't got all day.'

If I had known she had meant to come with me, I would not have said that I wanted the lavatory at all, but it was clearly going to be no good trying to escape now. I gingerly sat down and tried to forget she was there, as she stood, waiting, smiling her condescending smile.

After a few seconds she made a show of looking at her watch.

'Haven't you finished yet?' She must have known perfectly well that I hadn't even been able to start.

'I'm sorry, Miss Freeman; it's very difficult with you there.'

She sighed deeply, and eventually I managed to put her out of my mind sufficiently to relax my muscles, although she continued to sneer as she watched and listened to the soft sounds of splashing.

The instant the trickle stopped, she handed me a few sheets of paper and stood back to watch me again; I was to be allowed no dignity. I wiped myself carefully and stood up again. Miss Freeman frowned at me suspiciously.

'Are you clean now?'

'Yes, Miss Freeman.'

She sighed. 'I suppose I ought to check. I don't want you making a mess of Mr Winter's valuable desk. Turn around, girl, legs wide apart and bend over.'

She had seen everything, watched me closely. She knew the difference between ought and want.

'Please, Miss Freeman, I'm sure that's not necessary. I'm sure I'm quite clean.'

'Just do as you are told, girl.'

So I obeyed her, leaning down on to the cold narrow cistern with my legs spread as wide apart as the little cubicle would allow, I bent forward to expose my bottom to her scrutiny. Miss Freeman squatted down behind me and peered so closely I could feel her breath on my skin, right on the most sensitive area round my bottom hole, but then her sharp fingernails were digging into my delicate skin and I cried out and stood up. She just slapped me and made me bend over again.

Her fingers were pulling my lips apart again, and feeling between them right into the creases, deliberately rubbing at my bud as she probed and investigated me. She worked right between my inside lips and then, just as she had done in the office, she slipped a finger deep inside me and twisted it round before pulling back out again. I couldn't see what she was doing during the short pause that followed before she wiped her cold damp finger across my bottom and stood up.

'Humph. I suppose that will do. Come along, girl.' And with that she led me back the way we had come to Mr Winter's office, where he immediately made me get back up on the desk, so that he too could examine my sex and see if it was now clean and dry. Of course, as he pulled my lips apart and peered closely at me, and discussed what he had found with Miss Freeman, and pointed out slightly wet parts, and prodded at the small nub at the top, he handled me as freely as he could, and I could feel already that I was not going to be allowed to stay dry for very long.

He turned his attention to Mike, but his hand strayed underneath me and continued caressing my hanging breast as he spoke.

'I suppose you think it is somewhat unfair that Nadine, who after all is taking your punishment for you, should be the one to be required to undress. Do you?'

Mike coughed. 'Well, yes, I wasn't sure why it was really necessary, I mean . . .' but he tailed off.

Mr Winter's eyes positively gleamed. 'I agree with you. It would be unfair for her to take that part of the punishment alone, Mike. I think you should undress as well. Kindly do so.'

'Who, sir, me?'

'Yes, sir. You, sir!' and his tone made clear there was going to be no argument. At least it was clear to me, not to Mike.

'But Mr Winter, I . . .'

'Young man, I have already explained that you are quite at liberty to refuse my punishment whenever you like and to take the company penalty if you prefer to do so. You are not, however, at liberty to question my authority. Now, you had said you were ready to accept my decision in this matter, but if that is not so, then please say so straight away, so that we can all go home and need waste no further time here.'

There was another silence during which I dared not turn to Mike but knelt on the hard wooden desk, my hands clasped in front of me, gazing out of the window to the dwindling traffic as the car park emptied of all but one car, and trying to blank out the growing pressure that Mr Winter's continuing caresses were causing. Finally I heard the rustle of clothing, a zip, and further rustling. I could picture the scene that was unfolding, and the pictures formed in my mind sent more tremors down my body and through my limbs.

Finally there was silence again, and Mr Winter spoke. 'Good. Now, just turn to face this way and keep your hands behind your back. Well, Mike, my boy. What's this?' He was clearly amused.

This time I did look round. I had to. Mike was standing in front of his chair, completely naked and blushing bright red, but what immediately attracted my eyes, and, glancing round, was clearly attracting the eyes of everyone in the room, was his erection proudly presented in front of him.

Mr Winter was still laughing. 'Well, you can't stand there like that, my boy, it's shameful. What on earth are you thinking of? In front of Miss Freeman as well. Get rid of it.'

I glanced across at Miss Freeman and, although she was trying to look disgusted, it was an entirely unconvincing attempt.

Mike gazed down miserably at the source of this trouble for a few moments, then finally muttered, 'I'm sorry, sir. I can't, sir.'

'Would you like me to ask Nadine to do something about it?'

Mike was still staring down at the floor, but we all heard him mutter agreement.

So at last Mr Winter released my breast, but only so that he could slap my bottom yet again as he said, 'Go on, then, my dear, do whatever you need to. Just get rid of that.'

Then he went and sat back in his chair again, crossed his legs and waited. Miss Freeman too was lounging back in her chair and both of them watched as I slid off the desk and walked over towards Mike. The minute I reached out my hand to touch Mike's erection, it jerked as if I had given him an electric shock. Mr Winter laughed again.

'You had better use your mouth, girl. I don't want any mess on my carpet.'

I knelt down in front of him and, taking his glorious cock in my fist, my thumb stretched out along the side to massage under the head, I slid the swollen end between my lips and sucked him in. This was not going to take long, because I know what Mike likes, and already his fingers were tangling in my hair and his hips were starting to push against me. I ran my tongue under the rim and slipped the very tip into the tiny opening, and then, because I knew he wouldn't be able to resist it, I reached up to cradle his beautiful balls in my hand and to tickle – oh so delicately – at the skin just behind. Immediately his fingers twisted deeper into my hair and his knees bucked against my breasts and my mouth was filled with wave upon wave of his wonderful cream. I carefully swallowed it all down and gently ran my tongue around his shrinking organ again to catch every last drop and lick away the last traces. Mike's hands slid down under my chin and he leant down to kiss me.

'Thank you,' he whispered. 'Sorry!'

Miss Freeman sniffed noisily. 'How touching!'

Mr Winter was obviously equally unimpressed.

'That will do, girl. You are not here for your entertainment. Get back up here on the desk.'

I stood up, trying to avoid Mike's eyes as I made my way back to climb up on to the desk again where Mr Winter was pointing. I knelt as I had before and, as before, he manoeuvred me round until he had me the way he wanted. In the process he took the opportunity to slide his hands under my breasts, over my back and along the crease of my bottom; to squeeze and pinch my nipples, to tangle his fingers through my curls and slip his hand between my legs. He again moved my knees apart on the shiny wooden surface and ran his fingers up the inside of my thigh, this time making no secret as he peeled apart my lips and mocked the evidence he found there.

Having at last satisfied himself on all that, he opened the drawer of his desk and drew out a long wooden ruler which he smacked across his palm loudly a couple of times.

'Are you watching this, Mike? This is what happens to people who break the rules in my office. They have to learn the error of their ways.'

I heard Mike mutter an acknowledgement of some kind.

'Now then. Keep still, girl.' And with that the ruler came down on my bottom with a suddenness that made me cry out. The pain was terrible, much worse than I had expected, and I leapt up, but Mr Winter must have been expecting it, for his hand came straight down on my shoulders and pushed me back down on to the desk.

'Keep still, girl. I've hardly touched you yet.'

Then he brought down the ruler again, and I'm sure that he was aiming at exactly the same place. Then again and again. I know I was crying out at every stroke but, the longer it went on, the more the sensation spread out from the single target and I felt the heat and the blows almost like a fierce caress across my bottom, my thighs and my sex. When I laid my head down on my arms, I suppose it only raised my bottom and exposed the lips of my sex for him. He did not let this pass, although it was real agony as the flat of the ruler caught my thighs and swollen lips, and I quickly struggled up again to try to protect the tenderest parts between my legs. The next few strokes were marginally less painful and yet the feeling between my legs was growing stronger all the time, pushing me forward to get away from each stroke and pulling me back to welcome the arousal brought on by the next one.

Finally it was over; I don't know whether there was any fixed number of strokes that Mr Winter had reached, but he suddenly stopped and, as I lay sprawled across the desk choking back my tears, he replaced the ruler in his desk drawer and carefully shut it. Then he patted me on the shoulder.

'Very good, my dear, well done. As for you, Mike, you had better get yourself dressed again and we'll go and sort out the accounts that you've messed up.'

I watched Mike quickly scramble back into his clothes and, with a miserable glance at me as I lay naked on the desk, he followed Mr Winter out and down the corridor. I was wondering whether I could now get dressed, and had managed to work my hand down between my legs, when Miss Freeman's harsh voice rang out again. I had forgotten her completely.

'Get up, girl, and come over here.'

I carefully eased myself off the desk, trying not to rest any weight on my tender bottom, and shuffled over to stand in front of her. It no longer seemed at all unusual to stand naked before her while she sat eyeing me.

'Turn round.'

I did as she told me, and felt her fingers run down my back and into the crease of my bruised bottom.

'You know the position, my dear. Legs apart and bend over.'

Stretching myself out like that was agonisingly painful, but there was no question of refusal, and I delicately leant forward, holding on to my knees for support. Her fingertips traced across my burning cheeks for a few minutes before taking up their usual exploration between my legs, smearing up and then spreading me wide open. She laughed, bitterly.

'I thought so. You are absolutely sopping, aren't you?'

I said nothing; what was there to say? But she would not let me go.

'Kindly answer the question, girl. You are sopping, aren't you?'

'Yes, Miss Freeman.'

'Yes, indeed. Did you orgasm?'

'No.'

'No? No what?'

It was all coming more easily. 'No, ma'am.'

She laughed her mocking laugh again. 'Came pretty damn close, I'll bet.'

'Yes, ma'am.'

'Yes, I'll bet you did. And your clitoris is sticking straight out like a hat-peg. It's really quite some clitoris you have there, isn't it?' She flicked her nail across it twice, sending shivers rocking through me, as she continued. 'Does it get any bigger than that?'

'I don't know, Miss Freeman.'

'What do you mean, you don't know? You must know how big it is when you come, girl; don't try to pretend you don't know that. So, tell me if that is it, or if it gets any bigger.'

I slipped my hand down between my legs where my clit was indeed pushing out as she had described. I could feel the tip pushed out almost beyond the end of its cover, and I knew that sometimes, if everything was just right, it would get even longer than that. Not much, in all honesty, but maybe a little.

'I think that's about as big as it ever gets, Miss Freeman.'

'Pity. Stand up and turn round.'

She looked me up and down a couple of times before reaching up and moulding my breast in her palm, her thumbnail flicking at the erect nipple as she weighed up the options. Briefly she reached down and tugged at my pubic curls, then pushed the lips open again to prod at my clit from the front. Finally she made up her mind.

'Not the best, but I suppose you'll have to do. Kneel down. Closer than that.'

I could hardly believe what was happening, but she grabbed hold of my shoulder and pulled me up closer to her as she spread wide her knees and, with her other hand, pulled her skirt up over her thighs to expose the tops of her stockings and the stretch of white skin beyond.

'You know what to do, girl.'

'No, ma'am, I don't.'

'What on earth do you mean? Don't tell me you have never done this before.'

'No, ma'am, I haven't, honestly!'

She looked at me a moment, considering my words, then she sighed.

'You know what? I do believe you are telling the truth. Well, it's time you learnt. Use your imagination and I'm sure you will get the hang of it quickly enough.'

So I obeyed, and pushed her skirt up the rest of the way to reveal the full expanse of skin and then her knickers: white with little lace trimming round the edges. I gently stroked up and down the front of her knickers where they were pulled tight between her legs, but I didn't know what it was exactly that she expected me to do. After a few seconds, she snorted her annoyance at me.

'Don't be stupid, girl, you'll have to take them down!'

Nervously I moved my hands up her thighs and carefully plucked at the thin elastic waistband of her dainty white knickers. As I slid them down, she lifted her bottom up off the chair and, once I had peeled them down her legs and off over her feet, she pushed forward towards me, at the same time spreading herself even wider.

If outwardly in her office dress and manner she was prim and reserved, her sex more than compensated for it. She was entirely unashamed as she opened her legs wide to reveal a sex as abundant and warm, ripe and scented as a woman's could possibly be. She was also

36

amazingly wet: gleaming down both sides of her fleshy wrinkled lips while, lower down, just at the point where the two sides met again, there was a little shining pool that grew even as I watched. A single drop pulled free and trickled down towards her bottom.

Her scent was wonderfully strong and powerful and, to me just then, utterly enticing; her tangle of black hair, thick and luxuriant, was matted flat across her skin; her lips were as full and glistening as a peeled peach. Faced with such clear encouragement, it seemed perfectly natural that I should reach out my hand gently and touch her, letting the tips of my fingers run down her moist, swollen lips and then, as she pulled me in even tighter between her pale thighs, to push out my tongue and lap at her skin. Yet this was too timid for her; she squeezed me in tighter and, reaching her hand down, used her own fingers to part her plump soft lips and show me her thick pink clitoris, which was quivering proudly as it waited for my attention. Her middle finger flicked at it, and peeled away the hood.

I glanced up at her and found her staring down at me, her eyes glazed and fixed and her mouth open to allow the tip of her tongue to quiver between her tiny teeth, almost reflecting the tip of her clitoris quivering between her other lips. The firm pressure of her hand on the back of my head increased fractionally and I leant in nearer, my palms spread out on her warm inner thighs, and lapped at the swollen nub, licked at the shining juices that coated it, and circled my tongue around it. When she pressed my head in even closer still, I drew it right into my mouth and suckled on the smooth little nub like a baby at a nipple.

She sighed, heavily. 'That's the way, my little love, that's just the way.'

Her head was rolled back now and her eyes were tight shut, her hands clasping over her breasts, squeezing herself so hard she must have been making bruises. And, although I had never done anything like this with a woman, and I was humiliated and ashamed, I really wanted to bring her pleasure and I worked at it as hard as I could. I soon found what she liked, and slid a finger of one hand deep inside her warm tunnel while my tongue lapped and quivered at the entrance, sucking her clit into my mouth and almost nibbling at it as she quivered and heaved in front of me. She still had her eyes shut, and I sneaked my other hand down into my own lap and, kneeling with my legs splayed, I could tease out my own clitoris, run my fingertips round its slippery surface at the same time as my tongue circled hers. She was heaving so wildly that it was increasingly difficult keeping contact, and then she groaned and slumped down on me, repeatedly pushing her gloriously wet and pungent sex into my face, clamping her thighs around me as she twisted her fingers in my hair and sobbed words of real love through her clenched teeth.

When the waves had washed past her, she stayed slumped in her chair with her legs still spread wide and looked down at me, a serene smile on her lips. I knelt at her feet, staring up at her, my face smeared with her juice, and she tangled her fingers in my hair, sometimes running her fingertips across my glistening cheeks and lips to bring the flavour into my mouth. Once she dug her fingers deep into her own sex to retrieve more. She smiled approvingly as I lapped at her fingers, and finally I spread my knees even wider in front of her and brought both hands down to my lap, squashing fingers of one hand deep inside myself. With my thumb, I pushed forward my glistening swollen clit for her to see, and savoured the taste and scent of her juices that I sucked into my gasping, panting mouth, and bathed in her smiling gaze as I worked myself to my own shattering climax.

3

Rebecca's Tale – The Interview

It was the best of times, it was the worst of times, it was a vision of purity, it was a vision of decadence, she was practically naked, she had her back turned to me.

We were married on a glorious day in a shining spring of hope, when the world was bright and prosperity was everywhere; our house was new and gleaming and the perfect nest in which to pass a couple of years before starting to raise our family. We were young. We were in love. We had everything before us.

Eighteen months later I was out of a job and, as the summer days shortened and died, we entered a winter of despair. At first I was perfectly certain that it would not be long, a few weeks, a couple of months at the outside, before I found another job. After all, I was still several years short of thirty and had good experience and skills that allowed me to consider a variety of different trades. It was not until the middle of the fourth month, as I watched a television programme about the economy, that I realised it could be at least a year and maybe more before I started bringing in any money. I made discreet enquiries about selling the house but found we could get nowhere near enough to pay off the mortgage. In February we received our first chillingly polite letter from our building society.

All my attempts to find work were proving entirely unsuccessful, and our childish optimism was rapidly choked in the growing realisation that we had nothing before us. My skills were not needed on the job market and I secretly began to wonder whether I would ever find work again. I even made a joke about answering an advertisement in the local paper which said: 'Photographer seeks female models, 18+ for glamour work. No experience necessary.'

Beckie laughed too, and said, 'Well, I suppose I could do it.'

She was joking, of course, because although she's not a prude, she is definitely modest. When we had been to Majorca on holiday two years before she had not taken off her top on the beach, although she was almost the only girl who didn't. We had argued about that, which was silly because, as she pointed out, it was her body and her right to decide how much of it she exposed. All the same, she really is extremely beautiful, with thick, uncontrollable, shoulder-length brown hair, long slim legs and large and very round breasts. Yet it had been her eyes that had first drawn me to her; eyes so deep, so brown and so mournful that no one could look into her face without being smitten. Even me, after all these years. Overall, she is invariably the centre of much attention, and I am proud of her, and never tire of seeing the reaction in other men's eyes.

Still, she was not joking. I knew she was worried about the money, we both were, and, although this might have been a help, I was not prepared to let her do this or anything else that she would hate so much. However, she took the decision out of my hands because the following week the phone rang one evening as she was washing up and, although I wasn't listening to the conversation, I was surprised when she kicked the kitchen door shut to make sure that I didn't hear anything that was said.

She didn't come out straight after the call and seemed to be taking such a long time that I began to wonder if something was wrong; if the call had been bad news about her family. When she did return to the lounge, she was preoccupied. She came and sat next to me.

'That was the photographer.' I didn't know what she was talking about, having put the advertisement entirely out of my mind.

'I wrote in about the advert for the modelling.' So the story came out. The day after we had seen it, she had written in, sent a snapshot taken on holiday and said she was interested. The man had obviously been impressed and she was to go round for an interview on the Saturday. I offered to go with her and, although she put up a token resistance, she clearly wasn't even convincing herself so, after a brief struggle, she agreed.

We kept the topic well out of the way all through the rest of the week. I kept thinking about it, and I am sure that Beckie did as well, but neither of us put any of our fears into words. My principal concern was what precisely the man meant by 'glamour'; certainly at least underwear, but I thought it quite probable he meant topless, like the page three pictures in newspapers. I knew Beckie wouldn't go that far and I just hoped he wouldn't expect it and put pressure on her. It was possible that she knew already what was entailed – that it had been discussed on the phone and she had made her limits clear – but I didn't know for certain and couldn't face the consequences of asking her, in case she hadn't considered this and I only succeeded in worrying her unnecessarily.

Saturday loomed and, on the Friday night, we made love, something that had become much less frequent since I lost my job. It wasn't satisfactory and, although I had hoped Beckie would find it comforting, I don't think she did. She was too tense and too dry but, once we had started, neither of us could admit that it had been a mistake and so we struggled on until I managed a weak orgasm and she faked an unconvincing one. Neither of us slept well.

The next morning was no less awkward and, in the end, I left the house for a couple of hours just to kill time. When I got back at a little after twelve, Beckie was upstairs getting changed. I'd given no thought at all to what she should wear. She was after all attending a job interview, and yet the job requirements were unlike any other. I wanted to help her, to carry part of the burden, but did not know what advice to give, or what was required of her either at the interview or in the job. In the end, I left it entirely to her, and she came down dressed as she would be for any job interview: a mid-length skirt, a blouse and a long-sleeved sweater over the top. She had put on more make-up than might have been usual for the middle of the day, but she looked lovely and I told her so. She thanked me. We had a quick, light and almost silent lunch and then she fetched her jacket. Before we left the house I said, 'You know you don't have to go through with this if you don't want to.'

She smiled, unconvincingly, and merely said, 'No, let's go or we'll be late.'

I drove to the address Beckie had been given. Number 22 was a sombre house, with elegant brick chimneys and tall thin windows. It stood alone in a large garden, set well back from the road. There was a gravel parking area in the front but I parked in the road anyway; it seemed more appropriate somehow, and we crossed shyly to the three stone steps leading up to the front door.

Standing in the covered porch, we could hear the bell ringing somewhere inside, but at first it produced no response. The door was inlaid with highly decorated stained-glass panels but, having no light behind them, the atmosphere was bleak and intimidating. The big bay window beside the door was in shadow and, although the curtains were open, there was no shred of life within. Beckie reached across for my hand and I was glad she hadn't come alone. Finally a door was opened somewhere inside allowing light through the glass and making the whole house come alive, seem occupied and much more approachable. As a man's shadow loomed up larger on the glass and finally reached the door, I released her hand.

The man who opened the door to us was much older than I had been expecting; I had imagined someone of around our own age but he was probably more than fifty, and tall with thinning gingerish hair. He wore a sports jacket that hung loosely on him, and even a tie; admittedly a fairly shabby jacket and a dog-eared bow-tie but, all the same, more formal than I had anticipated. However, he was perfectly friendly and, although clearly surprised to see me with her, he welcomed us in and ushered us down a tall windowless passageway, past the melancholy clicking of a grand-father clock to his study at the back of the house.

It was a smaller room than I expected, or perhaps not smaller, simply less grand. Maybe it was too filled with furniture, the shelves too littered with books, the walls too cluttered with pictures, but it was a very powerful room – clearly his territory and his alone – where nobody else could ever be more than a brief visitor. The books, the pictures, the framed certificates and letters on the walls, all displayed his wisdom, yet it was a world into which we seemed to have stumbled out of our foolishness. In addition, although a big square bay window took up much of the far wall, this was two-thirds covered by maroon curtains so thick that most of the room was in darkness, except for a single bright patch in the corner where the sun sliced through beside his desk, making a distorted square of light on the floor.

The man introduced himself as Mr Cathart, but he

called Beckie by her first name and declined to use my name at all.

'Let me take your jacket, Rebecca.' He helped her out of it and hung it on a tall coat-stand beside the door then sat himself down behind his big mahogany desk, invited Beckie to sit in a leather chair in front of him, and finally waved vaguely at me to take the only remaining chair tucked away behind her in the corner.

Picking up what was evidently Beckie's letter, he read in silence, then replaced it carefully, neatly, on the desk before pulling out a fresh sheet of blank paper from the desk drawer. He peered up at her, over at me – briefly – then back at her. In the silence a mechanical wheezing started outside and the clock struck three. The gloom, the sound of the clock, the smell of wood polish, all combined to wash me back into the sensation of being called into the headmaster's study to discuss my end-of-year report, and I'm sure that I was just as nervous as Beckie was herself.

'Now then, er, Rebecca, you say you have never done any modelling before.' His words came slowly, as if he were unsure of his voice or perhaps of what effect it would have.

'No.'

'That's fine. It doesn't matter. We all have to start sometime. What I would like to do is just get a few details down and then take a couple of test shots of you. If that is all satisfactory, and I am perfectly sure that it will be, then we can make arrangements for you to come over at a later date for a proper session. All right?'

Beckie said, 'Fine,' but it came out so quietly that I don't know if he heard it, because he looked up at her and smiled – his thin lips stayed pressed together, but he altered the shape of his mouth to an expression that was clearly meant to be one of friendship.

'Don't be afraid, dear, it is not as bad as all that. Now then, I have your name here and your address and

44

telephone number. You work most days but are home by six-fifteen. Good. Now then, I assume it is all right to phone you on this number to make arrangements? Your young man does not object to that?'

'No, that is quite OK.'

'Good, good. Now then. A few details about you. How old are you?'

Beckie did not respond immediately so I answered for her. 'Twenty-one.' Mr Cathart's eyes flashed up past Beckie and blazed fire at my intercession.

'Thank you, young man, but I am quite certain that the lady knows all I need to ask, and if you don't mind I will take her answers.'

Beckie rescued me in the drumming silence that followed. 'Yes, that's right, twenty-one.'

'Fine.' He noted it down on his sheet of paper and turned back pointedly to address her. 'Height?'

'Five-foot four.'

'And, er, vital statistics?'

I saw Beckie shuffle her feet and sit up a little straighter. '34, 23, 33.'

He noted them down, but didn't look up. 'C cup?'

'No, B.' I was surprised at the amount of detail he seemed to consider necessary, and I think Beckie was as well, although in a moment of disloyalty, I wondered if she would have answered so honestly if I had not been there.

'Now then, eyes.' This time he did look up. 'Brown. Hair, let's say light-brown. I take it that is natural?'

'Yes.'

'And where else does it sprout?'

Beckie was evidently unsure what he meant, and after the last reaction I felt it better to keep quiet. Finally he carried on.

'By that I mean do you shave under your arms?'

'Well, yes.' Her bewilderment and indignation at the interrogation were quite evident in her voice and I wanted to find some way to comfort her, but he seemed not to notice her distress and simply wrote down the reply.

'And pubic hair? Do you shave that?' My eyes must have betrayed my incredulity at the intimacy of the questions that, in his belief, it seemed necessary to ask. I was on the point of getting up to say that we had endured enough and were leaving, but my slight movement caught the man's eye. He glared across at me with such malevolence that I stayed still.

Beckie shifted in her seat and said, 'No' very quietly. She was fully aware of me sitting behind her as she was verbally stripped bare by this man, and I'm sure that she must have been thinking – as I was – of the one occasion we did shave her hair as an experiment. She hadn't liked it at all, and we never did it again, but his questions brought up in my mind a picture, so detailed and clearly focused, of her hair and her pussy that, in spite of my anxiety and the bitterness I felt at his probing, I found myself starting to feel sickeningly aroused. I was returned to the dreadfully animated loathing I always experienced when I knew she was going to the doctor for an examination. Yet, if by right of being a doctor he could examine, by right of being a photographer and employer, could this man not enquire? They were, after all, only words. I wiped my hands on my thighs.

'Any tattoos, at all?'

'No.' Her response was a great deal easier on that.

'Fine. You can never tell with young ladies these days.' He glanced up to show us that he had made a joke. I smiled.

'There. That's that part over. Now then.' He turned over his piece of paper. 'The breasts. Let's start there.' He leant back in his chair, watching, waiting, it was not clear why, with the same arid smile on his mouth. 'Come along, dear, don't be shy. Just slip your top off.'

My heart suddenly stopped completely then went into

double time, my mouth went so dry that I could hardly swallow and sweat started to trickle down inside my shirt. The audacity of the man, the presumption, filled me with disgust and yet, at the same time, I could not deny that what had been a gentle pressure in my lap was quickly becoming a full erection. The man was quietly sitting there asking my wife to take off her clothes so that he could look at her breasts. I deeply resented his inexcusable intrusion, and for the moment that passed as we both sat in unmoving silence on our side of the desk, I could not tell what was going to happen. The man had no right to expect my wife to show him her breasts, but I found that I desperately wanted her to do as he asked.

For a minute Beckie didn't move, then, slowly, she reached down, crossed her arms in front of her, took hold of the bottom of her sweater and pulled it up over her head. She arranged it over her legs. Then her head went down as her hands started fiddling about at the front to undo the buttons of her blouse. I looked past her at the man sitting opposite, facing her, intently watching as her delicate fingers steadily unfastened her clothes. I could only see the back view and could only picture the movements and the progressive revelation. Finally she pulled her blouse out of the waistband of her skirt, first at the sides and then round at the back, before she slid it down her arms and placed it with her sweater. Her bare back was towards me, still showing some of the summer's tan and the neat white lines of her bra straps across and over her shoulders. She hesitated, then her hands, quivering, came round into my view and fumbled briefly but then unhooked the bra, slipped it off her shoulders and down her arms, and that too was carefully placed on top of her other clothes. There was a pause, silence, while the man's eyes devoured Beckie's breasts; her eyes stayed fast in her lap and I watched the smooth round back, pale and trembling.

47

The man stirred, breathing in deeply.

'Sit up straight, dear, you don't want to get a hunch. Why don't you put those clothes down? Give them to your young man to look after for you.'

So Beckie stood up and walked across to me, still keeping her eyes down, and I did not try to meet them either. Partly because I was utterly drawn by her nakedness – and I did glance up to her breasts, creamy and soft and so out of context in this dim, regimented and masculine room – but also because I knew my erection was clearly visible in the front of my jeans, and I was deeply ashamed of the effect that her agonies were having on me. She handed me the clothes but neither of us spoke before she returned to her chair.

He stopped her. 'Just before you sit down, could you come round to the light.' This meant of course to come round closer to him. 'Lift up your arms, right up over your head.' He swivelled round in his chair but stayed sitting and, placing his hands on her hips, twisted her round to face him as she raised her arms, the action lifting up her breasts almost as if she were offering them up to him, so round and enticing, her nipples hard, dark and tight.

Then he ran his hands up her sides, right up under her arms as high as he could reach and then down again, but, on the way down, he brought his palms round a fraction closer together at the front so his thumbs were raised by the swelling of her breasts, almost but not quite touching the raised circle around her nipples. Beckie was holding her head high, concentrating on a spot over his head, her eyes barely focused and her mouth open. I knew she was hating the entire ordeal; I despised him too and yet, hidden under the pile of her own clothes on my lap, I gave the head of my swollen penis a quick rub through the front of my jeans.

'Fine now, could you come forward and lean on the desk, just rest your elbows down.'

He said 'lean on'; we all knew he meant 'bend over'. Again the picture of the headmaster's study came flooding back to me: the terrible knotting in the stomach, the sweating palms and the utter dread of what might happen to someone so totally in another's power. This felt exactly the same – the dread both for me and for Beckie. For a minute I had an image of his fetching a cane and standing over her as he held her down across his desk.

She bent forward, arranged her forearms on the dark shiny surface, and laid her head down on her hands. Her hair tumbled forward around her, hiding her face entirely. He manoeuvred her round so that he could see the profile when she obeyed, when her breasts became slightly less round as their weight pulled them down into a smooth curve which was not so much interrupted as emphasised at the point by her nipples, still so erect and ripe. I could see the silhouette against the windows as he stood up, moved her along a few inches, causing her breasts to ripple, to sway. He was still ogling her, and all I could think of was my own selfish pleasure, of her kneeling astride me with those wonderful breasts in my reach.

He placed his hand between her shoulders and pressed down, making her back bow a little further. Then, without a word, his other hand reached underneath her and gathered up one breast, seeming to weigh it in his palm, his thumb flicking over her nipple, before moving on to the other. I took advantage of his total concentration on my wife's body to adjust the rigid erection in my jeans and stroke myself again.

He let her stand up while he sat back in his chair, still looking up at her: examining, considering, enjoying.

'Very good. Let's have the last few things off, shall we?'

I shut my eyes. How could this be happening? Why was I allowing it? How did I sit there, mute, passive and

acquiescent and permit this foul debasement to go on?
In despair at what I could do if she appealed to me for
help, I longed for her to do what was asked.

I yearned for it all to stop. I desperately prayed for it
to go on. I wanted to take her in my arms, wrap my
cloak around her and whisk her away to safety. I
wanted to watch her stripped of the rest of her clothes
and exposed utterly naked to this man.

I clasped my hands down in my lap; tried to control
my breathing, my pulse, my imagination. When I
opened my eyes again, there she was, not asking for my
help but, still standing beside the man's desk, already
reaching around to the zip at the back of her skirt. Her
naked back was still turned to me but, as I watched the
graceful movements of the muscles stretching and
turning, she kicked off her shoes and slithered her skirt
over her bottom, down her thighs and carefully stepped
out of it. As she turned to drape it over her chair, she
was held in profile and, for an instant, I thought I
caught the flicker of her eyes reaching across for me, but
she did not turn and I was too much taken by the
beauty of her standing there, leaning forward, her proud
breasts and her gloriously rounded bottom, too
mesmerizing a sight to notice subtleties. Then, all in one
movement, she slid off her tights and knickers and,
dropping them on top of the skirt, gave me a fleeting
view of her soft light bush before she again turned her
back so as to allow the photographer his uninterrupted
view of the whole of the front of her body. For an
instant, her hands clasped together in front of her but
then hesitated and fell back to her sides; she understood
what it was she was expected to reveal. I watched his
eyes, narrowing, stalking up and down and then homing
in on the centre. He now had everything: her breasts,
her little triangle of very fine pubic hair, and would be
seeing – doubtless enjoying – how little of the top of her
vulva it hides. I couldn't bear to imagine how Beckie

50

must be feeling. He pulled himself up, with an evident stiffness, out of his chair and came back round to her side of his desk and with one hand, casually, intrusively, placed on each shoulder, twisted her round so that for almost the first time she was facing me.

'Lean back against the desk.'

Her hands on either side nervously gripped the edge of the polished wood and she stepped back but, even after she was pressed against it, he still pushed back so that she had to move her hands almost into the middle of the desk to keep herself from overbalancing. Then he waited, his long bony fingers poised on her pale round shoulders, patient, confident, before his hands slowly began to slide forward. The movement was steady and hypnotic; a connoisseur evaluating an exquisite piece of art, fondling his latest acquisition. The final destination was inevitable and yet my eyes were held by the gradual descent across her skin, lingering briefly over the swellings of her breasts, the points of her nipples, down her ribs to rest on her hips. He paused then, and bent down himself before his hands resumed their fall and reached the tops of her thighs. Beckie was staring down at him, her mouth a fraction open, and her tongue flickered out and back again. Then, over his shoulder, I watched his hands begin the final move inward and his thumbs close in across her pubic hair to the lips buried between her thighs. Without even being asked, Beckie shuffled her feet apart to ease his exploration. He pressed his thumbs into her skin and stretched them apart, fully exposing her most intimate and secret self to his eyes. He stayed a moment, then released the folds, allowing them to close over her again, but in the split second before he did so, as his head moved aside, I glimpsed what had been plainly visible to him as he stretched her open. Beckie's vulva was pink and glistening, her clitoris was swollen out and, most telling of all, down one thigh was smeared shining proof of her

51

arousal. The sight was too much for me and, without even touching myself, shaking, gulping for air, desperately squirming to stay still, I climaxed into my jeans. They were both entirely taken up in their own theatre and neither noticed.

His hand was resting on her shoulder and pulled her back upright. 'Fine. I think you'll do just fine. Now I would like to take a few test shots of you and that will be that. I have my studio set up through here.' He indicated a door in the far corner that I had not noted before. Beckie didn't even glance at me but padded meekly after him, an innocent following the Pied Piper to eternal imprisonment. The door swung close behind them.

I waited, trying to visualise what was happening in there, trying not to visualise. On the leather chair was the little pile of clothes Beckie had left behind and I picked them up. Her knickers and tights were all bundled together and I disentangled them. They were still warm, and then, as I was laying out her knickers ready for her to put on again, I found more than warmth; clearly her excitement had begun long before she had taken them off. I crossed over to the far door and found that it was pushed to, but it was not shut tight and, although I could see nothing, I could at least hear them in there. I wish I could say that I turned away, but I didn't. I couldn't help myself: I stood there with Beckie's knickers – warm, damp and fragrant – clutched to my cheek and listened to the voice in the next room.

'Just push the chair out of the way and settle yourself down in front of the fire, would you? Good. Now lean back, lovely, turn a little more to face me. That's it, and lift up your arms. No, like this; good. Fine! Just like that! Now offer me your breast, yes, and give it a little pinch. That's right, very nice; and both of them, pull them out to me. Wonderful. Lean back a little further, sitting back on your elbows. That's it, bend your knees a little and your foot over here. And the other one out over there. Bit more. No need to be shy. Excellent! Hold exactly like that while I take one close in. Wonderful, you really are a natural at this. One more. Beautiful! Now up on your knees and turn with your back to me. No, on all fours. That's good, on to your elbows and bring your knees up the rug. Oh no! Not together! No, no, no! Keep them apart. Turn a bit more and face directly away from me. Good. A bit more, shoulders right down, and lift your hips right up. Now then, pull your cheeks apart. No, with your hands, so I can see right in. Beautiful! Great! Just one more. Can you manage just a little bit wider?

'Now over on to your back again. Yes, right over, and bring your knees up a bit, and hold on to your ankles. Wonderful. Oh dear, you're all a bit squashed up in there. I'll just ... arrange things for you ... down there. Goodness, you are nice and warm, aren't you? There. Beautiful! Like the petals of an open flower. How glorious! One more like that. Now. Bring your hands down between your legs; bit further, and open yourself up for me. All the way. Right open. Good! And the inside ones. You are a juicy little thing, aren't you? Wonderful! Now then, who have you got hiding up at the top there, eh? Pop him out for me. Ah! There he is! Oh yes, he's a perky little chap, isn't he? Beautiful! That's it, give him a little rub for me. That's the way.

'That's lovely, just carry on; pretend I am not here and do whatever you would do if you were all alone. Oh lovely! Very nice. That's good. Right up inside. And another one? Wonderful! Just a couple more shots, nice and close with your fingers in there, all wet and shiny, last one! Good.'

There was a pause, a silence, and I prepared to run back to my chair. Then his voice again.

'Now, one last little thing you can do for me. Come

over here by me, just here, now kneel down. There now, look what you've done to me. You know what to do with this, don't you? Yes, I thought you would. That's right, oh lovely.'

There were more breaths and sighs. Once I thought I heard a high squeal which could have come from Beckie; it was quickly followed by his voice, strained, gasping. 'No, stay ... there ... yes ... yes.' Then silence. I was erect again, and barely keeping from another orgasm. It was hearing his final words to her in that unseen room that pushed me over the top, guiltily massaging myself through my jeans so that I again ejaculated into my already sodden clothing.

'Now, then. I want you to come back on Wednesday evening at seven; can you do that? Good. And you see that big plastic sheet? Well, what I want you to do is to have lots and lots to drink that day before you come over and then we'll spread that sheet on the floor for you to use. All right? Fine.'

I returned to my chair, so shaken by everything that had happened to Beckie and to me that I didn't even care about the obscene wet stain down the front of my jeans. When, a minute or two later, Beckie came out of the room alone – still naked, her face and breasts flushed bright red – she didn't look at me and I couldn't expect her to. I fetched her jacket and held it in front of me as she quickly got dressed, and then Mr Cathart emerged and calmly showed us out.

We returned to the car in silence, drove the fifteen minutes home in silence, and still, without a word, walked back into our house. Inside, she finally turned her face to me, then grabbed my hand and ran, yelling, laughing, dragging me behind her as fast as she could up the stairs to the bedroom.

4

Alison's Tale – Wonderland

When I left London, I intended to see the world. When I reached Hong Kong, I stopped. This is all I have ever expected Hong Kong to be and, the moment I arrived, I loved it. It's bright and full of life and there's something happening all the time. I started off staying in a cheap little guest house that was all I could afford in a big warren of a building called Chung King Mansion at the bottom end of Nathan Road, Kowloon; I will never forget that. The place was stocked with interesting people of all nationalities, including Americans, Australians and New Zealanders. They all had big dreams and intended to achieve them or die in the attempt. I quickly started spending most of my time with one particular small group of Australians. While they told me about Oz, I reciprocated about the UK, and very soon I had so worked myself up that I couldn't consider going home without reaching Australia.

Chung King Mansion was where everything happened because, as well as my guest house, the block contained workshops, restaurants, travel agents and brothels. There were also rumoured to be gold and drug smugglers. It was also well known as a place for penniless European tourists to stay so, when a local film maker wanted some European extras for his film, a notice went up in the block and a dozen of us got four days' work on the film. I don't know what it was called;

I think it was a Kung Fu special for the local market, but it was fun and we got paid – a little. I was prominent in many scenes because of my thick blonde hair which was extremely noticeable in a society of entirely black-haired people. I'd never done anything like that before, but to me that's what Hong Kong is all about: doing things you would never get the chance to try at home. As I say, I love the place.

With the money from the film, on top of some that I had earnt as a waitress in a bar on Hong Kong Island, I finally made up the airfare to Sydney and I was ecstatic. I was so delighted that when we all went out to celebrate on the last day of filming, I told all the others that I would soon be off Down Under. It knocked me flat when they pointed out that the Ozzie immigration people would never let me in unless I could show I had enough money to support myself for the length of my stay. And I didn't. Nowhere near enough. I had reckoned on working when I got there, which I had been told was easy enough once you were there, but the difficulties of getting in had not occurred to me. I was not going to let this put me off, though, and answered gaily:

'I'll have to go back on the street, then,' and laughed, although I don't believe the flippancy hid my disappointment from anyone.

Afterwards, one of the other girls – an Australian called Julie – came up to me quietly and sort of half whispered, 'Did you really mean that? About going on the street, I mean?'

'Well, no,' I laughed. 'I don't think I'm quite that desperate. Not yet, at least.'

'Well, what would you do?' she persisted.

'How do you mean?'

'What would you do? How far would you go to make money?'

'I don't know. It depends. I certainly wouldn't smuggle coke into Malaysia, if that's what you mean.'

'No, it's nothing like that, but would you dance?'

'Dance? Just dance?' I had visions of some sort of formation dancing team.

'Yes, you know, in a bar. Topless or perhaps even nude.'

'Christ! I don't know.'

Would I? I really didn't know. Being honest, I know I'm reasonably good-looking and I had rather played on my natural charms when I was working as a waitress to ensure the customers appreciated me and tipped accordingly. Would this be any different or just more blatant? Then something else about Julie's question occurred to me.

'Why are you asking me? Hey, have you been doing that?'

'No – at least, I haven't yet. But I know this guy in a club here who said they were always looking for people, especially Europeans, and he asked me if I would. I said no, but really I could do with some extra money and if you were going along as well, you know, it could be quite a laugh.'

She tailed off when one of her friends came over and, while he was talking to her, I had time to think the suggestion through in a little more detail. I did notice that all the time they were talking, her eyes kept coming back to me.

There was a real attraction in the suggestion. I certainly was determined to go to Australia and this seemed to be a relatively easy way to get money. On top of that, there was another appeal. For many years I had harboured wild fantasies of exposing myself naked to strangers, sometimes of being laid and sometimes of masturbating in front of a crowd of strange men. Well, yes, I know everybody has similar feelings from time to time. I suppose for me it had just been stronger, and there had been one occasion when I had gone some way towards living the fantasy out.

When I was at college, I led a very full social life; in fact not so much full as wild. I enjoyed the freedom of being away from a rather cloistered home life and I made the most of it to have a good time, lots of friends, and I suppose I got a reputation for being pretty unrestrained. I never missed a party, and at more than one I had drunk too much and raised my skirts or opened my top for a dare or a bet or a joke. I used to get invited to a great many parties.

There had been one particular party at the house which my boyfriend shared. I'd got really rather drunk and had been dancing wildly, knowing that my full skirt was swirling up and showing my knickers; knowing that my partially unbuttoned blouse was flapping and offering glimpses of my braless breasts. As the party died down, I sprawled across a sofa, fairly drunk, fairly sleepy, but not really as much of either as I pretended. Well, my boyfriend obviously thought I was either asleep or had passed out as I lay there, and he commented to the others that he was not going to get much from me that night unless he took it himself, and that it wasn't fair because he was feeling randy. They giggled, but then, at the urging of some of the others, he started unbuttoning my shirt. He couldn't actually take it off me without sitting me up, which would (as he thought) almost certainly wake me.

Still, he carefully undid all the buttons down the front, gently pulled it up out of my skirt and laid it completely open so that my breasts were totally exposed for everyone else to see. The people there, I think there were about half-a-dozen boys and two or three girls, had made some comment about my breasts and, although I kept my eyes shut, I could feel my nipples erecting under their gaze. He might have been inclined to stop there but the others goaded him on and so he started on my skirt. This was very full, and he gently raised it up my legs, pulling it out from under my thighs

58

until it was lying across my stomach, leaving me lying in only some skimpy knickers. I think that even these had been partly pulled off, because someone said, 'Well, at least we know she's a real blonde!' And they'd all laughed. They then discussed whether they could get my knickers off as well. My boyfriend thought it would be impossible but one of the girls was sure she could manage. And I let her. I lay back with my eyes closed, listening to the tense silence as they all gathered round me, and revelling in being the centre of attention. I also liked the feel of her fingers gently working under the elastic waistband as she inched it down my thighs.

But then, when she had got about halfway, I suddenly lost my nerve and pretended to wake up as she started to pull them down. When she realised that I was starting to sit up, she threw caution to the wind and simply tugged at them, getting them down to my knees but not right off. It was enough to give everyone quite a show and they all cheered and it was all I could do to keep from giggling. I think now that if I'd been quite sure that they would just look, I would probably have let them go further, but at that age I wasn't sure.

I have relived that event over and over in my mind many times, and savoured it, often adding embellishments so that I've let the girl take my knickers right off. Since I am still showing no sign of life, she pushes my legs wide apart. Then they all gather round to look at me, and they talk about me, taking turns to touch me, gently inserting a finger or two inside me; even the girls do this. Sometimes they take turns to masturbate me or fuck me, trying to see if they can bring me to an orgasm without my coming round. Sometimes they tie me up. It has been the base for some of my most intense fantasies.

So, although I was not going to live out the whole fantasy – I wouldn't even be completely naked and they certainly wouldn't be touching me – a little mild flaunting, perhaps topless, couldn't do any harm and it would revitalise the dream.

When at last I was able to talk to Julie again, I took refuge by asking more questions, but they were not relevant, and I didn't even listen to the answers. In the end, I agreed.

'OK, I will come with you to talk to him, but I'm not making any promises that I will do it. How much do we get paid?'

'I've no idea. Only one way to find out.'

So we went round the next evening and Julie's friend, Eric, seemed pleased to see us both. He sat us down at the bar, gave us free drinks and then, after serving a few other customers, came back to talk to us.

'OK, girls, the deal is this. We have go-go dancing from the end of happy hour, at seven, that is, until eleven; after that it's topless and the nudies start coming on around two. It goes on like that until the club shuts, which can be anything from three o'clock onwards. It just depends what's happening, if we have any special bookings or whatever. The local girls are quite happy to be go-go dancers, but few want to go much further than that, so that's where you come in. Topless you get a hundred dollars a spot and you should do three or four in the evening. Nude you will get 350 dollars. You only do one nude spot in the night, but you should get plenty of tips and drinks. You get fifty per cent of any drinks bought for you and you keep any tips you can manage. Whether you go out with any of the punters is up to you. Some of the girls do. Some don't. The punter pays the usual bar fine of course, and that goes to the club. If Jackie (he's the owner, I just help run the place) catches you doing turns in any of the other clubs around here between spots, he will cut your tits off. I jest not. Do not cross him. Other than that, you don't need to worry. The place is very well protected. You can start any time you like.'

'Right,' I said, 'let's think about it for a minute.'

We talked it over for some time and, although I had considerable misgivings, I also felt huge temptations. In the end, I didn't exactly agree, I just failed to disagree so that when Eric came ambling back down the bar again Julie agreed for both of us.

'OK,' he said, 'come here at about eleven o'clock tomorrow and I'll arrange someone to take you over. Jackie will want to see you before he lets you on. In fact, no, I'll take you myself.'

'You mean it isn't here?'

'Here? Hell, no! This is an upmarket joint for tourists. No, you'll be working over at the Wonderland Club in Hankow Road. It isn't far, ten minutes. I'll show you. I'll have to. They wouldn't let a European in otherwise! If you have anything special to wear, bring it, but if not there is quite a wardrobe that other girls have left at different times. To be frank, what you wear is not as important as what you don't.'

I was a little worried about the reference to there being no other Europeans, but Julie seemed to accept it so I said nothing. And that was it, as simple as that. Julie and I moved on to a different bar where we had another couple of drinks and tried to act brave although I think even she was beginning to have second thoughts. After a couple of drinks, though, we were joking almost happily about it until I said:

'I'm not sure my disco style is quite up to date. Should we go to a club for a short while? For training purposes, of course?'

Julie was out of the door almost before I had finished speaking; she generally took little persuasion to go dancing. We danced together, in fact turned down the only potential pick-up who tried, and I felt a little reassured after that. Except for one thing. In the middle of one dance, I caught Julie looking at my bustline, and that reminded me why we were there. I glanced down at her boobs and, as I looked up again, caught her watching me. I knew (well, we both knew) we had been looking and trying to imagine what each other looked like under our respective tops and, I suppose, thinking that by tomorrow we would no longer be wondering, and it wouldn't be just each other that had seen them.

As we walked back to the hostel after that, nothing was said, although that Nothing walked along with us and stifled any attempt at chat. When we went up in the tiny lift, the Nothing pushed us into silent opposite corners, too embarrassed to speak. Finally, as Julie said goodnight outside her room, I decided to face the monster.

'Well, who do you think?' I asked.

'What? Who do I think what?'

'Come off it, Julie, you know very well what we have both been thinking. Which of us has the best boobs!'

'Boobs? Oh, you mean tits!' And she laughed, and the ice was broken. 'I couldn't decide. What did you think?'

'Come in,' I said and pulled her into the empty room. Then I turned away, pulled my sweatshirt over my head and tossed that and then my bra on to the bed. I turned back to face Julie. She looked at me, into my eyes, then down again.

'Well, what about you?' I asked.

She didn't even turn away; just unbuttoned the shirt, shrugged it off then reached behind and unhooked her bra. Her breasts sort of fell forward at me and I looked at them quite fascinated. They were certainly bigger than mine, but the nipples were quite pale, and rather flat and shapeless. Overall, I thought mine were better.

'You win,' I said and turned to retrieve my top.

'No,' said Julie, 'you do.' There was a trace of sadness and I think she meant it, and I felt sorry for her.

Julie and I spent the next day together, but I think we were both only too conscious of the steadily approaching evening. It hung over us like an anticipated punishment which I think was beginning to worry Julie even more than me. Anyway, when the time came we made our way back through the garishly lit streets to the club. Eric was behind the bar again but he called someone else out and, as he had promised, led us back through the middle of tourist Tsim Tsa Tsui and over a block further to where, in small letters, a sign on the side of a doorway proclaimed 'The Wonderland Club', and a doorman, or perhaps bouncer would be more accurate, leant against the wall watching. He nodded to Eric. Somehow this club looked a great deal less innocent than the one we had left. I suppose anywhere that advertises itself as little as that seems dangerous. It all looked like something out of a Humphrey Bogart movie, both squalid and romantic but at the same time undeniably vibrant. It was a world that I didn't know, had only ever seen on television and in films, and this made it so much more glamorous.

In any case it was too late to pull out and Eric gave us no chance to do so as he led us through a small door and up two flights of cluttered concrete stairs. He knocked on a narrow and grubby door, but when there was no answer he told us to wait while he went to fetch the club owner. He returned a few minutes later with a slightly older man, Chinese, who turned out to be Jackie himself. Jackie was not a likeable man. His hair was too thin at the top, too long at the sides and too greasy everywhere. His suit was obviously expensive but not very clean, and he was fat. He carried a cigarette almost all the time and his jewellery, watch and ring, were too big and gaudy. He looked like a man pretending to be a gangster, but then, from what Eric had told us, maybe he was not pretending. He unlocked the door and let us into a disgustingly cluttered and over-air-conditioned office, its most prominent features a large but grubby desk and a smaller but even dirtier leather sofa. He sat

63

himself behind the desk, pulled up an already overflowing ash tray, and started fumbling with cigarettes and an expensive-looking table lighter. He did not invite any of us to sit down, although Eric perched on one arm of the sofa. Jackie glanced at Julie and me briefly but did not address us directly.

'They know the rules, Eric?'

'Yes, Jackie. They understand. They want to do topless work, just for a few weeks.'

'I see. Right. They are a little better looking than the last girl you brought me, anyway. The main thing for you to understand, girls, is that this is my club and it has many rich and important customers. I will not have them upset or annoyed. If you think you recognise any of them in here you are mistaken. You don't, OK? All you know about them is what they tell you. Outside here, you don't know them at all. Girls like you I can get for a few dollars any time I want. The customers I cannot replace. OK?'

I nodded and I think Julie did too.

'Right, right.' He finally lit the cigarette. 'Take your things off.'

Neither of us moved; it seems stupidly naive now, but I don't suppose Julie was expecting that any more than I was. In retrospect we obviously should have been.

'Come on, come on. I can ask young Eric to leave, if you like.'

'No,' I said quickly, 'that's all right.'

I didn't say that I actually felt safer with him there. However, I turned around and took off my sweatshirt and bra, and my nipples immediately wrinkled up from a mixture of surprise and fear and also the sudden cold of being exposed. I dropped my clothes on to the sofa and Julie and I turned back to face Jackie at almost the same moment, but he barely glanced up, just said:

'And pants.'

I turned back, unzipped my jeans and pulled them off.

64

What did he mean by 'pants'? American, meaning trousers? Or panties as well? I caught Julie's eye also looking puzzled and I just shrugged and pushed off my knickers. I didn't want Jackie to have to ask again and nor did I want him to think I was afraid. Yet I was. It was not only the man himself; there was also something quite uniquely and intensely repugnant about having to undress in that cramped and dirty little room. It was so totally unsuitable a location in which to take off my clothes that I felt the atmosphere of the room itself touching me, almost groping me. It was somehow even more intrusive and so much worse than being only topless. The smell and squalor made me want to pull a protective covering tighter around me and yet I was less protected than ever, for being now completely naked. I faced him again but he sat impassively, saying nothing as he waited for Julie – on one leg and almost overbalancing – to finish taking off her jeans. When she was again standing beside me, he levered himself out of the chair and came round the desk. He stopped in front of us and leant back against the desk, pushing one hand down into his trouser pocket while he looked us up and down.

He moved up to Julie, and I remember noticing that, although this time her nipples had erected, they were still very small, little more than bumps on the surface of a wide flat saucer. I also realised that she had not taken off her knickers and I blushed at my stupidity. Jackie did not say a word but casually smeared his thumb across each of her nipples, almost as if he were wanting to see if they were real, and I saw Julie flinch, start to pull back and then stop herself. Working down, he hooked a finger into the elastic waistband of her knickers and pulled them down on one side to the top of her thighs, enough to reveal a thick growth of dark pubic hair, and then ran his finger along her stomach and through her hair across to the other hip to pull the elastic down on that side too. I was greatly relieved then that I had taken my own off; I wanted him to have no cause to touch me there. He stooped to peer closely at her breasts then came on round behind her, hooking his finger in at the groove between her buttocks to pull down her knickers below her bottom and then fondle her briefly. The elastic was stretched across her thighs but he gave the knickers another push down so that they fell to her ankles.

Then he moved across to me. I was standing facing him, my hands clasped together in front of me, but he took hold of my wrists to pull my arms away and I let them hang down at my sides. We were almost exactly the same height, and he stared into my eyes for a moment before he told me to turn round.

I found myself looking at Eric, who gave me a friendly and sympathetic smile, but could not keep his eyes from wandering down my body, back up to my face and then down again. I was conscious of Jackie moving behind me and then felt a cold and unpleasantly clammy hand settle on my shoulder and a slight tugging at my hair. The hand twisted me to turn sideways and then slithered down my back, paused on my buttock and spread out, took a handful and squeezed, squeezed hard. I was aware of his eyes examining me, waiting for me to wince, but I tried to betray no response. The hand lifted away and I thought that he was done when he suddenly brought it down on my bottom again in a slap that practically knocked me over. He turned me back in front of him again, and was smiling as he peered closely, first into my face and then down at my breasts. He sniffed and twisted me a little more to face him straight on, and still he said nothing; did not even glance up at me for permission or acknowledgement, as his cold hands lifted up and weighed first one breast and then the other. As he released each one, he let it slide out through his fingers until just my nipple stayed trapped

66

in his fingertips and he squeezed firmly. He leant back against the desk to get a better overall view, then flicked the backs of his fingers against the inside of my thigh. The command was clear, but even so I considered for a moment refusing; it was after all quite unnecessary as I would only be topless. Yet any refusal would only have acknowledged my humiliation, so I acquiesced, and moved my legs apart to let him see. He even bent down to peer more closely into the crease, but didn't touch me there. Still my hair is very fine and pale and, the way I'm made, I know my long inner lips would have been quite visible. Finally he straightened up, raised and dropped a handful of my hair, brushing it down over my breast a last time, and then returned behind the desk.

'Turn this way again.' He leant back in the chair while he seemed to compare us in his mind, looking very obviously from my breasts across to Julie's and then down at her pubis and over at mine. I'd brought my legs back together but, even so, I'm sure he had a good view. In fact, a few days later I saw Julie changing; she is much more compact than me – more like a little girl – and has much thicker hair, so there would have been little for him to see there. I suppose that was what had encouraged Jackie to take the time and the liberties with me.

I just stared at the wall above his head, trying not to respond, my hands hanging down at my sides while he looked us both up and down during half-a-dozen more drags on his cigarette. He had already seen everything, must have made his mind up already, and I'm sure this was only to let us know who was the boss.

Finally he stubbed out the cigarette and turned back to Eric. 'OK, OK, they will do. Take them down and tell Lee to put them on for a trial run tonight.'

As Eric led the way back down, he apologised for Jackie's treatment of us and I did think then he was genuinely sorry. He said he knew that Jackie was sometimes inclined to take liberties and that was why he had brought us over to the club himself, to make sure things did not go too far. Since then I have come to know Eric a little better, and I no longer believe him. I certainly think he knew that Jackie would take liberties, but I also know that Eric is afraid of him, and wouldn't dare to interfere in anything that Jackie wanted to do. I think he just wanted to be there to watch.

We went down one floor to the dressing room, a tiny dark corner, no bigger than a bathroom, and yet containing two elderly wardrobes made of a grimy dark-stained wood. A single bare lightbulb gave a little light. There was no window. Even so, almost half the floor space was taken up by a mound of cardboard boxes which looked as if it had lain undisturbed for many months or years. Eric suggested that we watch the first show so that we would know what to do and to make our own selection of what we should wear. He implied more than explicitly stated that there was no need to be unduly worried over the artistic merit; it was principally a matter of giving the customers a look at what they'd paid to see.

The club itself – the public part, that is – could hardly have been a greater contrast with the part behind the scenes. It was quite small, only twenty or so small tables and a bar down one side, but a considerable amount of money had obviously been spent on its decoration. The carpet was thick and soft, and the walls had been papered and dotted everywhere with tiny lights, like a Christmas grotto. The colours were all deep reds and gold, with ornate carvings and decorations up by the ceiling and around the bar.

In an alcove stood a tiny stage, little more than a platform raised a few inches, and about eight feet deep and not much more than that wide. Still, it was well lit and on this a Chinese girl was dancing. She was wearing a leotard, cut very high on the hips and, as she later revealed, very low at the back and front, altogether pretty stunning. Over the top of this she wore a T-shirt, loose but short, barely reaching her waist. She took the T-shirt off after a couple of minutes to reveal her breasts. They were nicely shaped and firm, but not very big, and she did no more than dance about, without playing to the audience; in fact she ignored her surroundings altogether. I was sure I could do better, and I wanted to do better, but then of course that was why he wanted some European girls, I suppose – fewer inhibitions. Peering around at what could be seen of the audience, I did not find a single European there. It frightened me a little, making it all seem that much more exotic and forbidden, yet it also induced a slight feeling of being a slave: owned and displayed in an Eastern slave market, the stuff of so much forbidden adolescent fiction. I don't know, maybe a psychiatrist could have a field day, but it certainly did nothing to reduce the intensity of my feeling.

Julie was still feeling a bit shaken by Jackie's treatment of us upstairs and so I agreed that I would go on first. After the girl finished, I followed her back to the dressing room but she said nothing to me, merely dressed quickly and pushed out of the side door, slamming it behind her. I took the opportunity to look through the wardrobe. There was quite a collection of different articles in a variety of sizes, colours and states of repair, including leotards, bikinis, short dresses, the lot. An attractive pair of emerald-green chiffon harem trousers rather took my fancy; they were quite sheer and in my slave-girl mood seemed appropriate, but in the end I decided on a short denim skirt and waistcoat. I did not button this up fully, but most of the way up so that I was, how shall I put it, decent but interesting. As the song played, I could undo the buttons and show off more. I have to admit that by this stage, I was beginning to look forward to the performance much more. It was an oddly liberating experience. Here I was preparing to do the very things that in any other circumstances I would have taken great care to avoid. Having accepted that, I was free: relieved of any responsibility to behave in anything like a proper manner.

I picked out the music I wanted, a fairly slow but quite smoochy song and, by the time it came to my turn and I was standing waiting at the side of the little dance platform – you could hardly call it a stage – while I was introduced, I was nervous certainly but also excited. Partly I was filled with the pumping adrenaline that would precede any performance but, as well as that, there was more: there was the thrill, the erotic excitement of being so displayed. If I never did this again, I would remember the performance until I died.

The music started, its slow tempo inviting a sultry and seductive swaying, and I ran my hands up and down my sides, up and over my breasts and down my hips. After a while I started pushing my hands up inside the waistcoat and over my hard bare nipples, so that it rode up and I unbuttoned it little by little until it was just hanging down the sides and acting as a frame for my breasts instead of a cover. A couple of times I dropped down to a squat, so they could see up the short skirt to my white knickers, wondering as I did it whether they could see the damp patch that I could feel must be there. I was paying no attention to the time but I was noticing the audience and they were definitely noticing me. The difference between this reception and the one that had been given to the last dancer was enormous. They had stopped talking, stopped drinking and were watching me, watching every move. As the song came to an end, I turned my back on them all, then shrugged the waistcoat down on to the floor. I stood with my legs apart and stared at them over my shoulder, then ran my hands slow and hard down my buttocks and slow and hard back up again, pulling up my skirt on the way, to show my round cheeks in their thin covering layer of tight white cotton. As the sound died away, I bent down to pick up the waistcoat, showing off my breasts to their best advantage. The applause and cheers were all I could have hoped for, and I knew that I would have no trouble holding down this job.

Over the next few weeks I worked at the club two or three nights a week, and gradually developed quite a loyal little following. I never did a nude spot, but kept myself in demand by always holding something in reserve and yet behaving each night as if this might be the one that I showed it all. Many evenings my dances had finished to calls for me to take the rest off although, in all honesty, there had often been little left to take. Money had been thrown up on the stage and even more had been offered me afterwards. Several men had asked to take me out. I had turned all these down. Being honest, I know that to a large degree my colour helped me, because Julie stopped coming before the end of the first week and after that I was the only European there. Julie hated it, and could never get used to the leering and the cat-calls, whereas I had no trouble with that. I did not mind being chatted up, patted as I got on and off the little stage, even groped at times as I passed.

It was well worth it, not just for the money I was making but somehow it was the very foreignness of it – the side that so disturbed Julie – which helped me. She felt the meanness and squalor clawing at her and infecting her. For me it was the opposite. It was all so far removed from my real life that it didn't even reach me. I was no part of it, simply immune. Jackie often came down, watched from the bar and sometimes he followed me down to stand in the doorway of the dressing room and, although I ignored him and carried on as though he was not there, he often watched me changing. In fact he saw less in the dressing room than he would have done when I was on stage, so I really don't know why he bothered. He never exactly groped me, but he often put a hand on my shoulder in a way that was clearly possessive and, on the occasions I came off stage wearing only a G-string, he always patted my bare bottom as I passed. He offered me drinks, which I accepted, and dinners, which I refused. Generally though, the club was, as Eric had said at the beginning, well protected, and if Jackie was one of the worst, he was bearable.

I was starting to feel settled in, and thinking that I really had earnt enough to move on, when I got a message just as I came off stage one night that Jackie wanted to see me in his office. You didn't cross Jackie, so I went straight up, still in the G-string but I pulled on a sweatshirt and pants.

His office was as squalid as the first time I'd seen it, and as cold, with the air-conditioning droning away in the back wall. Another man, Chinese, was sitting on the settee, and although Jackie didn't introduce him, I had a strong feeling that I'd seen him in the newspapers and on television.

Jackie looked up as I came in.

'Ah, Ali. Now you have been here a month, right?'

'Yes,' I volunteered a little hesitantly, unsure where this was leading.

'Right, right. But you've never done a double. I think it's time.'

The 'doubles' were laid on for occasional special evenings mostly when a particular member was entertaining guests. Then they went much further than a stripper, and would have a couple, mostly a man and a girl but sometimes two girls, to perform on stage. Jackie had asked me at the end of the first week if I would do one – a lesbian show with a Chinese girl – but I'd turned it down then. He asked again a couple of times and, although I declined, I suppose I never quite refused. The money he offered was always good, but between what I was getting already, plus the tips and the drinks, I was getting enough without that.

'No, I don't want to.'

Jackie fumbled with his cigarette for a moment, then, glancing, almost as if for approval, over at the man on the settee, he simply shrugged and carried on.

'Well, I think it's time. My customers have seen your tits plenty of times. Now they want something more. Besides, this gentleman has heard good things about you, and although he has never seen you dance, he wants you to do a double.'

I looked round to see who this man was who held such authority, someone who even Jackie treated with such respect. He sat quietly, and barely glanced at me, yet there was something about his silent power that melted my resistance.

I said again, 'I don't want to,' but it came out too weak and, when Jackie made no response, I asked what he wanted.

'What kind of a double do you mean? Another girl?'

He shook his head.

'No, a man. I have someone I think will be good. He is also English, and he has worked here before once. He is always popular.' Jackie smiled. 'He's a big man, you know what I mean?'

I blushed.

'Right, right. Friday, then. One other thing. The gentleman has never seen your act here. You'd better show him what you've got.'

'What, here?'

'Yes, here. Quickly, now.'

I looked round at the man sitting calmly on the settee. He was about fifty, going bald on top and neatly dressed in a well-fitting suit and silk tie and wearing thick black-rimmed glasses. Altogether, he looked entirely unremarkable and I figured it could not be every day that he had the chance to watch a twenty-year-old girl undress, and certainly not a blonde European girl, so I expected to see eager anticipation on his face. Instead it was completely devoid of any expression beyond a very slight impatience. He was clearly not used to being kept waiting.

The dirty little office was still cold, and the rumbling air-conditioner underlined the expectant silence of the two men. I had just come from flaunting myself in only a tiny G-string in front of a couple of dozen men downstairs, so it seemed silly to be coy. Yet here was completely different. The nakedness of being in a private setting made it much closer and more personal than when I was in public. Even as recently as a month ago, when I had first undressed in that dingy little room, it had been, in theory at least, because I needed to show I had got what they needed for the job; there had been some kind of justification. Downstairs on the stage, it was all an act; artificial and made up. And I was the performer. I was the one in control. Now it was different. The man sitting behind me simply wanted to see what I looked like with no clothes on; wanted to see all the private parts of me that he couldn't see when I was normally dressed. Now he was the one in control and the choice was simple: obey or leave.

I pulled the sweatshirt over my head. My breasts were still shining with sweat after the exertions of the dance, but my nipples immediately erected under the gaze of the two men, and the cold from the air-conditioning. I laid the sweatshirt down on the settee, and then pulled my sweat-pants off, laid them down too and stood up to face the silent visitor.

He looked me up and down, but still said nothing, and it was finally Jackie who spoke.

'Turn round.'

I turned slowly to face Jackie, feeling the strength of the gaze on me and, knowing that I looked good, feeling the effect of the exposure. My mind was still full of the exhilaration of the stage act that I had only just finished and, with that to build on, I could feel a wetness growing between my legs that the skimpy G-string would be quite unable to absorb. Having the visitor sitting no more than a couple of feet away from me while I showed him my breasts and bare bottom was unendurable. Jackie looked me up and down, as he always did, then told me to turn back, facing our guest.

'Take that thing off.'

The man was looking into my eyes as I was given this instruction and, although I tried to show no reaction, he must have seen the fear and the excitement that I felt as I heard it. I reached down to slide the little scrap over my hips and down to the floor.

I stood up again, and the man looked down, focusing on my neatly trimmed blonde bush. He would have been able to see my inner lips hanging down below my pussy, and I could feel the moistness already glistening on them, but still Jackie was not satisfied.

'Let him see the rest.'

I knew what he meant, and I hated myself for wanting to show it, but I had come so far that just standing there naked would be insufficient. I shuffled up to the settee right in front of the stranger and lifted my foot up on to the seat next to him. Then I leant back and rolled my knee over to open myself completely to his wide unblinking eyes. Even that was not enough, and with my fingers I pushed my lips apart, not just the thick puffy outer ones, but also the long inner ones which were hanging wet and slippery beneath me. I peeled them right open to display the pink inside my opening and, just at the top, the erect stem of my clit. With my other hand, I even pinched that between my fingertips, squeezing it out still further into plain view, and rubbed my fingers over the delicate round tip. I was so sopping it was almost as if I had wet myself, so I rubbed again, and then reached back to dip my finger into the warm wet channel that I was holding open for the man, and then slowly withdrew it, slurping as my inside muscles tried to hold on to the penetration.

When I spread my lips open again, they stayed smeared flat by the thick juice that was spread all over my pussy. Now at last there was a reaction from the man for the first time. He glanced up just briefly, then reached out and his finger traced slowly along the ridge of my lips and over the livid pink nib of my clit. His fingers felt cold and hard against my wet skin and, as soon as he stopped, I pressed back down again and then rubbed again at my clit until it was all too much. I shut my eyes and stood in front of him and masturbated, less than two feet from his eyes, until I climaxed in a deep groan of pleasure that pushed another dribble of juice out of me as my muscles clamped tight around my fingers.

He looked up at me again and nodded slowly, saying something in Chinese to Jackie.

'OK, Ali. That will be fine.'

By the Friday, word had got round and the customers knew they were due for something a bit special. My partner for the show, John, turned up an hour or so before our spot was due to start, and I immediately took a dislike to him. He sauntered into Jackie's office and threw a small holdall on the settee then looked over at me.

'This the little girl I have to fuck, Jackie?' He walked over towards me and hooked his finger into the scoop neck of my T-shirt. Then he pulled the neck out and peered down inside at my breasts. It was only for a moment before he released me.

'Shouldn't be a problem.'

Jackie left us after that, and John and I worked out a rough plan for the show. He was a little less cocky without Jackie to play up to, but still arrogant and bossy.

The show started with two songs for me alone: the first one quite fast, so I could really throw myself about, but the second was back to the slower beat that was my style and which let me caress myself slowly in a way that seemed to be well liked. During the first one, I stripped off everything above the waist, tossing my clothes on to a flimsy chair on the side of the stage. My boobs are the right size to look good if I'm really dancing wild, and tonight I was; I gave a completely unrestrained display, almost animal, that left me glistening with sweat by the end. During the second number I slid out of the skirt and very slowly out of a pair of knickers but I still kept a silky red G-string. By the end of the second piece that was all that was left and, although it covered very little, it nicely focused all attention on the centre of interest. I did not take it off as the song ended, but instead retrieved the shirt and slipped it back on to the sound of the most muted applause I think I had ever received. The boys had not seen what they had been led to expect and they were not going to hide their disappointment.

As I finished rebuttoning my shirt and went to gather up my other clothes, the music started up again, loud and fast, as John strode out on to the little stage. I pretended surprise at first as he strutted around in time to the music. When he grabbed my arm and included me in his dance I obliged with what was an evidently forced tolerance. When he swung me round so that I was facing the audience and held tight against him, he ran his hands up inside the shirt, then slowly he tore it open, ripping off the buttons one by one until my breasts were exposed again. He rubbed me, caressed and pulled harshly at my nipples, but I did not respond, just stared out at the men in the darkness, who were attentive now, sitting silent and barely sipping at their drinks. Only one thing interested them at that moment: my sexuality.

77

That is what I wanted to show them, the final scrap of me that I'd always kept hidden. We circled again, but this time when he grabbed me, he caught only the sleeve of the shirt and, as I spun round, it tore and slid off, leaving me back in the little red G-string as John tossed the shirt off the stage. We were almost fencing now, circling round, half bent over, my breasts swaying from side to side as I tried to get past him and away. When I darted by, he caught me again, pinned me up against the side of the stage and rubbed his fully clothed body up against my naked one.

The audience had quietened down now; we had definitely got their total interest. He spun me around and clasped me back in front of him again, but this time my hands were both held tight behind me, leaving my front in full view as he rubbed up and down and pulled my nipples out to a very full erection. I wriggled convincingly, but he was not going to let me get away. Finally his hand dropped down my belly and over the G-string, up again and back down inside it. He pulled the top down a little so that the audience could see the top of my neatly trimmed blonde triangle and, although it wasn't much to see, it was more than they'd ever seen before. His fingers pushed through a little further between my legs, and he would certainly be in no doubt of my excitement. I could feel it too, beginning to seep down. John let out a short low moan beside my ear, a sign of appreciation for me alone that nobody else could hear, and which showed that he understood and approved of my arousal. I turned and kissed him long, letting the audience see my tongue running up into his mouth as he continued to run his fingers up and down inside the tiny bit of cloth. What were the men thinking as they watched this? They could not doubt now that this was for real, that this time they would see all they wanted, perhaps more than they dreamt of. I pulled away, realising that I was starting to lose control.

I dropped down to my knees and turned to undo John's belt then his fly. Somewhere above me I was dimly aware that he was unbuttoning his shirt, but I was not really interested in that. I reached inside and pulled out his prick, half erect and, as Jackie had said, already huge. After a few quick strokes with my fingers to let the audience see that this was the real thing, I slipped it into my mouth and pulled his jeans right down his legs. Several times I pulled back and, holding his thick rigid shaft in my fist, smeared the glistening head over my lips and cheeks and up all over my face.

He suddenly pushed me away, turned roughly and tipped all my clothes off the chair. Bringing it a little nearer to the centre of the stage, he sat down, legs apart, and motioned to me to stand up. I pretended not to understand. He repeated the gesture. I obeyed, slowly and timidly, and he pointed at my G-string and, when I didn't move, he waved at it, irritated at my delay. He meant me to remove it, this tiny scrap of cloth, the last covering I had. The gesture was clear enough to the men beyond the lights. I was aware of their craning round expectantly to see better and perhaps it was this that changed the mood. I was suddenly deeply conscious of the room full of strangers, silent watchers, whose eagerness reached out like tentacles towards me and emphasised their presence and their concentration, gazing at me, pushing forward, trying to bore through the thin veil of my skimpy covering to the only treasure they had not yet seen. I shuddered, and a blush burned its way up from my throat and over my face then down to my chest, further inflaming my breasts and nipples. I began to wonder whether I would be able to go through with the display after all. Certainly this was the enactment of a fantasy that I had cherished since I don't know when, but the reality was different: harder and so much more intimate.

I looked to John for support but his expression

immediately dissolved my freedom of choice. He was as absorbed as I had been and if my role as slave had been getting the better of me, his as master had already taken him over. His glance at me was cold: all his arrogance had returned, and he was totally confident of my obedience. He would not let me stop.

Without fully being in control of what I was doing, I reached round behind my back and undid the hook, peeling the string down from where it was caught well up between my buttocks, and timidly passed it into his outstretched hand. Without a glance, he tossed it down at the back of the stage and I stood there, completely naked and motionless. He looked me up and down, slowly, disdainfully, and when I reached down to cover myself, he stretched out and viciously snatched my hands away again. He gestured to me with both hands to expose myself to him and again I delayed and he had to repeat it before I slowly complied.

This was the hardest moment of all, and yet I was now so deeply immersed that it needed no conscious decision. My hands dropped between my legs, felt for the puffed and slippery lips, and pulled them open. My forefingers met, pushing forward the hard swollen pea of my clitoris and, as I did so, rubbed it slowly but firmly, a gesture that only he could see. My lips were so engorged they almost ached. I felt so full, so engrossed, that the dancing of a few minutes before could have been another person. That seemed now to have been no more than showing off, a mild and immature flirtation. This was harder and fiercer, a desperate animal arousal.

The way I was standing, sideways on to the audience, the other men could not see all that I was revealing but they could see more of me than they had ever dreamt of seeing. They saw me being humbled: a woman, and more than that, a European woman, forced to behave obscenely, to do things she clearly found humiliating. John grasped my hips, twisting me round to face them and holding me a minute. I could only look down at the floor as I held my lips open for their inspection but, even so, I pushed my hips forward a little; I could not help it. Then he pulled me round yet again, in front of him now so that I presented my back to the audience, and he made me stand with my legs wide apart; actually kicked them wider so that I almost overbalanced.

The men directly behind me would now be able to see my swollen lips, hanging, dark and red, no doubt glistening in the spotlights. Were they actually dripping? His hand on top of my head, John pulled me down towards him until my head was right in his lap and I sucked the bright end of his huge shaft into my mouth. I had to steady myself against him as my hips were pushed out behind me, further displaying me – more of me – to the men. John's hand ran beneath me and between my legs, his middle finger digging deeply into the groove before pushing up far inside me. Two, three, wide circles and then out again and up across my buttocks. For a dreadful second his wet finger paused over my anus and I feared he intended even to penetrate me there, but slowly he moved on, to leave a cold glistening trail across my buttocks.

Then he threw me flat down on the stage, spinning me around until my feet were again towards the silent watching men. He towered over me, standing level with my shoulders and his thick thighs and long jutting cock filling my vision. He took hold of his own cock and rubbed himself a couple of times, as if he would ejaculate all over my body, but then squatted down, grabbed my knees, paused and then steadily pulled my legs up and apart. I swear I could hear a deep slurping as my lips were peeled open and I could certainly smell my own juice; even over the beer and smoke and sweat, there was no mistake. Looking down my body, I saw the cluster of faces gathered round, straining to devour me, and I could only pull my legs a little wider and a little higher to let them see. A slow trickle of juice was running between my buttocks and I couldn't keep myself from reaching down to my clitoris, from pulling the hood back, pinching it between the tips of my fingers, flipping the tip with my other hand. John did not interrupt me at first, just let me lie there under the lights, under the public gaze, and masturbate.

Down beyond my hands, framed dimly between my thighs, the watchers had given up their chairs now and were all crowded directly in front of me. Their eyes were no longer caressing my nakedness but now rasped over my body. I could feel them running over my skin, around my breasts, but always returning to concentrate between my legs, on hands and fingers and cunt. I raised my hips off the floor to offer them more, to offer everything, as I felt deep, deep within me the slow beginnings of my orgasm. John pulled my hands away.

He was still standing over me and he bent down and pulled my inner lips so wide I could feel the cool air rush in, far up inside me. Then I felt his fingers trailing up and down the lips, then two pushing in, until his knuckles rammed against my lips and the hard base of his thumb was pushed up against my clitoris on every downward stroke. In and out he thrust his hand obscenely, but I was meeting him push for push.

My own hands reached at my breasts, pulled at my nipples but, again, just as the rhythm was beginning to build up, John stopped. Moving round between my legs, he pushed my knees over and down on to my shoulders then ran the head of his huge cock up and down my groove before plunging it straight into me. The feeling was so deep – I have never been so full – and yet still it was not quite enough, and I had to reach down between us to work my clitoris some more, bringing me to the verge of an explosion. John was still holding off. His thrusts were energetic enough, yet the expression on his face, the refusal to look me in the eye, showed he was struggling to maintain his control. He finally pulled out again and stood over me, his massive prick seeming even longer and thicker as it shook in front of my face. He pulled me up to my knees in front of him and offered his gleaming prick, glistening with my own juice, to my mouth. According to our script, I was supposed to pretend reluctance but by now I could not. I just grabbed it with both hands and pulled it into my mouth while I sat on one foot and worked my heel into my cunt. I licked his full length, sucking it as far as I could into my mouth and then out until only my lips touched the tip. When he grabbed my hair, I knew we were past the point of no return, pumping harder, faster, sucking deeper; he shuddered and his knees almost knocked me over as he bucked at me with the first gush. Quickly I pulled back a little to let them all see the rich spurts arc through the air and splatter on to my face, in my hair and some in my mouth, driven by my pumping hand.

As his orgasm died away, I could no longer hold off. I let go of his prick and fell back to dig both hands hard into my cunt, pinching my clit as hard as I could; it was so over-stimulated; the orgasm had been building for so many days of anticipation. But I still wanted the men to see me and, before losing all self-control, I turned to face them square, then, kneeling on the gritty floor, spread my legs wide to invite them all within. I could hear the groans in my throat as if from another person somewhere above me. I was so deep inside myself I was no longer the face or the hands or the legs, not even the breasts that squirmed on that stage, just the contracting tunnel and womb that gripped at fingers and sucked at pleasure and washed over me and through me and away.

5

Helen's Tale – Cat and Mouse

The alarm clock started shrill and commanding, but when neither of us moved it quickly lost its self-confidence. The tone dropped and the pace slowed, eventually fading through a discordant croak into silence. It was a Saturday, when we would normally have a lie-in, but David was due to play golf with his boss, Geoff, and it was unthinkable that he should be late. For a few minutes I lay still, staring into the back of David's head and willing him to move. Finally, faced with his refusal even to acknowledge that he was awake, I got up and went to make the coffee.

That particular morning we were both even more drowsy than usual. Ros and Mike, friends from a long way back, had come round for drinks and dinner and more drinks the previous evening, and had stayed until well past one o'clock. Even then, when we did get to bed, David had wanted to make love. I don't want to complain, because our love-making was always good and David was always careful to ensure that I had an orgasm, but sometimes his carefulness irritated me. I wished he could be more relaxed and enter into the feelings rather than treating my body as a machine to be worked. Although I was satisfied physically, sometimes I wanted something more emotional that would have been no less pleasurable. Of course it was impossible to say anything to him about it, although I had tried occasionally. Often it was easier simply to accept the mechanical orgasm with him and then sneak away to masturbate later and lose myself in fantasy and a deeper orgasm on my own. I have a vibrator that David had bought for me because he likes to watch me using it, but I never use it when he's not there. It's all too quick, too mechanical and efficient, and I prefer the softness and understanding of my own hands.

Last night Mike had brought along some magazine with him, one of the 'girlie', 'top-shelf' type, I forget which one it was, but it meant we had got on to the subject of sex almost as soon as they arrived. They are both much less inhibited about it all than I am. I mean, we have a varied sex life and I don't mind talking about sex in general, but I don't like to discuss personal details with other people, not even with friends as close as Ros and Mike. Those two seem to feel no such inhibitions and, since we'd all had a lot to drink, the conversation was very free; I didn't join in much. After they'd gone, and left the magazine behind (it would not surprise me if this had been agreed between the boys), David dragged me into bed with a jovial confidence that was heavily fuelled by Mike's description of games, conquests and encounters, which I suspected were heavily exaggerated. All taken together, poor old David seemed to think he had some kind of challenge to meet. He had worked away at me attentively and, even though he was a bit drunk, he went at it with even more determination than usual. But he was so determined and so efficient that I was put off, and although I did have an orgasm in the end – he would never have stopped if I had not at least pretended to – I still felt unfulfilled.

I saw David off to his golf and then made another cup of coffee while I pottered about the house in my dressing gown. It was a bright summer day, but with a sharp breeze blowing up from the bay, and I had the patio doors open to get rid of the stale air while I started clearing up glasses and dishes from last night. I came across the magazine left over by Mike, and casually started reading while I finished my coffee. I started with the letters section and found one from a woman who had met two boys – or maybe young men is more accurate: they were about nineteen or twenty – while on holiday in some Spanish resort. While her husband was sunbathing only half a mile away, she had made love to both of them at once on a lonely bit of beach. I strongly suspected that it was all invented, but I was in the right mood for it to hold my attention and, after a couple of paragraphs, I stopped; I made a fresh mug of coffee and settled down in comfort with my dressing gown undone and my nightdress up around my waist to start reading again from the beginning. I wanted to take time to enjoy the morning, the description and the feelings that it brought. I was wet almost straight away, but I relished the feel of my fingers caressing between my legs and occasionally I would slip a finger up inside for a moment. I was in no hurry, deliberately prolonging the pleasure.

It was so easy to visualise the two eager young men, fresh and inexperienced, but so enthusiastic. I could imagine the feeling of having one inside me and tasting the other on my tongue, exactly as the woman described. Many times I brought myself to the brink of orgasm and, when I was nearly there, I withdrew my fingers from the cleft, stroked instead the inside of my thighs and my thick bush of hair. I tasted my fingers, and liked the taste. It was so intimate; the boys would have savoured it too, tasted it themselves, and I would have tasted it on their fingers, on their lips and on their stiff young pricks. Still I didn't let myself climax; I wanted to make this one last.

A few pages on from that letter was the set of photographs which had been the centre of so much of the conversation last night, showing a girl on a beach.

She too was masturbating, or pretending to anyway. The difference was that she had shaved her pubic hair, and she looked stunning. Mike had mentioned once having a girlfriend who shaved, and how much he had liked it, so, when David admitted that he never had, he seemed sad.

With their comments in mind, I took off my dressing gown and nightdress and tried to imagine what it would be like. It was hard to visualise, so then I went up to the bedroom and stood in front of the full-length mirror, trying to see myself as someone else, a man, would see me. I tried to picture how I would appear if I didn't wear that conspicuous dark triangle like a badge in the centre of my body. I've a thick growth of hair and I have always been pleased with it because, although I had not been to bed with many men before I was married (and with none since), the one man that I'd lived with previously had often said how much he liked it. He thought the hairier a girl was the better, and I suppose this had led me to assume that all men felt the same. Up until last night David had not expressed an opinion either way, but his initial reticence during that conversation unveiled more than a curiosity about a novelty. He was clearly intrigued, and when Ros pressed him, he admitted that he did find the effect appealing. I was proud of my own rich bush but, at the same time, there was no denying that this other girl was thoroughly alluring.

If I shaved, I would be completely different. Hairless, I would look more feminine and sort of vulnerable and accessible. My thoughts went back to the two boys in the letter and I sat down on the edge of the bed. Like that, with my knees together, you would not be able to tell anything; but then I slowly spread my legs wide apart and settled back on the bed, all the while savouring the show in the mirror. I could see myself clearly now, puffed and full, and could picture how it would look shaved bare. When the lads wandered by, they would just glance at me at first, as they probably did every girl on every beach, but then they would see something special, see I was not just like every girl on every beach, and they would stop and look again. Without the hair, my vagina would look more inviting; the lips were swollen and I could see the tip of my clitoris projecting out from under its hood. I pretend I haven't noticed them, but I'm secretly watching through my sunglasses and, while they're standing there, I unthinkingly brush off some sand that seems to have blown on to my stomach, and then let my hands drift lower.

The boys watch. They are so young, blond, clean and sort of brand new; self-confident and yet innocent and completely gripped by this sight: a spectacle outside their most far-fetched fantasies. Casually I raise one knee to brush the sand from the crease at the back of my thigh, to open my vulva further to their gaze. The lads like that. They move in closer, see that I know they're watching, and that I don't mind. They come right up to me then, want to look closely, impatient to learn, and I'm impatient to teach them. I have them kneel between my thighs, naive little pupils whose eager faces press close so that they miss nothing, their breath agitated and impatient on my skin. The whole area begins to glisten slightly as my fingers slither down the folds, then glide back up the plumply rounded sides, turn in and dive down either side of the long puckered lips, squeezing them together before my fingertips slide out at the bottom, then join together to travel up the middle to splay and display the gleaming focus of their attention.

I would make one of them caress my breasts, my nipples lifting and hardening between my fingers, the palm of my hand rubbing over and over across my whole chest, squashing my breasts down and almost bruising me; they would be so new but so keen; they would do it too hard, their slim bodies tanned and hard against me, pressing down on me until it hurts: impetuous hands reaching down over my smooth stomach, between my thighs, pulling them apart, roughly parting my legs, my fingers pinching my clitoris, their pricks/my fingers pushed deep up inside me and still one hand rolling my nipples to and fro as I urge them to fuck me as hard as they can; to drive their pricks deep into my cunt, hurting me, torturing me with the pleasure; I would be helpless – they are so much stronger than me – and they would make me take them in my mouth; make me taste the cream of my own arousal on their pricks on my fingers, and they would force open my mouth as they had my thighs and make me take them deep into my body, far down my throat and at the same time high up into my cunt, their sperm shooting up right inside me, invading me time and time again as I thrash about gripped beneath their tightly muscled limbs, and still they would go on, they fuck me and fuck me until – until at last my whole body melts, my nerves on fire, exploding between my legs and up over and through my whole body, taking me over and numbing my brain.

Slowly my feet slithered back down to the floor and my eyes focused again on the bedroom and on the mirror, on my naked body sprawled open on the bed and on my fingers still gently caressing out the last few twitches of pleasure, still half dreaming.

It was all too strong a dream to be discarded, too glorious and rich, and I knew that if I ever wanted to live such a dream then I needed to shave too; I could hardly blame David for not being the lover that I wanted if I were not the woman he wanted.

I fetched some scissors and went into the bathroom, where I sat on the bidet and carefully snipped off as much as I could. Then I fetched my make-up mirror, a new disposable razor and some shaving soap, and lathered up the remaining stubble.

As I picked up the razor, the doorbell rang. I sat still and waited for the intrusion to go away, but it rang again, longer. I cursed as I pulled the dressing gown back on but still hoped it would be something I could ignore. Cautiously, I peered out through the bathroom window and, just as I did so, Geoff's wife, Patti, peered up from outside. She saw me.

'Hi, Helen. Come on, let me in. I'm bloody freezing down here!'

I smiled as sweetly as I could and suggested silently she might put on something more substantial than a little vest, and cursed again as I sat back down on the bidet and rinsed off all the shaving foam I had so recently and so carefully applied.

I don't like Patti; I never have, and I don't think she likes me, though she won't admit it. She's not really one of our group, because whereas Geoff, David and I are all of a similar age, a couple of years over thirty, Patti is barely twenty-five. Yet, even despite being much younger than any of the other managers' wives, she always acts as if she is the senior member of the group; as if she is more experienced and knowledgeable than any of us and that we should appreciate her guidance. She is thoroughly spoilt and she makes-up, dresses and behaves exactly the part of the trophy wife; she only manages to be taller than any of us by wearing such ridiculous heels. She plays the boss's wife perfectly – always friendly to the staff, always 'one of the girls' – but she intrudes where she isn't wanted. She's always on about Geoff this and Geoff that, and I don't believe it's because her husband really features so large in her life; I think she just wants to keep reminding me of the power that her husband has over mine. Some of the other wives call her Barbie, because she has such big pointed breasts and thick blonde hair on her thick blonde head; we have suspicions about the breasts and the hair.

As I dried myself hurriedly, I wondered whether I had time to dress, but decided against it; she would complain if I took too long and, besides, a dressing gown would show clearly she was not expected to stay. I tied the dressing-gown belt tight, put on a smile and opened the door. She pushed straight past me.

'Sorry to be so early. Did I get you out of bed? Geoff's sodding car won't start again. He's only had the thing six months. It's ridiculous. Anyway, wifey had to get up and dress and drive him down to the golf-club. Christ, you look shattered! Did you have a late night last night? Sorry! You probably had the same as me. A couple of drinks on a Friday night and dear old Geoff is chasing me all round the house.'

I think I blushed, but I led her into the kitchen.

'Coffee?'

'Oh, yes, that would be great. We had to leave in such a rush I didn't have time for anything this morning. Still, I thought I'd look in as I was passing. Well, to be honest, Geoff asked me to call. Apparently David has some magazine that Mike had left here last night that Geoff wanted to borrow. Or something. I honestly don't know why they don't get one each. Stupid kids, they are sometimes. Is it around?'

'Oh yes,' I said. 'I think it's in the sitting room.'

I was making the coffee and she wandered through. I could see the room and immediately realised that not only was the magazine in there, lying spread open on the floor at a full-page picture of a naked girl, but my nightdress was draped over the settee next to it. I hoped Patti wouldn't put the two together. She did.

'Hello, what's all this? Smutty pictures and clothes strewn around the room? Has our Helen been having a quick feel while she was all alone? I'd better ring David and tell him to get home quick! Hey, you haven't got someone upstairs, have you?'

She was trying to make a joke, but I was still

92

embarrassed at her deductions and annoyed at her insinuations.

'No, of course not,' I called back.

'Shame!' She sat down and I could see her picking up the magazine as I poured the coffee.

'The boys kept talking about this shaved girl this morning. She is very pretty, don't you think?'

I said nothing, but Patti was not to be put off. She called again.

'Helen? Do you think she looks pretty?'

This was too direct to ignore.

'Well, yes, I suppose she is rather.'

'Yes, so do I.' There was a pause. 'Have you ever tried shaving?'

'Er, no. No, I haven't.'

'No, I suppose not. I don't imagine you have enough down there to be worth it.'

It was typically Patti; said to sound like no more than an offhand comment, but still intended to wound.

'Actually, you're quite wrong, Patti.'

She looked up, surprised, perhaps even shocked at the sharpness of my tone as I returned with the mugs.

'Sorry, Helen, love, I didn't mean to be rude. So you were shaving, were you?'

I didn't want to answer, because I don't like lying and I couldn't see that it was any of her business. Of course she meant to be rude, and we both knew she did but, by pretending otherwise, she could prevent my responding.

'Here you are: coffee.' I practically thrust the mug into her face.

She was still sitting in the armchair, the magazine open beside her, but she didn't take the mug.

'Let's have a look. Was it difficult?'

'No!' I said, and I almost laughed. I wasn't entirely sure whether she really expected me to take her seriously. 'No, you can't!'

'So you *were* shaving! Come on! Let me see!'

93

And there was nothing I could do. I was standing with a full mug of hot coffee in each hand and she simply reached out, took hold of the hem of my dressing gown and lifted the two sides apart. She stared in at my pussy and laughed.

'That looks absolutely awful, Helen! Like a half-plucked chicken! You can't leave it all like that!'

'I didn't intend to actually, Patti. I hadn't finished when you turned up.'

'Oh well, I see. I suppose that might explain it. I'll give you a hand then, if you like.'

'No, it's all right, thank you. I can manage quite well on my own.'

'It's no problem. That's what friends are for.' Then, still holding the dressing gown open, she looked up at me with a half smile and leant forward even closer, wrinkling her nose.

'Rather a strong scent here, Helen, if I may say so. It seems to me that you were doing a bit more than shaving while you had the chance all on your own, weren't you?'

She smirked up at me as I felt the scarlet blush blaze right across my face.

'I don't know what you mean.'

'Oh, yes you do; little Helen's been having feelies!'

She finally dropped the side of my dressing gown back and took one of the coffee mugs. I turned away, trying to close the dressing gown with one hand, and sat opposite her.

She laughed at my embarrassment. 'Never mind. Don't worry. I'll make sure Geoff takes your David to one side and has a quiet word with him. Get him to be a bit more attentive in future. We can't have you left to do it all for yourself!'

'Don't be ridiculous, Patti. There's no need at all for anything like that.'

'Oh, don't be so uptight, Helen. I'll be ever so discreet.'

'Please, Patti, just leave it.'

She stared at me a moment. 'Well, all right, I won't say anything about that if you let me help you finish shaving. You must let me do my good deed for the day.'

'I really don't need your help, thanks all the same.'

She smiled still, there seemed to be nothing that would stop that, but there was determination in the smile. 'One or the other, Helen. What will Geoff say if I have to tell him that you were so unfriendly and wouldn't let me help out where I can? Now, which is it to be?'

She knew she had me cornered, and must have realised that there was only one choice I could make. I tried to make the best of it.

'All right. If you could help me shave, that would be kind of you.'

'Good. I'm only too glad to be able to help.'

She took out her cigarettes and waved one in the air. 'You don't mind, do you?'

'Well, actually I would really rather you didn't.'

'Oh, all right then; I'll open the window.' She took out her heavy gold lighter and lit the cigarette.

'Now, let's go and finish you off. In the bathroom, were you?'

There was going to be no way I could stop her, so I followed her upstairs and into the small bathroom off our bedroom. The shaving brush and cream were still prominently laid out beside the bidet.

Patti looked round the cramped little bathroom, twittered, 'How sweet!' and then took up a seat on the edge of the bath, directly in front of the bidet.

'I'll sit here, so we can chat while you do it. Take off the dressing gown. You'll only get it wet.'

I was tempted to refuse, but in truth there was little point in keeping it on, since I would have to unfasten it and sit with my legs open anyway. I turned and untied the belt, slipped it off and hung it on the back of the door. When I turned back completely naked, Patti smiled with almost triumphant good cheer. I quickly sat down on the bidet and took up the shaving brush again.

Patti sniffed, squinting through her cigarette smoke, and nodded down at my breasts.

'Your tits aren't very big, are they? I'd always imagined they would be bigger than that. Still,' she went on, 'that's often the way. You expect people to be one sort and they turn out another. Don't you find that?'

'I don't really know what you mean,' I replied. I sat with my legs clamped tightly together, making myself busy working up a lather in the shaving bowl.

'Well, don't you and David wonder about other people? Heavens, Geoff and I do it all the time. Normally we get it right, but sometimes we are utterly wrong. Take your David, for example. We both assumed he would be circumcised. Don't know why; he just seemed the sort.'

She saw me looking at her in horror and laughed again.

'Oh, don't worry! I haven't been to bed with him or anything. No, Geoff checked him out in the showers after some office football game. He's not very long, I gather.'

She took a sip at her coffee mug, watching me over the rim, and waved airily in the direction of breasts again. 'What size are you?'

'36,' I muttered.

'But a B?'

'Yes.'

'Yes, you see I would have thought a C, from seeing you dressed. You must have very ingenious bras! Geoff will be surprised, because I bet he takes them for a fair bit bigger.'

'I don't see that he will ever know.'

'Oh, I have to tell him!'

'Why?'

'I tell him everything; after all, he's my boss too.' She laughed gaily and, while I was still working out the ambiguous meaning of her remark, she leant forward without a word and quite brazenly took hold of my breast in her hand, scooping it up and squeezing me painfully.

'Bit floppy though,' she added as she continued to roll and knead my breast. 'You should do more exercise. That would tone them up.' She finally released me and sat back before she curled her middle finger against her thumb and then flicked, hard, at my nipple. I was utterly shocked and horrified, not just at the pain but that she could so casually be so cruel. When I cried out, she merely giggled and did it again on the other nipple, and smirked again.

'It makes your whole tit wobble. You really should firm up your muscles, you know, before they get even worse. A bit of regular exercise, instead of lying here masturbating, would work wonders.' She sat up straight, pushing her own chest out. 'Like mine, see?'

'Yes,' I said. 'I see.'

Eventually I had to accept that I'd worked up as much of a lather as I could possibly need and so I started gently brushing it round and over the stubbly remains of my hair. I tried to ignore Patti sitting there, and concentrate instead on soaping myself, but she must have understood my intention and, since she couldn't stomach being ignored, she reached over and grasped my breast again.

'They are ever so soft, though. Even the nipples.' She pulled at them both in turn, twisting and pinching until she had succeeded in working them both up to erect points. I wished she would stop, because callous and brutal though her action was, no one can sit unmoved for long while their nipples are fondled.

Finally she sat back and surveyed the results. 'There. They respond well, don't they?' She tossed her cigarette into the lavatory and didn't bother to flush it.

I put down the brush and started on the main triangle with the razor. It was surprisingly easy, and cut long clean swathes through the dark hair until very quickly all the front was done. This left the part I was dreading: the area between my thighs and along my lips. If I'd been alone, it would have been no trouble, but I couldn't do this area without opening my legs wide and displaying myself entirely to the conceited meddling woman sitting so close in front of me.

What was even worse, was that after the personal comments she had made about my breasts, I expected her to be even more insulting about my vulva.

Again, I had no choice if I was going to get this dreadful business over and get her out of my house as soon as possible. I pushed my bottom further forward, opened my legs and tried to cover myself with my hand. It didn't work, because Patti leant forward again to get a clearer view as I scraped the razor across the dip between my thigh and my pussy and, as more of the lather and the hair was removed, more of my vulva was revealed.

'Good heavens, Helen. What massive lips you have! And your clit. It's almost like a little cock! How wonderful! Geoff would love that. He will be intrigued.'

'Look, Helen, I really wish you wouldn't tell him about this. It doesn't concern him in the least.' I was so desperate, I even tried some simpering bribery. 'Let's just keep it between the two of us. Between friends.'

'Oh, don't be silly. He'll love to hear.'

There was no point in continuing, so rather than give her the satisfaction of having me beg, I stayed silent as I sat in front of her with my legs splayed obscenely while she sat opposite and watched. In spite of her, the effect that was emerging was all I'd hoped for and, when I managed to put her out of my mind, I could appreciate the sleek sensuality of being so smooth and accessible. Finally I shaved away the last few strands and rinsed myself off.

Patti bent down to look closely and even reached forward to push my knees further apart.

'You know, that does look very pretty. You've ended up making quite a good job of it, and it really does make it look much more attractive, even yours. You know what? I'm even tempted to let you trim mine as well. Just the edges, and right underneath. I don't want the whole lot off, because mine's quite fine, light and silky, not at all like you, but a little trim might be fun.'

I wanted to protest, to tell her she had no right to ask me to trim her pubic hair but, without waiting for any response, she stood up and started unfastening her belt, kicking off her shoes and suddenly it all became too late. She slid down her tailored slacks and knickers in one go and that was it: she was standing naked from the waist down. I reached for my dressing gown, but she stopped me.

'Don't put that on, Helen. Stay as you are.'

'If you don't mind, Patti, I think I'll put it back on now.'

'No, Helen. I've asked you to leave it off. You look fine naked, and I prefer you like that; it seems more fitting somehow. Besides,' she added with an innocent shrug, 'now that I've seen you, what's the point?'

There was a real coldness and determination in her voice that intended to be obeyed. I hesitated and then hung the gown back on its hook.

She took my place sitting on the bidet, and then told me to stand in front of her and bend forward. At first I couldn't work out what she meant, but I leant forward a bit until she told me to hold my hands behind my back and lean forward as far as I could.

When I stood like this, it was clear what she wanted. When I leant forward my breasts swayed down and she reached up to squeeze and fondle them, even lightly patted one breast on the side and we both watched it quivering. Then she smiled up at me and, as I automatically smiled back, she slapped me, really hard on the side of the breast and then backhanded across my nipples. I know I cried out and pulled back, protecting myself with my own hands, but she ignored my protestations.

'That'll remind you not to disobey me again. Now,' she continued, immediately back to her bright cheerfulness, 'time for you to trim my little puss.' And she sat back and opened her legs wide, gently teasing at her thin blonde bush. 'You see. My hair is very fine and ladylike. Not at all like you were, see?'

The stinging in my breasts was beginning to subside and, although my eyes were blurred by tears, I looked down where she said. Her hair certainly wasn't nearly as thick as mine and I could see the crease of her neatly closed vulva perfectly clearly through it. The hair itself was almost golden and contrasted with her tanned skin, a tan which extended all over, and I remembered her saying once that she and Geoff both frequently sunbathed nude.

'Now, you'll have to kneel down here in front of me, so you can reach properly.'

When I was in a position that she considered satisfactory, she opened her legs and pulled the outer lips apart with her fingertips, still smiling at me.

'There! My little lips are much more delicate and feminine, see?'

So I looked, and could see every detail of her body, and the vision burrowed under my protection. I'd never seen another girl's body like this before – had never even seen my own as clearly as this – and though I couldn't help being excited, I was also embarrassed and found it difficult to look her in the face. But, most intriguing of all, she was so different from me. When she released her lips, whereas my pussy stays open like a grand flower, hers closed up like a shell so that no part of her vulva was visible except the long straight slit.

'Now,' she said, then lifted her feet up on to the sides of the bidet, gripped hold of the basin to keep her balance, and spread her legs wide. This not only exposed her vulva again, it also pulled open her tiny little inner lips so that I could see the pinkness inside and even a drop of dew gathered at the join. Her clitoris was covered by a long thin hood that ran almost halfway down the length of her crease, and although her inner lips were very skinny, it all still seemed puffy, and the scent of arousal was clearly no longer coming just from me. She held her lips open again, and casually brushed her thumb over her clitoris a couple of times.

'Fetch the shaving brush again, and just do the sides, down here and along the lips.' She indicated the insides of her thighs and the outer lips, all lightly covered with a fine down, where she wanted me to shave.

'Actually, hold on a mo.' She grabbed hold of the basin and carefully lowered her feet back down to the floor. 'I need a wee.'

I started to move back discreetly, but she stopped me. 'No, stay there, Helen. I want you to watch.' And so, while I was still kneeling directly in front of her, she spread her knees again, and as my eyes were automatically drawn to the gap between them, a thin golden stream of piss shot straight out into my bidet, splashing noisily on to the clean shiny surface. She just sat there smiling and unabashed while I knelt in front of her and waited, trying not to look.

In the middle of the flow, as we sat listening to the steady stream, she jerked her chin towards the basin.

'Which is your toothbrush?'

'The green one.'

She picked it out, studied it a moment and then her actions seemed almost like a film in slow motion. I just knelt there, unable even to move or try to stop her, as she deliberately lowered it between her thighs, to dip it directly into the thin yellow arc of pee flowing out of her. I bowed my head, utterly hypnotised by the slender fingers that slowly twirled the handle around until she was satisfied that all the bristles were completely soaked. As the stream began to slow, she lifted it out and shook it briefly, so that drops of her urine flew off on to her thighs and on to my breasts. Then she sat and held it up, looking at the brush, looking at me, and saying nothing. Even so, I knew – we both knew – what she required, and the silence somehow developed its own command; finally I relented. I leant forward and opened my mouth so she could push the brush into my mouth and I could suck off the last few bitter, sour drops.

Then she dropped it back into the tooth mug.

'There!' Her voice was as light and jolly as if she were a young dental nurse. 'Now you'll think of me whenever you clean your teeth.'

I just knelt in appalled silence with my head hung down, horrified at my own weakness. As the trickle finally stopped, I looked up to find her sparse blonde hairs were sparkling with golden drops. She sighed.

'That's better, but rather smelly. You had better rinse me off first. Have you got that flannel?'

She was sitting looking straight at my face flannel still lying across the bath where I had put it, so I wiped her carefully, vainly trying to ignore the low soft ridges of her lips that I could feel through the cloth.

'Right, now you'll be able to do it better.'

I took up the brush again and lathered across her open crease and down the sides. In the middle of this, she suddenly caught hold of my chin, raised my head and giggled.

'God! Just look at your boobs! You can see my handprints as clear as anything, right across your nipple, look!'

She absent-mindedly traced her finger round the hot outline of her handprint as I finished applying the lather. Finally, glad to be nearing the end of this grotesque charade, I took the razor and shaved down the insides of her pale sinewy thighs. Moving on to the actual lips, I reached forward and pulled the lips out, stretching the skin tight and carefully shaving the length of each soft puffy roll. Although I tried to be as precise as I could, it was impossible to avoid touching the inside of her lean pale lips, and even the narrow central rise over her clitoris. I found myself thinking that if it had been anyone but Patti, I might have been tempted to take longer and make more of it, but with her I just wanted it all to be over.

At last I was done, and rinsed off the final flecks of soap. Although the covering had been very light, now that it was all gone, the slim delicacy of her lips was fully revealed and there could be no denying the seductive fragility of so sweetly closed a fold.

She peered down but it seemed nothing ever satisfied her.

'Get the mirror. I can't really see much from here.'

When I offered it to her she didn't move, just waited for me to hold it up for her and angle it so she could examine, as if she were at the hairdresser's, the results of my efforts. Then she cocked her head to one side until at last she had seen enough.

'Yes, that's very nice. Well done. I'll have to come back and let you do it every time. This is much better than going to that dreadful place in town.'

She was still bobbing her head from side to side as she spoke and her slim fingers were opening her lips to examine the inside.

'It is surprising how different we are, though, isn't it? I mean, you can hardly see my clitoris at all, it's completely covered, but yours is so huge, and so visible.'

She was bemused and engrossed, suddenly seeming concerned as if she had only just considered the possibility that in some way I might have bettered her.

She pushed the mirror away and sat up demurely with her knees together.

'Show me yours again. Sit up here on the bath and let me see.'

'Please, Patti, I think that's enough. You helped me shave and now I've done you. I really must get dressed and, besides, the boys will finish their golf and be back soon.'

'Helen, I'm not asking you; I'm telling you. Just do as I say. After all,' she continued innocently, 'I haven't yet decided whether I really ought to tell Geoff that I caught you masturbating.'

There was steely cold in her eyes as she stared at me, and no doubt that she intended to get just what she wanted by whatever means she needed to use. When I didn't move immediately she casually leant forward and took hold of my nipple tight between her thumb and forefinger and simply pulled, twisting viciously as she did so. I tried to brush her off but she wouldn't let go, so I had no choice but to scramble up and sit in front of her where she indicated. Only then did she release my nipple, but she immediately grabbed hold of my knees and angrily yanked my legs wide open.

'That's better. Now I can see you properly,' she said.

She stared a moment before she leant forward again and, in that dreadful moment, I knew that looking was no longer going to be enough. She had already touched my breasts, but now she was going to want to touch me more, touch me deeper, more privately. She reached out and took hold of both my inner lips together in her hand and squeezed.

'These really are huge. I've never seen lips as loose and floppy as this before. I mean there's practically a whole handful.' She looked to me for some comment, but I ignored her. I could say nothing that she wouldn't twist and turn to hurt me further.

Although she let go eventually, she still stayed

examining me closely and then neatly laid my inner lips apart, peeled them open, pinching me between her thumb and forefinger and stretching the lips out and apart.

'I can pull you right open, and your clit hood is so loose. I can roll it right back so practically your whole clit is visible.'

She pushed the hood upward, exposing my clit, and then scraped her finger lightly across the tender top, making me immediately pull away.

'Sorry!' She smiled cheerfully. 'Is that sensitive?'

'Well, yes, of course it is.'

'Oh.' And she did it again, but harder, almost scratching at me with her fingernail just to watch me flinch, and I snatched hold of her wrist and pulled her hand away. She laughed as she inspected me again, then frowned and finally stretched over to fetch a single sheet of toilet paper, folded it into a neat triangle and dipped the corner into the very mouth of my opening. She held it up, smiling triumphantly.

'There! Look! You're already wet!' She laughed as she watched me blush even redder – laughed that same victorious chuckle which I was growing to hate – and carefully laid down the evidence. 'I wouldn't be wet if it were me. I'd just be embarrassed.'

'But I am embarrassed,' I protested.

'Maybe, but you can't deny that it's made you wet, can you? Not just damp, but absolutely creaming, as we used to say.'

'I'm just not used to being so exposed.'

'But it excites you?'

'No,' I whispered.

'And me being here, making you do all this. That excites you.'

'No!' I repeated.

She continued, 'But what I wonder, Helen, is if your pussy' (and here she paused, and in case I was in any doubt what she meant, prodded her fingers up and down the lips, cheerfully flapping them from side to side) 'is as puffed out and wet as this now, what on earth is it like when you're really stimulated?'

I could find no way out of her traps and stayed silent.

'I know. Fetch your vibrator.'

I was astounded at her bluntness but answered immediately. 'I don't have one.'

'Yes, you do, Helen, don't tell lies. David told Geoff that you have one. Go and fetch it.'

I stood up and went through to the bedroom. It seemed almost normal now to be walking about naked at her command, but I started when I looked up to see she had followed me into the bedroom. She'd even had the nerve to put on my own dressing gown, which she was tying as she walked in. Quickly I retrieved the vibrator and closed the drawer of the bedside table before she saw the handcuffs in there and started asking about them too.

She took the vibrator from me, obviously fascinated as she turned it over in her hands, switching it on and off before offering it back to me again.

'There you are, then. Lie down on the bed and masturbate again.'

I stared, probably open-mouthed. I must have looked a complete fool, but this was too much. I knew I'd already allowed myself to be pushed further than I should, but I still had some self-respect and I stood up straight and finally found the courage to look her in the eye.

'No, Patti. I'm sorry, but there are some things that I won't do.'

'Don't be silly, Helen. You've already done it to yourself once today. I can see no reason why you shouldn't do it again. Unless you want everyone at the office to hear about it, of course. And about this.' She waved the vibrator in the air.

I took it from her, embarrassed at the way she brandished it about so carelessly.

'Why do you want me to?'

'I just want to see what you look like. Obviously it's not something I ever do, and I'm interested.'

She sat down on the end of the bed and patted the mattress. 'Come on, lie down here.'

Unable to think of any way out, I did as she said, settling myself down on the mattress, my legs sticking out towards her, but ashamed of how naked I must look now that I was completely shorn.

Patti almost sniggered as I stretched out in front of her.

'Your tits practically disappear when you lie down, don't they? They go so flat there's not much more than a nipple left.' She poked and prodded at the soft flesh, eventually taking hold of my nipple again and dragging it up, twisting as she did so to watch the tears come back to my eyes as the skin was stretched so tight. 'Doesn't David mind you having such floppy tits?'

'If you must know, David rather likes my breasts.'

She scoffed again. 'Breasts? Those aren't breasts, Helen. I have breasts. Those are just tits.'

I shut my eyes and tried to fathom what on earth had let me allow her to find the wretched magazine and, after that, how I'd allowed each step to follow each dreadful step. I couldn't move, I couldn't bring myself to masturbate here in front of her for no reason other than that she wanted to watch me humiliate myself. I dropped the vibrator down and covered my face in my hands.

'Of course,' Patti said, as if continuing a conversation, 'I could always tell Geoff that you paraded around in front of me naked and tried to get me into bed. He would be surprised, but when I told him all the intimate details – about you answering the door wearing nothing but a dressing gown; you asking me to help you shave;

107

you sitting in front of me with your legs wide open; you showing me your vibrator – well! I know which of us he will believe.'

I swallowed and almost sobbed as the spiteful twisted words slipped so calmly from her honey mouth, for I knew that she would do exactly as she said if she did not get her way. Then I reached down and took up the vibrator again.

Normally I dislike using the vibrator because it's so fast and efficient, but I felt that now that would be an advantage. I switched it on, still just low, took a deep breath and then slid it into the warm damp crease between my closed thighs. Patti snorted with irritation.

'That's no good. You'll have to open your legs again or I can't see a thing.'

'This is how I do it,' I said.

'I don't believe you.' Patti's comment was not a challenge, just a simple quiet statement of fact as she inspected my quivering fingers.

I slid open my legs but Patti leant forward and, without warning, slapped me again, as hard as she could, across my thighs. Before I realised what she was doing, she took hold of my knees and wrenched them apart, bending my legs right up to expose me completely. Then she ran her hands right up the inside of my thighs and pushed her thumbs into my pussy. I felt them penetrating roughly inside me, both together, before she moved on to spread open my long inner lips and push back at the hood of my clit again. I could feel tears beginning to well up, from the surprise and sting of the slap, but also from the shame and disgrace of what she was demanding. But her eyes were still alert, waiting for another chance to punish me, so I quickly brought my hands back to my pussy and started to fondle my own swollen lips, and seek some consolation in a more familiar and delicate caress.

I thought she was done, but a smile came back to her

face and her hand crawled steadily back up my thigh to the open lips at the top. Then she carefully lifted the delicate loose skin from over my clit until, holding just a tiny fold lightly in the very tip of her finger and thumb, she pulled it up free.

'Remember, Helen dear –' and she raised her eyes to my face '– if you disobey me, I have to hurt you. Don't I?' As I lay under her gaze, we both knew she was going to hurt me, and we both waited for her to do it. Ever so slowly she nipped the little corner of skin tighter and tighter, and when I gasped she ignored me, and when she had it pinched just between her nails, I cried but still said nothing. When her nails were steadily digging right into me, harder and deeper, I finally gave in and she stopped at once. After all, it was only the begging that she had really wanted to hear; the begging and the sobs.

'There, now don't be silly. Carry on.'

This time I slipped the vibrator down the full length of my crease, then brought it back up to catch just under the tip of my clit hood. Now that I'd accepted the task, it was shamefully easy. Even following so quickly on the earlier, glorious and private release, there was no resisting the steady low trembling of the machine. The effect was immediate. I could feel my lips swelling even more, and the moisture that had already been seeping down from deep up inside me began to flow more freely. As my clit hardened, I felt it pushing forward even further, reflected by a look of eager desire growing on Patti's face. She was clearly longing to touch me again, looking for any excuse to continue her exploration of my sex. I ran the tip of the vibrator in circles round the thick skin over my clit and then into the entrance to my vagina. It felt good there, so sensitive, so moist and so tempting, quivering just far enough away from my clit to stop me overdoing it but just close enough to feel the vibrations there too. It was all so tantalising, quivering at the very rim and, holding the lips wide open with one hand, I could slide it in gentle circles round the whole opening. My thighs and bottom clenched automatically as I twisted my legs together and focused on the quiverings growing deep within me.

My mood was shattered by Patti, snorting with impatience. She snatched the vibrator from me and, with no preparation, shoved it straight up inside me. 'There! Fuck yourself with it.'

When I didn't obey immediately, but just lay there with the object buzzing obscenely inside me, she grabbed it again and brutally thrust it in and out, deliberately hurting and bruising me until I managed to get the thing back from her and continue more gently.

I pulled the slippery round shaft almost out and then pushed it in deeper until I felt the whole length filling me but, as I slid it slowly back and forth, the loathsome mimicry intensified the stimulation. When it was in deep, the vibrations were much more muted, but when I gripped it tight from inside they seemed to spread out right through me, unbearably intense so that I slowly drew the glistening stem back out again, and ran it round the outside of my lips.

Patti's piercing attentive eyes never left my circling fingers, but she could barely stay still, squirming as she stared avidly. A couple of times her hands slipped down into her lap and under the dressing gown, so that I wondered whether she was about to give in and join me on the bed, but the fear of a loss of control was evidently greater than the pleasure to be gained. Still, she did reach up hesitantly to my breast again, and this time gripped me more gently, stroking me with something much more like a caress than her previous cruel rasps.

She practically whispered, 'They're so soft, your breasts, such velvety nipples. Now,' she said, and leant down to plant a light kiss on my nipple and rest her hand on the top of my thigh, just suggesting she could reach out and touch me if she chose. 'Now,' she whispered, 'make yourself come.'

I looked up at her then, to take in and build on the curious superiority that glowed from behind her eager malicious eyes as she surveyed the display she had orchestrated. Still she held my breast, squeezed painfully at it and smirked as I winced, but I reached up to squeeze the other one myself, and pushed the vibrator right up against the underside of my clit, directly squashing down against the delicate tip and the sensitive little spot just beneath. As I pressed harder and traced tiny rings round my bud, my breath groaned out in long drawn whimpers, and I was rocked by waves of such strength that I clamped my legs together again, holding in the pressure flowing from inside and clenching the vibrator tight into the crease while I sobbed out the strength of the shame, the exposure, the release and the pleasure of the degrading spectacle that I had been forced to present at the command of the smug grinning bitch who sat so placidly beside me and watched.

I finally turned off the vibrator and drew my legs back together, feeling the stickiness squeezed out and trickling down on to the bed-cover. Patti was still gazing at my bare sex as she pulled my dressing gown more firmly closed around herself.

'Yes. Good. That looked really nice,' she said. 'When I come back for my next trim, I think I'll have you do that to me. Only I don't think I'd really want the vibrator; that seems too mechanical and efficient, somehow. I think I'll want you to use your fingers. And maybe your tongue.'

6

Carol's Tale – The Reflected View

I'm still not certain whether Robert believed that the carriage was empty or not. Robert was facing me, and the other man was in the next bay behind him and on the other side of the carriage. Certainly he was out of Robert's line of sight, but he was in front of me and a little to the right, on the opposite side of the aisle. You get the picture? He wasn't particularly attractive, rather bald, but I think prematurely so, because I do not suppose he was much over forty. He had an appealing face, very round, kind and understanding but, taken altogether, nothing very remarkable. I'd noticed him when we got on at Waterloo because he was right by the door and we had to climb past his luggage, but we hadn't spoken to him. In any case the train hadn't stopped anywhere for him to get off so, unless Robert had forgotten about him entirely, he must have known he was still sitting there. Overall, I think probably he did. I want him to have known, so, in my memory, he did.

It was Robert's birthday and we had been to London to have a meal out and see a musical and were now heading back home. The whole day had been a treat for us, one that we had both been looking forward to for many weeks and which had completely lived up to our expectations. It had been warm and sunny during the day, and London still held enough visitors to retain some of its holiday atmosphere. Robert had held my hand while we walked and I like that. In fact we had both been very affectionate all day. I was feeling completely at ease with myself and content with the world at large.

I had bought some new clothes specially for the day and I felt elegant and attractive, all dressed up in a way that Robert liked and that showed me off well. I wore a very pale green silk blouse and a matching greenish-grey skirt and jacket, which buttoned down the front and was fairly tight. The skirt was long – about mid-calf – and loose. At Robert's request I was wearing no bra, and stockings, the sort that stay up by themselves, rather than tights. Actually, he looked good sitting there too, wearing what we always called his interview suit, much smarter clothes than he would normally wear. Don't get me wrong, I like his usual style, but this made a nice change and it suited him. Even though we'd been living together for more than three years, I found myself sitting there and thinking, I fancy that man. Quite silly, really.

But in fact our love life had been subdued recently. It wasn't simply that Robert had been working very hard and often late into the evenings, indeed that may well have been a result more than a cause. Over the years that we'd been together it had lost much of the fire that it had held in the early days. It was satisfying, physically satisfying, that is, in that I always had an orgasm, but it was all so comfortable, so predictable and uninterest-ing. Consequently, it was also much less frequent; our sex life was growing middle aged before we were and, although nothing was ever said, we both knew. It needed shaking up somehow, given a new vitality, made less predictable and more dangerous.

However, this was Robert's birthday, and I knew, and he knew, and we both knew that the other knew, that we would make love when we got home. All day long, from when he had watched me getting dressed, there had been an unspoken anticipation, surreptitious kisses in the theatre and gropes on the underground. It had all been unrestrained, undignified, with an adolescent carelessness of being seen kissing; a steady build up which we knew this time would be consummated.

The evening was still warm but it was getting dark and, as the train rattled along behind the rows of Victorian houses, we could see all the windows lit up as we passed. The lights glowed warm and yellow and cosy and the glimpses of domesticity in the kitchens and living-rooms showed a world at peace. Even the few curtained windows seemed tranquil; the curtain being not so much a barrier excluding us as much as a demonstration that there was an enclosed family within. The flickering on the train windows reinforced the security and serenity of it all so that sitting there just with Robert (the other man was deep in his newspaper) I felt almost as if I were at home in front of the flickering fire, comfortable, secure and, I suppose, quite romantic.

The train slowed to a gentle lollop and passed under some of the roads that cross the track a few miles out of Waterloo Station. As we ambled beneath one of these, the sudden darkness of the brickwork outside offered a perfect reflected view of Robert sitting there looking at me. I do not suppose he could see my reflection but I could secretly spy on him. His expression was very loving but he also kept glancing down at my breasts and, as I leant over towards the window and the train jolted along, they must have been well shown off. I leant forward a little further.

When we moved out from under the bridges, and the reflection had dissolved, I turned to look straight at him, and he smiled at me warmly, lovingly and, in this mood, I leant across to kiss him and really that is what started it all going. Of course, when I leant forward,

Robert slipped his hand inside my jacket and gently cradled one of my breasts. I am quite proud of them, to be honest; they have often been admired and when I lean forward they seem quite big, bigger than they really are. My nipples are very sensitive and responsive to any attention they receive. Well, we kissed for quite a time, his tongue darting into my mouth, tasting of wine and coffee, and I started to anticipate other routes it might follow later. He stroked me all the while and my nipples perked up pretty quickly and, after a short while, I was beginning to feel more than a little damp between my legs. When we broke off and I leant back again, the other man was still hidden in his reading, so I smirked at Robert seductively and licked my lips.

'Go on,' he whispered, 'show us your breasts.'

While I certainly did not intend to go that far, I did feel loving enough, or perhaps securely wicked enough, to put on a bit of a display, so I undid my jacket and spread open the front. Then I smoothed my blouse down tight across one breast so that my very full and erect nipple was clearly outlined, the darkness showing through the thin silk. I also gave the nipple a quick couple of extra rubs because I know that seeing me do that really gets Robert going; in fact he had often asked me to let him watch me go all the way, but I never did.

'Show me,' he begged. 'I want to see.'

So, with another quick glance across the carriage, I unfastened the top two buttons of my blouse and pulled it around so that I could poke a nipple – a very rosy and eager-looking nipple I should say – out at him. A couple of tweaks to keep it erect and provocative.

Robert let his breath out. 'And the other one. Let them both out.'

I honestly don't know what came over me then. I suppose in part it was that I knew there was only one other person there and he certainly wasn't paying any attention (I checked to be sure) so, I thought, why not?

Give the boy a birthday treat. Well, all right, to be honest, I rather wanted to do it for myself as well, I mean, how many women can honestly say that they have never had slightly exhibitionist fantasies? This was probably a unique opportunity for me to indulge myself in total safety, in a place that was very obviously public and yet a little compartment that we had made our own and from which the darkness and the glass excluded the rest of the world. Even the presence of the other man, within the carriage but outside our circle, emphasised rather than reduced the security of our cocoon. And maybe I wanted to see how far it would be possible to go without his noticing anything.

Slowly and teasingly, I unbuttoned the blouse down the front, keeping the two halves together. Then, from waist level, I slipped one hand in and ran it up my side, pulling the blouse wide open as I went. When I reached the top, I circled the breast a couple of times before centring on the nipple and rolling it between finger and thumb. Robert then leant across to me and he kissed each nipple before moving up to my mouth and we kissed again, this time with his hands rubbing on my bare skin. It felt so intense that I was almost ready to slump down in front of him, to follow as far as he wanted to lead.

Halfway through the kiss I opened my eyes and met the gaze of the other man, staring at us. I don't know for how long he'd been watching and I just continued to kiss Robert, all the while watching this man watching me. He didn't blink or quickly look away, nor did he smile. He just sat in his seat calmly watching us.

Then I suddenly realised two things. First, I realised that when Robert stopped kissing me and pulled away, my blouse would be open and the man would be able to see my breasts, and second, I realised that the prospect of this happening was making me wetter and more excited than I'd ever been in my life. I suddenly wanted him to see me. I wanted my boyfriend to stop kissing me so I could expose my breasts to a stranger. Somehow I feel the patient, unresponsive stranger knew this too.

Robert went on kissing me and then I did something dreadful. I, Goody Two-Shoes Carol, ended the kiss. I simply pulled back a little so Robert, who obviously did not appreciate the consequences, sat up straight and looked at me and smiled. Then the man looked across at me, and *he* smiled, glanced at my face and then stared at my breasts. And I smiled; I mean, why not? As I settled back in the seat, I could feel the strength of the other man's eyes directed at me. It was a physical heat that radiated out and made me glow. I even looked across at Robert and let a few seconds pass before I rebuttoned the blouse – rebuttoned it a bit anyway.

Then Robert whispered, 'Show me some more. I really like it when you show yourself off. You're so beautiful.'

Well, I was partly looking at Robert and partly looking at the other man (who, obviously, could hear what we were saying and by now was quite openly listening). I swear to you, the other man nodded.

I said nothing. I was torn. Half of me was disgusted at how blatantly sluttish I had been already, but the other half was very aware of the growing wetness between my legs – matching the dryness in my throat – and of the faster and louder heartbeat. I knew too that I would never see the other man again and so, being quite logical, it really didn't matter one bit if he saw me or what he thought as a result. No, that's wrong, it *did* matter what he thought. It mattered very much that he liked what he saw, that he appreciated me, and on that there could be no real doubt. It was perfectly clear from his expression that the man liked what he saw very much.

I glanced across at him again and this time he did quickly look down at his paper, a totally futile gesture since we both knew that he had been watching. He was desperate not to do anything too intrusive; he wanted to witness everything and yet to remain invisible. Should I let him see me? Being blunt, he was not particularly good-looking, but neither was he too bad. He was a bit older but I suppose if Robert looked like him at that age I shouldn't complain. I quickly looked away again, afraid suddenly that Robert would be reminded of his presence, because, although Robert liked me to dress attractively and seductively, he could also be extremely jealous.

I whispered, 'You've already seen my breasts. I've already shown you my breasts. What else can I do?'

'Show me again. Show me everything. Show me all of you!' He smiled, and tried to look casual, but he was very serious beneath it, a deep-seated and quite desperate seriousness.

I just smiled back at him, fiddled with the buttons and wondered what the hell I was going to do.

'Please?' Robert begged.

'Well . . .'

I pulled the top open and looked down at the top of my breast, and at my nipple pushing out bigger and darker and harder.

'Well,' I whispered, 'I have to admit it does look nice.'

I licked my lips, undid the buttons once more and pulled the front forward a little. It was not enough for Robert to see much because I kept my hand in the way, but it was enough to show the stranger what he wanted, sitting there staring open-mouthed and completely caught up in my display. Did he know that I was letting him see deliberately? Did he know that I was displaying to him what I was hiding from Robert?

As I lay back there, I held the two men in the palm of my hand. One was a man who had seen my breasts, had seen (had touched, caressed and kissed) every inch of my body, hundreds of times. The other was a complete stranger, just a man, but any man or maybe Everyman. All I had done was allow them a glimpse behind my veil and it had put them both totally under my spell. What a power! It made me feel so sexually alive, how could I doubt myself, or doubt my sexuality when these two were living breathing (panting) proof? What woman would fail to feel the glow of pride and self-confidence in that situation? Their faces were so eager, like little boys gazing in a toy-shop window, and yet it was really desire, desire for me, that I was seeing reflected in their eyes. I felt it, I felt it in my heartbeat and I felt it in my womb. It elevated me to a height I'd never known before and would probably never reach again.

It was suddenly understanding that aspect, that nothing like this would ever happen again, that made me realise this high was not quite high enough. Nearly, not quite. I needed to go just one stage further. Tonight I needed to show them how high a woman could really soar. I just needed one more confirmation, needed them to sink down one more step to grovel at my feet.

I asked, 'Is this what you want to see?' and slipped my right hand inside my blouse, pinched the nipple between the tips of my fingers, and then spread the two wings of the cloth all the way open to my shoulders.

Robert gasped, 'Yes,' his eyes fixed on my gently caressing fingers. I looked across at the stranger. He was looking me straight in the eye. I fractionally raised my eyebrows and then he nodded again, no question this time.

'You must promise only to look, not touch,' I said, and that took Robert about a millionth of a second to agree.

So I leant back, diagonally along the seat and into the corner and shrugged the blouse right off: this was not a time for half measures. I rubbed both hands down my breasts and back up again, then cradled them in my palms and caressed the nipples with my thumbs. I licked my fingers and ran them slowly around the nipples. I pinched them as hard as I could bear and pulled at them. I did everything I like to do when no one is there to see me, and I did everything I had ever seen the girls doing in films and in Robert's magazines. I was one of them. I was as good as the best of them. No model, no stripper, anywhere had ever held the attention of her audience more totally than I then held mine. Robert was entirely fixated by the sight. He had never seen me go as far as this before. When I dared to glance over at the other man, his expression was the same as Robert's. He didn't know whether to believe what he was seeing, whether he could risk blinking in case it stopped, whether to watch surreptitiously from behind the paper, pretending he was not there, or whether he was allowed, invited to see whatever was to unfold.

I kicked off my shoes, raised one leg up on to the seat and let the skirt slip down my thigh. They could both see my stocking tops and my knickers but still I just caressed my breasts all the while, sometimes licking a finger before returning to encircle a hard nipple. Then, slowly I let one hand drop down to my lap and on to my bare leg, ran it slowly up to cover my crotch and let it lie there. I paused. Slowly I pressed the heel of my palm into my pussy: round, and up, and round, and down. Again: round, and up, and round, and down. So, so slowly, so entranced, the images surging in front of my eyes of this free and totally uninhibited woman; not a lady, but a woman.

I swivelled round straight along the seat, and raised both feet on to it so that my right knee fell against the back of the seat. I slipped my hand up my skirt and down inside the waistband of my knickers; they were almost dripping. I pushed down through my little thatch, across the top of my clit (gently, I would not be able to stand too much) and deep between my thighs until I could dip my forefinger far up inside me. It was like a cauldron, so hot and so wet. Suitably moistened, I rubbed my fingertips up, over and down beside my button.

The men could now see my arm and wrist moving up and down inside my knickers, and they could imagine where my fingers were digging. But they couldn't actually see, not yet. My other hand moved down to my waist, unbuttoned and then unzipped the side of my skirt. Both the men gasped and I think it was only at that moment that they realised that this display was not going to stop. In fact the skirt was so bunched up around my waist that it hid nothing, but still somehow it suggested modesty; it was a link to respectability, and I wanted none of that. I pushed it down my hips, lifting up my bottom to let it slide down my thighs, over my knees and, hooking my thumbs into the tops of my stockings, I dragged them down with it, letting the whole lot tumble into a pile on the filthy floor.

I settled back again, pushing back into the corner where the coarse covering of the seat scraped across my back like a lover as I twisted against it. Naked now, except for my knickers, I continued palming up and over my nipples. And as I continued, I slowly let my left knee sag down towards Robert, although as I knew quite clearly, I was giving the stranger an even better show. When the leg was flat against the seat, they could both see the outline of my fingers quivering inside my knickers.

I withdrew my hand and then pulled the knickers up tight into my crease. The hair was splayed out on both sides, matted and glistening, and the sheerness and wetness of the material can really have not been much more than a token covering.

I pulled both knees up together again and glanced at my audience. They were completely, utterly hooked! I think if I'd decided to stop then they would have raped me but, in all honesty, I was no more in control than they were. Again I lifted my bottom and slipped my knickers down my legs, slowly, let them wait for me. When I pulled them over my feet I brought them up and (Christ, actually I am quite embarrassed about this bit) I sniffed them. Well, then I let both the men see the huge wet stain before I rubbed the crotch down my throat and chest and right across my nipples, round and round and leaving them even more erect and glistening than before. Then I flipped the knickers across to Robert, I believe he still has them.

From then on, I had no inhibitions at all. I had passed that point by such a margin that there could be no pretence. I was lying there as completely naked as the day I was born. I could hide nothing. I knew what they both wanted to see and I wanted – I more than wanted, I needed – the admiration, almost the reverence they gave me for showing it to them. I thrust my hands down between my thighs, pulled my legs apart and rubbed hard and rough over my clitoris and my lips, lips so puffed and full and almost burning, my clitoris pushing out, hard as a nut and ready to burst. I dipped one finger up inside and out again, then two, then three. I was panting and twisting and I just wanted to let go.

But there was still one thing I had not done and I was holding it back and savouring it. There would come a moment when I would let this audience actually look full at my pussy, no, my cunt. A moment when I would show the audience my cunt. I could clearly imagine it, peeled open, a glistening, swollen, glowing invitation. I half sat up, and turned back round with both my hands clasped between my legs, almost as if I were trying to keep from wetting myself, rested my left foot across on Robert's seat, the other foot on the floor. I parted my legs so wide that my thighs ached. Then I took my hands away, drawing one up each side, along each thigh so that my lips were pulled wide apart and everything I have was displayed to the world, so ripe, so red and dripping, absolutely dripping.

And it suddenly all became too much. With my eyes shut, I just had the image of lying there, totally naked, legs apart, pussy lips wide (was there anything else I could do?) while two men watched me. They saw me as I wanted to show them: unsophisticated, unrefined, slutty, oversexed, such a whore, and that image was just enough to tip me over the edge. I started to come and shoved fingers – I don't know, two, three, it could have been a hundred – deep, far up into my pussy while all the time rubbing my clitoris as hard and as fast as I could. I was pushing my hips up harder and further to offer them out, for someone, anyone, to take me, to fuck me, oh please, to fuck me.

When I'd come back to earth a little, I looked across at Robert and his erection was thrust unashamedly out from his trousers but was already starting to wilt, and the back of his hand and his fingers were wet and gleaming. My other admirer was holding his newspaper across his lap, but as I watched he screwed up his handkerchief and put it back in his pocket. The effect had been the same. I had given them both a show that had pushed them beyond their self-control. Robert said:

'I love you, Carol. You are so beautiful, so amazingly beautiful and so . . . I just love you.'

The stranger didn't look at me again although it was several minutes before I sat up, retrieved my clothes and put them back on, most of them; the stockings were ruined.

I sat back beside Robert and, with his arm around me, I dozed for much of the rest of the journey. When I woke up and had pulled myself back together again, it was nearly time to get off. We had stopped at three or four different places by then and at one of them my other, unknown, untouched lover had got off (and thinking about it, surely Robert must have noticed him then).

Since then I have let Robert watch me masturbate several times, but nobody else has ever seen me and, although Robert referred occasionally to that night on the train, neither of us has ever mentioned the other man. Sometimes I want to ask, but I'm afraid of what his answer might be, so I live in the doubt and the hope and whenever my fantasies turn back to that evening I remember Robert's exact opening words: 'Show us your breasts.' Not 'Show me,' but 'Show us,' and then I believe he knew.

7

Gemma's Tale – The Sales Pitch

'Well, how did it go?'
  'I got the order.'
  'And?'
  'Full commission, I reckon the order's worth practically £20,000!'
  'That's brilliant! So why are you acting like that?'
  'Like what?'
  'Well, I don't know. Odd. Guilty.'
  'Well . . .'

I sat in the car for a few minutes before forcing myself to go up to the house again. Firstly I was not completely convinced that I had understood correctly, and if I was wrong, then I was probably doing myself no good at all. However, there had been so many hints, veiled to varying degrees, but taken altogether there seemed to be only one meaning. Secondly, even if I was right in understanding what they meant, I was very far from certain that I wanted to go along with the suggestion. There were attractions, of course there were, but this was new ground for me. Barry had revealed a few fantasies along these lines, but I was uncertain whether that meant he really wanted me to act them out. However, the choice was clear: go up to the house and play this through to the end, or start the car again and drive away. Yesterday I had been the innocent, but that was not a role I could play now that I understood.

My hands were visibly quivering as they gripped the steering wheel and I could feel sweat trickling down my back. I couldn't go through with it. Then I remembered Barry's face that morning when the credit card bill arrived and the way he'd turned away from me and said nothing; it hurt to see him so worried. I pulled the sheer cotton blouse tighter over my breasts, tucked it firmly into the short skirt and stepped out of the car.

When I'd made this same journey yesterday, it had all seemed so very easy. This had promised to be a good call, and that was something that I badly needed because my quarter's figures were way down. The couple had just retired with a lump sum that they intended to spend on home improvements including double glazing the whole house. Best of all, this was not just a lead from one of our canvassers but a direct enquiry on the basis of a recommendation from friends. They had made me very welcome when I arrived. Mr Gifford was tall and slim, greying just a little but a man with great dignity; he could easily have been a retired army officer, while his wife was perhaps a little stout, with a round face and short permed hair, but she was motherly and friendly. They were both very open and direct and I knew at once that this was not going to be one of the many wasted evenings with people who are merely browsing. These two knew what they wanted and clearly had enough money to buy it.

However, as the presentation progressed, it had not proved quite so straightforward. It had started well, as I had spread out the brochures and samples of glazing styles, of frames and locks on the floor of their living room and went through my usual speech. I had kept to the familiar thread of my talk and the couple had shown sufficient interest, so that by the time I reached the end, they had evidently already made some choices but there seemed to be no real enthusiasm. I actually got the distinct impression that Mr Gifford in particular was spending more time watching me than looking at the demonstration pieces and that he was mainly hoping to see up my skirt. He had very little chance of that because I have always taken care to wear sensible skirts of a proper length when working.

At the end, Mr Gifford had cleared his throat and spoken. 'Yes, all very nice, but I haven't yet seen anything I particularly liked. How about you, dear?'

His wife had agreed. 'No, not really,' she said, and then after a pause she added, 'Not considering what a big order it would be. I suppose your commission would be more than a thousand pounds.' She had glanced over at me, and I read her expression at once to mean she anticipated a very big discount on an order like this. That was quite normal, because after all the total list price was well over £15,000 and there was certainly some room to negotiate.

I smiled my enticing smile. 'I'm sure I can do something to improve the price once we've sorted out the detail of your requirements and then we can see what the total book value of the order might be.'

Mr Gifford had sighed and looked across at her again. 'The cost isn't really the point. I don't think you dealt with our friends the Williamsons, did you? That was a young lady called Melanie, I think.'

I almost shuddered at the mention of that name. Melanie was the only other woman on the sales team and we hated each other; had done so from the moment we first met. Melanie was very outgoing and made no secret of the fact that she frequently flirted with the customers in order to get commissions and she generally used her sexuality in a way that I considered to be thoroughly unprofessional and even a little sordid. However, she was undeniably good at the job and got excellent results.

'I'm sure that I can match any terms she was able to give your friends,' I said gaily.

'Oh good,' Mr Gifford had said again. 'I understand that she was most helpful and, as I say, I haven't yet seen all that I expected.' This time his attention had been quite clearly fixed on my bosom, and he was making no attempt whatsoever to disguise it. I was starting to feel uneasy. They both sat waiting for my next move so I suggested they go through the catalogue in detail so I could mark down exactly what they required and start to work out how much discount I could offer on the list price. The suggestion clearly did not interest them, for they exchanged glances before Mrs Gifford spoke.

'Look, my dear, why don't you leave these brochures with us for now, just overnight so that we can have another look? Then you go and work out all the sums, the prices and commissions and everything and perhaps you should have a word with your friend Melanie about it all and then pop back tomorrow, and we will see if we can get it all sorted then.'

I had no intention at all of speaking to Melanie; she would only have tried to pinch the sale, but once I got home I did start working out the cost – it came to at least £18,000 including all the extra features they wanted and the prospect of a commission on that scale was very attractive.

It was not until I was standing in the bathroom in my nightdress – looking at my reflection as I washed ready for bed – that I began to get a glimmer of their meaning. Melanie was known to dress very provocatively, and obviously the old man had hoped I would flash a bit of thigh for him – like Melanie had no doubt done for his friends. Bizarre as it seemed, the more I thought about it, the more it seemed to fit. He'd said he'd not seen anything he liked – had not seen what he expected. Even Mrs Gifford had stressed the value of the order and the commission I would earn on it. She was obviously aware of her husband's little whims and ready to go along with them. It suddenly all became crystal clear. Then something else came to mind: he'd said the cost was not the problem. Maybe they did not intend to ask for a discount, although for an order as large as that, I would have been prepared to give away up to half my commission. I went back into the bedroom and was about to ask Barry whether he thought this could be remotely possible, but he lay staring up at the ceiling looking so tired that I changed my mind; he had enough to worry about already.

All night I turned the ideas over in my mind. I wasn't Melanie, but I wasn't going to let her get this order. If it meant a little mild flirtation with an old man, well, I could live with that. He was certainly not unattractive and there would be no danger of it getting out of hand with his wife there.

So the next evening I came home and dressed specially for this call. I wore one of my shortest skirts which finished well above the knee, and even some hold-up stockings. I picked out a specially lacy bra which was just visible through the slightly see-through cotton top. In all, I think I was looking quite alluring, so after that brief hesitation, I pulled the sample case out of the back of my car and walked steadily up their path.

Mrs Gifford answered the door.

'My husband is just making a couple of telephone calls and will be down in a moment. Come through, while I finish clearing up in the kitchen.' She poured out a cup of coffee for me and looked me up and down while she stirred it.

'Did you speak to Melanie?'

'No, I couldn't get hold of her,' I lied. 'I think she may be away for a while.'

'Oh. Pity. I would imagine she must be one of your most successful sales people.'

'Yes, she certainly seems to get good results. She's often the month's top earner.'

'Perhaps she has a good understanding of what it is the customers are really looking for in this sort of transaction.' She looked at me, hoping I would follow her meaning. When I made no response, she came and sat down opposite me at the little breakfast bar and folded her hands carefully in front of her.

'May I be quite frank with you, Gemma? May I call you Gemma?'

'Oh, yes, please do and please be as frank as you like.' I wasn't actually sure that I was ready for too many frank admissions, but it's difficult to say no to that question.

She hesitated. 'You look really charming tonight, very summery. I think many of your potential customers would appreciate that.'

'Thank you, that's very kind of you but – and if I may also be frank, Mrs Gifford – I'm not sure that I entirely know what you are getting at.'

She hesitated again. 'I did rather wonder whether that was perhaps the problem, and that was actually why I suggested that you speak to Melanie about it. Well, let me see. How shall I put this?' She seemed almost embarrassed and hesitated before looking firmly into my eyes and continuing. 'Melanie is a very attractive girl, as of course are you, but, to take one example as I understand it, she does not generally wear a bra when she is making her calls.' When I said nothing, she added, 'But you do.'

I could feel myself blushing. This line of conversation seemed much too personal, even with another woman, even when we had agreed to be frank. I considered her remark for a moment.

'Are you suggesting that it might be better if I followed Melanie's example?'

'Yes, dear, I do believe it would. Look. My husband

won't be down for a minute or two; why don't you nip into the loo before then and see what you can do? I'm sure it can do you no harm at all. Do remember that my husband is intending to give you a contract worth a very great deal of money, and he likes to feel his business is appreciated by those who gain from it.'

I put down the coffee cup carefully as I made my decision, although there was not much to decide. Safely locked in the lavatory, I undid my blouse, took off my bra and stuffed it in my bag. To be honest, I only wear a bra for decency as my breasts really are not big enough to need one for support. For a moment I looked at myself in the mirror, wishing that I were a little bigger; wishing, I suppose, that I were more like Melanie. I replaced the blouse, even leaving one extra button unfastened in the front. If Mr Gifford wanted a little treat as a condition for giving the order, I was prepared to go along. The dark rings of my nipples were just visible through the material, and they were pushing out unmistakable points which could not be missed.

Mrs Gifford was still in the kitchen when I came out and she gave me a little smile as I stood in front of her.

'I see you are getting the idea, my dear. Now, may I suggest something else that may help you?'

She didn't wait for my agreement but reached over and unfastened another button of my blouse, then a second before she smoothed the front of the blouse down, in the process running her hands across my breasts. I pulled away from her touch, although I'm sure it was accidental, but I hardly needed her to adjust my clothes for me.

'There. You'll find that's much cooler and I think you'll also find it helps your sale. Shall we see if my husband is ready yet?'

She showed me through into the living room again, where her husband was already sitting in the easy chair on one side of the fireplace, just as he had done the previous night. Again Mrs Gifford took her place beside me on the settee on the other side of the fireplace facing him.

Mr Gifford smiled across at me. 'This seems a little more promising. Let's see if you can show us something more to our liking this evening. I've made a note of the various things we would require and perhaps we could now price them.'

So I stretched out my legs, exposing a long length of thigh, and ran through the various choices again. On the pretext of picking up a profile sample, I even hitched the hem up a little to show the dark band at the top of my stockings. I smiled at the two of them as I launched into the speech and fluttered my eyelashes a little until I felt I was in danger of out-doing Melanie. I also gave some clear hints that the price could be fairly negotiable. I ended with one of my usual questions.

'Well, Mr Gifford, is there anything else I can tell you to show you that this really is the best choice?'

He looked a little wistfully at me, then very definitely dropped his eyes down to my chest.

'To be honest, it still doesn't seem as interesting as I'd expected. I really think it might be better if we asked that other girl, Melanie, to take the order. You wouldn't mind if we did that, would you?'

He knew very well I would mind; he knew what that meant as to who earnt the commission. He was still looking pointedly at my chest but, glancing down, it must have been obvious that I was not wearing a bra and Mrs Gifford had unfastened enough of the buttons for him to see a generous expanse of skin. My breasts are not large, and I don't have anything you could call a cleavage, but I did push my arms together to try to create a little fold in the open vee of my blouse.

'I would really like to be able to help you with this order if I can, Mr Gifford. I certainly would not like to think that Melanie was better than me in any way.' I made it sound very ambiguous, made it sound like a joke, and I laughed but received only a very polite smile in return. He sighed and turned to his wife.

'What do you think, Margaret?'

'I believe she just doesn't have the same experience as Melanie but I'm sure she would be quite happy to let us guide her. Wouldn't you, my dear?'

'Well, yes of course.'

'That's right.' She spoke almost as if she were dealing with a child, and mimed undoing a button on her blouse, as she smiled and looked pointedly at the front of my blouse and raised her eyebrows. I understood her meaning and nervously unfastened yet another button, but when I looked up she only repeated the gesture, so I undid the next below that, and finally the last three. At that she smiled.

'That's better, sweetie.' And then she leant over and slipped her hand right inside my blouse and ran it over my bare breasts before pulling the front wide open to expose me to her husband, and pulled it out of the waistband of my skirt entirely. I don't know why I didn't stop her, but she was just so calm and assured that her gesture did not seem as out of place then as it should.

As soon as she sat back, I glanced down to see that the caress she had already given me combined with the sudden exposure had caused my nipples to ripen and erect. I blushed, and started to pull the front of the blouse together again, but she stopped me.

'Oh, don't cover yourself up, sweetie, you have the most beautiful little breasts, doesn't she, Gregory?' And again she reached over to smooth the open blouse off me, and in the process first to rub her open hand over me and then actually to take one of my nipples between the tips of her fingers and pinch it to an even firmer erection. I was still shocked and, although I was ready to close up my blouse again, she brushed my hands away, making it quite clear that would be the wrong thing to do. She sat back.

'There!' she said. 'Gorgeous. You're just so tiny!' Then she leant over and whispered to me as her fingertips traced round the circle of my nipple. 'I really do wish I had such sweet little breasts myself, and I'm sure Gregory does as well.'

Mr Gifford simply smiled, and did not deny the suggestion, but he still said nothing direct about the fact that I was sitting in his living room half naked.

'I think I've decided about the windows now. Shall we move on? Are there any other adjustments you would like to make before we discuss the next part of the contract?'

'Well, no, I don't think so.' I hoped I did not sound as uncertain as I felt.

It was again Mrs Gifford who stepped in, by taking hold of both my hands and whispering to me to stand up. She moved me round straight in front of her, all the while looking me right in the eye and smiling. Her hands were resting on my hips, but they slid down the sides of my legs until they passed the hem of my skirt and then climbed back up the sheer stockings under my skirt to my waist. Her gaze was hypnotic; I could feel her fingertips moving up my legs, moving off the stockings and on to my skin, but my eyes were still held in her gaze, in her smile. She had reached my waist, where she took hold of the thin elastic waistband of my knickers but, without hesitation, she changed direction and slipped them down my legs, still smiling, still gazing into my eyes so that in spite of myself I lifted first one foot and then the other to let her take them right off.

'Now let's carry on, shall we?' Mr Gifford was so obviously and so determinedly ignoring what was going on that it was impossible not to follow his lead. He picked up the brochure that I had left him the previous evening and turned again to the section on outside features.

He was talking about various items and I tried to answer his questions, getting up and down to find the different fact sheets and the various lock styles from the sample case to show him. Every movement emphasised my nakedness so that after a few minutes it seemed quite obvious that my blouse flapping about unbuttoned and untucked was just a nuisance, so I slipped it off and laid it across the arm of the chair next to me.

'That's good, dear,' muttered Mrs Gifford, although her husband gave no indication that he had even noticed the change in my appearance. All the same, the casual decadence of the situation, the real naughtiness of it, was quite unexpected and yet very appealing.

He continued the discussion and then sat back in his chair, leant back expansively with his hands clasped, and gazed across at me, his eyes at last taking in my naked breasts, my nipples still pushed forward towards him. I crossed my legs to give him another glimpse of my thigh but then I noticed Mrs Gifford squirming in her seat next to me before she very obviously uncrossed her legs and sat with them apart a little. The implication was clear and I followed her example, aware that in doing so I was letting Mr Gifford see right up my skirt, certainly to the very tops of my stockings, and perhaps even to the bare skin beyond. Sitting there beside his wife, I suddenly wondered whether she too was naked beneath her skirt, and whether I should take more of a lead in this. I glanced across at her, hesitated and then dropped my hand on to her thigh and ran it up her leg but, immediately, Mrs Gifford moved to clamp my wrist tight, lifting my hand off her.

'Don't be impudent, my dear.'

The game was clearly not entirely as I had thought and I clenched my hands between my knees trying to work out the rules. Mr Gifford was still saying nothing, still waiting, still watching me with a look of disappointment on his face as he glanced down at my hands clasped between my knees. It was obvious what I should do, and although half of me was desperately trying to think how I could get out of this terrible situation, the other half was already relishing the idea, anticipating the pleasure that the next stage of exposure would certainly bring.

Mr Gifford turned over the final page. 'Well, I think I'm clear now what we will require.' He paused. 'If the terms are right, that is.' He stared at me again, and let his gaze drop down into my lap. He was making no secret of what he wanted and I laid my hands down flat on to my thighs and slowly spread my legs apart a little and pushed my bottom lower into the chair. When I stopped, he waited a moment then he closed the brochure, and sighed deeply.

I understood him and, putting down the price list I was working on, I stood up, kicked off my shoes, unzipped the back of my skirt and slipped it down my legs. I followed this with my stockings and turned to face him, entirely naked now, and sat down again, staring down at my hands in my lap.

For the first time in all the conversation since I had been there, Mr Gifford smiled and acknowledged my display.

'Lovely, my dear, quite lovely. I do think it's such a shame for beauty to be covered up at any time, and when it's a beauty such as yours, it's even more of a crime.'

Mrs Gifford muttered her agreement and then, while one hand reached up to stroke my cheek, she leant over and kissed me, gently at the corner of my mouth. It was not unpleasant – she tasted slightly of peppermint – but then her hand slipped down my throat and across to my breast and stroked me, her thumb rubbing softly across my nipple. The next kiss was more direct and, when I turned towards her, she placed her lips directly on mine and her tongue emerged briefly. Her hand dropped down my body to my lap and snaked along my thigh to my knee before starting to pull that over towards her. I did resist this, it was too much, but she leant back again and smiled at me with such easy encouragement that I stared at her, feeling my face burn up to a bright crimson, as I allowed my legs to be drawn steadily further and further apart, and opened myself entirely to the scrutiny of her husband sitting opposite us.

When she kissed me again, I responded almost instinctively, opening my mouth to receive her gentle tongue and turning my shoulders to let her reach my breasts more easily. When she pulled away, she sat smiling at me and traced her fingers lightly down across my stomach until at last she reached my pubic hair.

'There we are,' she murmured as she curled it between her fingers. 'What an adorable little bunny you have. Such soft silky fur!'

Her fingers continued teasing at my hair, but occasionally dropped down to spread it out either side of my crease. I'm sure this was just to ensure her husband had an unrestricted view. Her fingers stayed down there, running lightly along the crease itself, along the edge of my lips and finally dug down among the folds for my clitoris. Her fingertips were never still, but quivered up and down the length of my vulva, sliding along the lips on either side, and then pausing so that she could actually dip her long fingers inside, right deep inside me, and spread the wetness out over my lips. She pinched at me and stretched my lips out as far as she could, keeping on returning to the very top, tracing little rings round my clitoris and tweaking at it with her fingertips. All the while, she continued kissing me, her tongue running round inside my mouth and her strong arms holding me tight against her. I was squashed up against her bosom, so much bigger and softer than mine that I wanted to experience that too. I half expected to be stopped again, but I lifted my hand once more and rested it on her ample breast. This time she didn't remove it and I squeezed gently, to be rewarded by a gentle sigh. So I carried on, first squeezing and stroking, and feeling the nipple hardening beneath her clothes, and then I felt for the buttons on the front of her blouse, unfastened two of them and slipped my hand inside on to her bare skin and then squeezed my palm right down inside her bra.

The nipple felt enormous to my fingers, I mean I'd never touched another woman's breasts before, and yet this was wonderful. It was so soft and luxurious and voluptuous that it was wasted being so restricted by her clothes.

I pulled away from her kiss. 'Please,' I whispered, 'May I kiss you? Kiss your breasts?'

She smiled kindly at me. 'Of course, my dear, if you'd like to. That would be lovely.'

Between us, we undid the rest of her blouse and I reached round to unhook her huge white bra. When she peeled it off, and her breasts emerged, full and pale and ripe and so sensual, I leant over and lifted her whole breast in my hands, and kissed and licked at her, my lips grabbing at her nipple, round and dark and huge as an egg yolk, and then suckled like a child.

She lay back to give me total access to her for a moment, cradling my head against the deep cushion of her soft breasts while her one palm covered the whole of the little mound on my own chest, and her fingers toyed with my tiny nipples; they must have seemed so ridiculous, like a doll's, compared with her own. Eventually she lifted me away, though I was sorry to leave the comfort of her breast, where her nipple now stood proud as a strawberry and shining wet from my tongue.

'Now stand up, dear, and turn round. Let Mr Gifford see your sweet little bottom.' She helped me stand and turn my back on her husband, and then pulled my shoulders down so that I was bent forward, first leaning on the cushion next to her, and then drawn further down until my head was almost resting on it.

'That's right, dear. You know he rather likes bottoms.' Her voice was little more than a whisper, as if this were some private conspiracy between us that he could not hear. 'Now, why don't you stretch your little round cheeks open. Let him see right into your pretty little bottom hole. He will love that! Yes, can you see? He's smiling now.'

'Good girl. Now come and sit back down by me again, and see if you can manage just one last little thing.' Mrs Gifford turned me round again, and eased me back to the settee next to her. This time she made me keep my bottom on the very edge of the cushion and pushed me almost flat on to my back. Then her hand travelled back down to my legs, eased them wide apart again and slid down into the wet crease between them.

Half leaning over me, she kissed my breasts, nuzzling and sucking my nipples up between her teeth as her hand continued rubbing determinedly, rhythmically, insistently, up and down the full length of my crease. Occasionally she would dip her fingers back inside me and, although I squeezed at them, she pulled out to spread the slipperiness all over my outer lips and round the clitoris itself. I could feel myself getting wetter all the time, and when I looked across, Mr Gifford was studying me so closely. Our eyes met for a minute and I was ashamed.

'Please,' I asked Mrs Gifford, 'please stop. I don't want him to see me. Not see me come.'

'Nonsense, my dear. That would be a quite wonderful thing to see and I know he would love very much to see your climax.'

'But please, Mrs Gifford. Please . . . I think . . . I'll . . . I sometimes spurt. It'll go everywhere.'

'That's fine, child. Don't be embarrassed, just let yourself go.'

Her fingertips were now even more concentrated on the little point over my clitoris, and I knew I couldn't hold on. I tried to sit up.

'Oh no, please stop, please stop, I will be so ashamed with him watching me.'

She ignored it, merely pressed me flat again and returned her mouth to my breast and sucked at my nipple as the pressure steadily increased in a way that I knew would soon be unbearable.

Still she continued, though I kept begging her to stop, but each time she pushed my thighs apart again until finally she worked one finger right up inside my vagina while her thumb continued circling over me until it was too late and I turned against her, to bury my face and muffle my cries as I felt deep tremors break all through me and the flood that I had been afraid of gushed from me, and I shook and screamed out into the wonderful deep soft pillow of her bosom.

She let me down gently, still softly kissing my little breasts and my mouth, although her hands insisted that I keep my legs spread wide apart so that I'm sure her husband could see my soaking wet lips and probably even the glistening tip of my clitoris itself.

Eventually she allowed me to sit up. 'Now, run along and get dressed, my dear, and then we can sign these documents.'

So I quickly gathered up all my clothes and my handbag and went along to their loo where I could get dressed again and repair my make-up and my hair. When I returned, Mrs Gifford was also dressed and there was no sign of what had just taken place, except for a wide dark stain on the settee next to where she was sitting. They signed the order forms, not once asking for a discount on the list price, and I explained that our production manager would be in touch with

142

them in a few days to arrange suitable installation
dates.

It was left to Mrs Gifford to show me out, but I
couldn't just walk away as if nothing had happened. I
stopped on her front step.

'Was that all right, Mrs Gifford?'

'Yes, my dear, that was very good indeed. You see, I
knew you would be able to manage perfectly properly
once you were shown how.'

'Thank you. I mean for showing me. And for
everything.' I hesitated, uncertain how to phrase what I
needed to ask. 'Will you want anything else from me at
anytime?'

'Oh, I don't know, dear. We had been thinking about
a conservatory because we are really quite cramped with
only that little sitting room now that Gregory is also
home all day, but conservatories are so expensive.'

She paused and glanced over her shoulder towards
the sitting-room door. 'On the other hand, if perhaps
you and Melanie were both to come and talk to us, we
might be tempted. I am sure that the two of you
working together as a team could be most persuasive.
Do you think you could arrange that?'

8

Linda's Tale: A Family Secret

Weddings are the fires on which emotions are brought
to the boil; how many marriages – and divorces – have
their inception in that overcharged overdressed atmosphere? The young look forward, the old look back, and
unspoken beneath the delicate icing and the white lace
simmers the knowledge that the entire festival is a
celebration of a sexual desire about to be consummated;
a white-robed virgin is led to the altar and there passed
over to the eager male who will despoil her. It can be no
coincidence that the groom wears a tailcoat. I shivered
and huddled deeper into the corner, trying to avoid
being noticed and dragged out to dance.

Stuart was working his way across the room towards
me, and I managed to catch his eye and smile; my
objection to dancing does not include everybody. He
flopped down into the seat next to me.

'Hi, Linda. How are you these days? Good do.'

The 'do' was my sister Helen's wedding, and I think
Stuart and I were both feeling a little sorry for ourselves.
He and Helen had been 'courting', as our mother liked
to call it, for several years and it had always been taken
for granted that they would get married. But then the
relationship just seemed to go flat; not cold, but stale,
and they drifted apart. Helen took a job down south
and met someone else; he stayed behind and seemed to
shrink. Even so, they had remained good friends, and so

it wasn't surprising that he should be invited to her wedding. I had mixed feelings about the break-up; it could lead me to lose touch with Stuart and I didn't want that; we'd grown close during his courtship of Helen. He'd always treated me kindly and not just as the irritating baby sister, even though I'd been no more than a teenager then, and at that age eight years was a big difference. Even so, when some new boy of my own age was roughly trying to push his hands inside my clothes, it was not England but Stuart that I thought of.

On the other hand, the break-up did mean he was available again.

No, be sensible, all that had been years ago and, now into my twenties, obviously my childhood crush was over.

We sat in the hotel banqueting suite as the reception began to wind down around us, drinking a little, talking happily enough and watching the dancers begin to thin out, the families starting to move away and the hotel staff beginning to clear the tables. It had been a good wedding but maybe we both would have liked to have been participants, not guests.

I was halfway through an account of my car's MOT test problem, when I realised that Stuart was not listening at all. He was looking over at a nearby table where one of the waitresses was wiping the table top. She had her back to us and was bending over the table, her short black skirt stretched tight over her slim bottom and the material pulled up to reveal an expanse of black-nyloned thigh.

I teased him. 'What are you thinking, Stuart?'

He blushed and grinned, as he picked up his glass.

'A man can dream, can't he?'

'Not what you were dreaming, he can't! That's illegal in this country!'

He laughed again. 'No, it isn't!'

'Well, no all right, it used to be.'

'That was not what I was thinking.'

'Liar!'

He just shook his head, and turned away to put his glass down. Something in his manner convinced me that he was telling the truth, but perhaps not the whole truth.

'What then? Stuart, tell me, please?' I looked at the waitress again. 'Do you know her?'

He looked up then and shook his head slowly, and although he saw I wasn't teasing anymore, he was still unwilling to reveal anything. I leant over closer in the little corner and coaxed him with the phrase we had used all those years ago, when he needed my advice about Helen, and I asked his about my new boyfriends.

'Family secret, Stuart, I promise.'

He smiled at the recollection of the childishness, how we used to call each other brother and sister at one time, but he saw too that I did mean it. He carefully stood the almost-empty pint glass down on the table and sat turning it in his fingers, gauging how much he could tell me, how well he knew me.

'I was thinking of tying her wrists and ankles to the table legs, lifting up her skirt, pulling down her knickers and caning her.'

'Christ!' This was not what I expected from Stuart, whom I'd always thought of as kind and gentle. He'd never been anything else to me.

He smiled sadly. 'You're shocked.'

'No, surprised, that's all. No, I'm lying. I am shocked. Is that what you do, you know, with girls?'

He picked up the glass again and laughed. 'No! Not normally! I mean, well, I have done it sort of, just once.'

This was too much to let by. 'Who was she? When did it happen? Describe it all.'

'Oh no, Linda, I don't think I should tell you all that.'

'Please, Stuart.'

He laughed again then. Maybe he was relieved at having someone to share this secret. After all, if it had been me, I couldn't think who I could have confided in – except Stuart.

'When I was at university, I was going out with a girl who kept messing me about, cancelling dates at the last minute and so on. One time I went to pick her up from home, where she lived with her mother, and it turned out she had gone off to Manchester with a gang of friends. I was quite upset and Margaret, that's Julie's mother, invited me in and we were talking about Julie. She said she reckoned I ought to put Julie over my knee and give her a good spanking. She said she deserved it.

'I was very doubtful, but then Margaret said it had never done her any harm when she was young, that girls needed it at that age, and perhaps when they were older too. It was very ambiguous but I realised she meant at her own age. She must have been over forty, at least twenty years older than me, and yet she made clear what she wanted. I was still pretty unsure about it and said I wouldn't know what to do and finally it ended with Margaret stretched across my knees while I smacked her bottom. Then she had said, "You must always make it up afterwards, and don't pretend you don't know how to do that." And she led me upstairs to her bedroom. We met again a few times after that, but secretly because she didn't want Julie to find out.'

'Did you smack Julie?'

'No, I never did. After that evening, I kind of went off her. I have never smacked anybody since then, but sometimes I think about it, if I see a girl who has a really nice bottom, really round and attractive . . .'

'Like that waitress?'

'Yes, like the waitress, then I . . .'

'Or like me?'

There was a second's pause. 'Yes, someone with a bottom like yours, I suppose, then I might . . .'

'Have you thought of caning me? Not a girl with a bottom like mine, but actually mine. Caning me?'

148

He swallowed. This was new ground for both of us.
'Yes.'

A week later that conversation was still careering
around inside my head like a wild animal, crashing
across my mind, breaking through every other thought,
dominating every consideration. Every night when I
went to bed and at different times during the day the
images surged up into my brain blocking out all other
thoughts, of work, of friends, of anything. I had barely
slept, even after I'd finally settled to try.

I pictured myself, dressed as a waitress and leaning
over the table; I saw Stuart squatting down to tie
lengths of rope around my ankles; I felt the coarse
texture of it rubbing against my skin and then jerking
tight as he fastened the knots. It would cut in, but hold
me so tight that I would be unable to move. He would
move up to my arms and I would be able to see the top
of his head as he bent to tie first one wrist then the other
to the remaining two legs of the table. I would be held
there, stretched across the table, powerless, entirely at
his mercy.

And it was that part which affected me the most, the
powerlessness. I couldn't visualise what would happen
after he moved away, the whole scenario was so utterly
foreign, but I could feel the intensity of being so
vulnerable as I pictured him, standing back and
studying me as I lay across the table. He would look at
the mound of my bottom, fully covered by my skirt at
this stage, and know that he could expose it whenever
he wanted to. He would know that he could do
whatever he liked: could kiss me or hurt me; could hold
me there or release me; could caress me or beat me. It
would all be entirely his choice and I would not be
consulted. It was terrifying and alluring and repellant
and irresistible.

By the Friday, I was a wreck. One of the other girls

149

at work had asked if I was ill because I seemed so washed out and unable to concentrate. All week I'd been running off to the toilet every day and emerging flushed and shaking; I couldn't tell her the reason was not what she assumed. In the end, I gave in and went home early. I was exhausted from getting so little sleep all week and went straight to bed.

But a few hours later I awoke with the same images dancing in front of my eyes, twice as large and three times as consuming. I tried to settle down, to think about work, about how to reduce my credit card bill, whether I could afford to buy a new car, all the things that should have exercised my brain.

I even put my nightshirt on, but it was no use. The image just seemed so totally open and erotic. No silly games, no wondering what you ought to do next, or what he thought, what he wanted, what was right. Just pleasure. I was picturing being pulled down across his lap, and manoeuvred into place. He would lift up my skirt and pull down my knickers and see my bottom. Then he would spank me; whatever I said or did, however much I shouted and protested, he would be in control and I would have to suffer whatever he decided.

I reached out from under the warmth and dropped my nightshirt down on to the carpet, then rolled over into the cold side of the bed on my front, stretching my legs out to feel the contrast of temperatures and textures from my skin brushing over the cold sheets. I scissored my legs out and slowly drew them in, pressing my whole body down the length of the bed to get the sensation across my tummy and my breasts. Then I came up on to knees and elbows, lifting my bottom to the world, parting my knees, fingering my lips apart and waiting. What would it be like if I were really waiting for a cane to come whistling down on to me? The sting and fire and then another wait. Another whistle. Another crack.

Another wait. It was the same scene I'd been picturing all week, but these were the same fingers, and it was not enough.

I needed to face this, to talk it over with someone, but I couldn't think of anybody I could trust with something so immense. The last time I'd been so consumed about sex worries was as a spotty teenager, and then who did I ask? Well, Stuart himself.

I still had his phone number, although it was several years since I'd last used it. 23:14 blinked at me in red from beside my bed. It was far too late to call anyone.

He would be out, bound to be on a Friday night. If he is out, it doesn't matter if I call; he simply won't answer.

So I climbed out and padded naked along the passageway to fetch the phone back from the cold living room and then climbed back into bed, setting the telephone down in front of me.

I stared at it, although it was barely visible in the darkness, willing it to give an answer to the questions that I did not dare to ask. I fetched some milk and a piece of cake and brought them back too and then sat cocooned in my huge duvet, as I sipped milk and nibbled cake and tried to gain courage. The world was so still, the occasional passing cars barely intruding into my flat and the light from outside street lamps diffused and gentle through the curtains. I have always loved my bed.

Finally I set the empty glass back down beside the telephone, lay back down again, then stopped, then hesitated again. I knew what I wanted to do and I realised that I would have to do this sometime, or I would never be able to carry on with my life. I dropped my hand back down between my legs to try to generate extra courage for myself. My sex welcomed me; it was only my brain that was still afraid.

I could actually hear my heart beating as I picked up

the receiver; it was louder than the beeps of the telephone. I decided to let it ring four times; if he hadn't answered by then, I would hang up.

He answered immediately.

'Hello, Stuart. It's me, Linda.' I hoped my words were sounding better at his end of the line.

'Linda! How nice to hear from you. Everything all right?'

'Fine. Sorry to ring so late, I hope you weren't asleep. Or anything,' I added suddenly, realising that if he was in on a Friday night it was probably because he was not alone.

'No, no. Just watching a video.'

'Ah. What?'

'Just rubbish. Nothing you'd know.' He said it too quickly. 'Is something the matter? You sound a bit funny.'

'Stuart, I've been thinking about what you told me at Helen's wedding.' There was silence at the other end.

'I'm sorry, Linda, I know I shouldn't have said anything. I feel very silly, actually. I'd probably drunk too much. Could we just forget it? I really didn't mean what I said.'

'Yes, you did, but I don't mind. That's what I wanted to say, that I haven't been able to get it out of my mind; I find myself thinking about it all the time.'

'Thinking what?'

'Well, thinking of you, doing that. Stuart, would you really want to do that to me?'

'No, Linda, obviously I would never hurt you; I'm very fond of you. Please, just forget I said anything.'

'I don't want to just forget it. Don't dismiss me, Stuart, I'm not a child anymore.'

'I know that, that's why I feel so stupid.' There was no doubting his tone. I recognised this whole business as something which could make him try to avoid me, that his shame would destroy our friendship and my bringing the subject up again would increase the pressure even more, unless I pressed so hard I burst it open entirely.

'Can I tell you something in return?'

'If you like. If you think it's a good idea.'

'Every night since you told me that, I have lain in bed masturbating while I pictured it.'

The silence from his end showed I had finally reached him. I continued.

'Not only at night; even during the daytime at work. Twice.'

Still silence.

'Stuart, I want you to do it to me.'

'Well!' He hesitated. 'You should try being naughty!' He was trying to make it sound light, but it wasn't working.

'No, I don't want silly games like that. Just do it because it's what we both want. But not smack me, but like you said about the waitress at the wedding.'

'What did I say at the wedding?'

'You said you would tie her down and cane her. Do that.'

'Linda, are you really sure about this?'

'Yes, I am. Completely. I have been thinking about nothing else for the last week. I need you to do it.'

'Well, all right. I suppose. When?'

There could only be one answer to that, even if it was getting on for midnight.

'Now. I'll be at your house in half an hour.'

I washed quickly, my face, under my arms and between my legs. I found the right clothes, a pair of plain white knickers, and plain bra, hold-up stockings, a full, mid-length skirt, a sweater and finally a pair of low-heeled shoes. It was all thoroughly sensible and I could have been going to work.

I rang Stuart again.

'I'm just leaving. When I get there, please don't ask

me if I'm all right or if I'm sure, or what I want you to do. Don't ask about anything. Just do what you want. Do you understand?'

'Well, all right, Linda, if you're certain, but if you want to stop at any time just say so.'

'No! You mustn't take any notice of anything I say. I don't want to have any control, that's the whole point. Just do anything you want. Anything. Do you understand?'

There was a pause at the other end of the line before Stuart answered quietly. 'Yes, I think I do. See you in a minute.'

The roads were almost completely empty but I had to force myself to concentrate. The initial excitement was beginning to die away and, when I was on to the dual-carriageway and had more time to think, I wondered what on earth I'd let myself in for. I'd never done anything remotely like this before, and I suddenly felt entirely out of my depth. It was going to hurt; it would probably hurt very much. I slowed the car. What if it hurt too much for me to stand? I had told Stuart to do whatever he wanted.

No, I couldn't pull out now. I needed this. I could trust Stuart. I did trust him, completely.

It was just twelve o'clock as I pulled up behind his car in front of his house. The porch light was on, and Stuart must have heard me because he came to the door before I reached it.

'Come in.' It was almost formal, his greeting, and he was wearing a dark-green turtle-neck pullover and grey trousers with black leather shoes. It seemed unlike him at first, but then he had dressed for his part just as I had dressed for mine, and no doubt for the same reasons. He was serious, and determined, and I couldn't meet his eyes, but neither did he seem to be looking to meet mine.

In the middle of the living-room floor stood his heavy

oak table, but the top had been taken off, leaving a solid square frame at hip height with a ledge all the way round the outside. Laid along it were a coil of cord, a thin cushion and a length of bamboo cane. My throat was constricted and I tried to swallow down but I was too dry. The table stood there innocently waiting for me, the few things neatly lined along it seeming so innocuous. I licked my lips again: still too dry.

'Do you think I could have a drink, please?' It was not my usual tone with Stuart.

'Certainly. What would you like?' It was not his usual tone with me.

'Water would be fine.'

While he was gone, I tried to compose myself, to control my breathing, my heartbeat and to look around the room, but that length of bamboo cane and the tidy coils of rope kept dragging my eyes and thoughts back. The waistband on my skirt was too tight, as was my bra – both the strap and the cups seemed all too small. My nipples ached.

'Here you are.'

The glass was damp and I gripped it hard, concentrating on working my fingers so as not to let it drop. The water seemed to slip over my tongue and down my throat without wetting me. A sickening fluttering of fear and anticipation tumbled through me when I finally conceded that the glass was empty.

'Ready?' And I nodded.

He took my shoulder and led me up to the frame. He swept up the cord and cane in one hand and pushed the cushion into the centre.

'Stand right up against the edge and bend forward.'

The hard rail dug into my hipbones but my head and shoulders were able to rest on the cushion. Between them there was no support, so my breasts, swollen and aching, were suspended in the void.

Stuart worked in silence, taking hold of one wrist and

pulling it out to the corner of the table, where he held my arm as he looped the cord twice around my wrist and knotted it, before tying the other end round the top of the leg. I watched the careful working of his fingers as they stretched and flexed, fingers that would soon pick up the cane. He pulled the knots tight and glanced at me, about to ask if that was all right, but he stopped himself in time. He moved around to the other arm and tied that the same way.

Then my legs. I'd been standing with my feet together, but he pulled them apart a short distance and, from the edge of my vision, I watched the top of his head as he tied first one end of the cord and then the other to the bottom of the table legs. He stood up and moved back into my line of sight, collected the cane and laid it on the edge of the table right in front of my eyes, then circled back and checked all the knots again.

He picked up the cane and flexed it. 'I shall give you six strokes.' His voice was flat, just a statement, an announcement of a minor decision as I watched the bamboo curve and straighten. He glanced down at me and then replaced the cane in front of my face before leaning down, and I felt his hands at my waist, pulling my sweater up over my ribs. His hands moved to the back and his cold fingertips fiddled with the clasp of my bra. I heard myself sigh as it came undone and my breasts relished the release. He reached underneath me and eased my breasts out of the bra, then, for a moment, caressed my puckered nipples, turning and twisting them in his agile fingers, even pinching at the hard and erect tips, tugging, squeezing and stretching.

When he released me, he moved further down and I felt him take hold of the hem of my skirt and drag it steadily up my legs, over my bottom and lay it flat out, a weight across my back. Then his fingers hooked into the waistband of my knickers and pulled them down, still steady, in no rush, the elastic scraping across my skin, all the way down my thighs until they finally dropped to my ankles.

His hands moved across my bottom now, fingers digging in and kneading at the cheeks. He was not the first man to admire it, but he was the first man I had said could do to me anything he wanted. Fingertips circled the perimeter and then ran delicately and lightly down the centre crease. I tensed my muscles to try to hold myself together and protect myself but he just stopped and waited wordlessly until I relaxed again. He would not be prevented and had all the time he wanted. His fingers slowed and hesitated as they passed lightly across my anus, but carried on.

Then he was fiddling around my ankle again, and I felt the rope loosened and removed. He lifted my ankle and slid my knickers right off over my foot before retying the cord, but this time he pulled my foot right over to the table leg. He repeated this on the other side, pulling my legs so wide apart that I felt the chill air slide right into the crease of my bottom and the folds of my lips, all the colder because they were so damp. Again his hand ran up the inside of my thigh and cradled my open sex. He almost lifted me up like that, one finger raised a little so that it concentrated the pressure directly on my clitoris as he slowly seesawed his hand through me, milking the gathering moisture and opening my lips, gauging me, taking me to the edge, teasing and waiting.

He knew what he was doing, and I was sure that the continual starting and stopping was deliberately planned to keep me on edge. Every time he picked up the cane, I wondered if this would be the time he really used it; every time he put it down, I wondered what further rearrangement he wanted.

Strapped face down, I couldn't see his face, but he seemed satisfied now; nothing more needed to be done. My body was exposed naked to him for the first time, stretched out helpless in front of him and he could do with me whatever he liked, whatever his fantasies were, whatever his darkest secret desires, I had told him to carry on. Yet, although we both knew what it was that we both wanted, and how we both wanted it to be played out, with a directness and a formality that enhanced the imbalance of the relationship, the slow progression in preparation was as important as the execution. His palm gently ran across my tight bottom, the skin damp with apprehension, and ran down between my legs again. His fingers spread my lips apart and coaxed at my clitoris, smearing my juices over my skin and back through the crease of my bottom. He pushed a core of fingers up inside me and twisted as he pulled back again while his other hand again scooped up my breasts and squeezed them in his palm.

Then he let me go, moved round in front of me once more, and picked up the cane yet again. This time it was for real, he didn't play at bending it, I had already seen that trick, and his next one needed to be the actual performance.

He stood to one side of me and tapped it lightly on my bottom but then stopped and I felt his hand again. I was quivering; it was cold and I was afraid, but there was also the anticipation and hope and desire. His hand slipped underneath me again and his fingers wormed between my swollen lips and pushed deep into me, then ran out and pinched slipperily at my clitoris before his hand came back and slapped down across my bottom with a suddenness that made me cry out. This was almost immediately followed by the first stroke of the cane. The intensity was so strong that I had barely registered it when the next came, and only with that came the full realisation of the pain that I was suffering. I realised I had screamed, but already Stuart's hand was working at my vulva again and his fingers circling and pinching my clitoris with a determination that outweighed the suddenness of the pain. His thumb worked its way up inside me as his fingers continued to rub and his hard knuckles pushed their way across my tender skin.

Although I could feel the tears running down my cheeks as I sobbed, I could also feel the free running of my arousal down my thighs. When his hand was withdrawn again, I couldn't stand it. I was teetering on the edge and the flash of pain that seared through me with the next stroke of the cane passed straight into me and imploded deep inside my sex. I was utterly on fire, across my bottom, through my nipples and my lips and my clitoris. The next stroke was even worse, concentrating spasms of such depth and intensity and suddenness all through my nerves that the pain was excruciating, magnificent and irresistible. The next one was the same, as I writhed my hips against the table to try to scrape stimulation to every other part of my over-sensitised flesh, and another stroke – the last, the hardest, the greatest – came and I screamed and climaxed as he dropped the cane and plunged his fingers into my gaping sopping cunt, and the other hand kneaded at my hanging breasts and twisted my nipples as the waves raced through me and washed me, loosened me, released me completely. I closed my eyes again to hold in the sobbing panting gasps of exquisite agony until they faded away.

It was a relief to feel his cool fingers working at the knots again as he released me and helped me stand up. Then he wrapped me in a dressing gown and led me upstairs, where he laid me down on his bed, delicately kissing each cheek of my upturned bottom before carefully pulling the sheet over me. I watched him through my tears, moving around the room as he undressed and, when he slid naked in beside me, I hauled myself up to kiss him on the lips at last, my girlhood hero.

'Thank you, my love,' I whispered.

As he leant over to turn out the light, he carefully laid the cane down on the bedside table in front of my eyes. Ready for the morning.

9

Philip's Tale – A Private Party

I suppose you find similar people in all offices; certainly looking back now on all the different offices where I've worked, I can see the same basic types of characters cropping up repeatedly. The ages obviously vary and even the sexes too sometimes, but the essential characters, or maybe just caricatures, remain the same: the jokers, the flirts, the mother- or father-figures, they are all there. Anyway, that's not really relevant except to the extent that I suppose I would have been less surprised had I appreciated the fact then. Well, that is true of everything; if we had known in our twenties what we know now!

I had come to a small town, not too far from Melbourne, and to the job straight after leaving college. On the whole the job had been quite good to me. The company was not especially competitive and had no great aspirations to be an international force. It was actually quite efficient, more by chance than intention, but it didn't have very high expectations of its workforce. This suited me because it meant that I didn't have to work very hard, and I wasn't very ambitious, while the slightest exertion in that weak competition produced an unexpectedly high result so I was often held in very much higher esteem than I deserved. I didn't mind. At the beginning I was treated as just 'the lad', but as I got older, and as people even younger – or at least newer – than me joined the firm, this changed and I was treated with a little more, well, respect I suppose; being a relatively small office (of a fairly small company) it took quite a while before a new recruit was entirely accepted.

Two women worked in the general office, dealing with all the incoming correspondence and contract enquiries, assigning them to the proper customer files, and so on. They were both much older than me, had both worked there for many years, and had always teased me. I think it was intended at first to keep me in my place, to show me that they knew the ropes and I did not, but it was almost continuous and sometimes harsh. In particular they tried to embarrass me sexually by being coarse. It did shock some other people in the office, but although I'm cursed with a rather babyish face, I have led a sufficiently varied life to make me really hard to shock. Gradually, as the weeks went by and I did not rise to their baiting, and nor did I try to push my weight around too much, the tone changed a bit and then they were not so unpleasant. In the end it amounted almost to a continual flirtation and, although it was always the two of them together against me on my own, it was all harmless and good natured.

In fact, as the weeks turned to months, I acquired a name for being quite wild and immoral. I enjoyed the reputation although it wasn't one that I deserved as much as I pretended, nor as much as I would have liked. Most of the conversation included the usual banter and double-entendres which I expect goes on in most offices and shops. On several occasions they would say they were looking for files and that they would come and search me, and then I would start to undo my trousers as if to help them and they would giggle and egg me on but, of course, I stopped a long way short of doing anything improper. I didn't fancy them at all; I was in my mid-twenties and they were in their late thirties, I

162

suppose. Linda was divorced and Ann's husband was a salesman dealing in some kind of agricultural stuff so he was very often travelling up country. It meant they were each quite independent and would sometimes go out together in the evenings. They were both reasonably attractive and, from photographs I'd seen taken at some dinner they attended, were capable of making themselves up very glamorously when the situation warranted it. Even so, the great difference in our ages was enough for me not to take the flirtation seriously. I had no conscious attraction for older women and confined my attention to women around my own age or younger. Besides, I was trying to make out with one of the typists who was of an age that I took to be more appropriate and was also, by any standard, stunningly attractive. It all went on like that for a couple of years.

One Christmas party things went a bit further than usual, and while I was dancing with Ann – I was pretty smashed – I reached up inside the back of her jacket and undid her bra. She made vocal but insincere protests and when the dance finished she encouraged me to dance with Linda and do the same to her, which I duly did. It went no further; I started dancing with someone else who was more of my age and to my liking and who had obviously had enough to drink to make her randy. I left the party with her.

One Monday morning not very long after that, during a summer heatwave, I made some joke about having been sunbathing nude in my garden over the weekend, that I had overdone it and got burnt. I was exaggerating a little, though the basic facts were correct; I had!

Linda immediately said: 'Let's see, then. Come on!'

I started to undo my belt but I stopped pretty well straight away. Ann said: 'You know what, Linda, we'll have to lock him in here one lunchtime and debag him. Then we'll see if he's got as much to be proud of as he claims!'

So I said, and even now I am not really sure why, just trying to sound unworried I expect, 'Oh, you wouldn't have to lock me in; I'll show you, if you are interested.'

'Go on, then,' said Linda.

'All right, sometime I will.'

'Show us now, come on.'

'No, but sometime, I will.'

'Do it now. There's no time like the present.'

'Not here, in the office, I won't,' I said. 'It would be spread all round the firm in no time; I would never live it down!'

They greeted this with jeers and 'Chicken!' so I said: 'No, I'm not frightened. I do quite a bit of swimming and so forth in the nude. It doesn't bother me having no clothes on.'

'All right, then, show us.' Linda was persistent.

'I suppose I could show you some evening if you like.'

'All right then,' said Linda, 'you're on. When? This week?'

'Well, what about Thursday?' I said.

'Fine.'

I turned to Ann. 'Are you free on Thursday?'

'Yes!'

'Right then,' I said, 'Thursday it is. I'll come round to your house, about eight o'clock? Look, I want this kept just between us. If I find that you've told a whole crowd of other people, it's off.'

They agreed to that, so I then spent the rest of that day, and the next few as well, wondering what I'd let myself in for. In fact, I did swim and sunbathe nude quite often, as the two of them knew, so I genuinely wasn't specially worried on that score. On the other hand, lying nude on a beach was completely different from standing up in front of two women and taking my clothes off. I thought of saying, 'I will if you will', but that would have been a very weak cop-out and I didn't want that. I was quite certain that it would end up with them naked in any case, so I decided to make it a bit of a striptease and see how it went from there; to be honest I found the prospect exciting.

I've always thought that imbalances have great potential. This evening, with an unequal number of people and one who would be stripping naked for the other two to watch, looked extremely promising. Additionally, I'm enough of an exhibitionist – and voyeur as well – to find myself anticipating the event with some impatience.

All the same it would need careful planning if it was to go the way I wanted it. Linda was the more outgoing of the two and Ann was likely to follow. Ann was conscious of this and didn't like to seem 'green' so would be likely to obey me. Also she would be embarrassed more easily, and that in itself would be exciting. Anyway, I spent a considerable time planning what I would do, and how I would set about it, and even practised bits in front of a mirror. As I said, I had not previously considered the women from an erotic angle, but now that I did so I was not disappointed. Ann had one child but Linda had none, and in fact, during those days of waiting, I found myself raising my estimation of them. On reflection, they both seemed a good deal more attractive than I had thought. I don't think I was merely trying to convince myself; I'm sure that every woman is attractive in her own special way, and in such an erotic setting would be even more so.

For the two days intervening, I tried to avoid being alone with the two women in the office, but before I left on the Thursday afternoon I went and confirmed the address and made sure our date was still on. In the evening I had a last quick rehearsal, then a shower, and at about 7.30 set off, stopping on the way to buy a couple of bottles of wine.

The directions Linda had given me were quite clear and I quickly found the dull modern estate where she lived. When I reached her house I could hear music and found Ann already there. It was a bright evening, and very warm, even with all the windows open. They had both changed out of their office clothes and looked as if they had been drinking for a little while; that suited me well enough.

I opened the wine for Linda and we all started drinking and making small talk. The room was smaller than I'd been anticipating: French doors on one side looking out on to a spread of grass which was all that the garden comprised, and then a low fence before the same pattern for the next house. I suddenly realised that we, or I, could be visible from there. That was something else that I'd not taken into account in my planning. Furthermore, the space available in the living room was quite limited; Linda was sitting in an armchair and Ann was facing her on a settee. There was one other chair that I could have used but it was tucked out of the way in the corner; I wondered whether it had been moved there deliberately. On a garish rug between the two girls was an oblong coffee table and, along one wall, opposite the French windows, stood a modern home-assembly-style wall unit.

Things were a little bit tense to start with but I thought I should not wait too long or I would lose control of the sequence of events, and I'd worked out quite precisely how I wanted it all to progress. When I stood up to refill the wine, I gave them both their glasses and then said:

'Well, we should get this show on the road.'

There was silence from the two women, a slight shuffling of their feet. I put down my glass on the wall unit and moved away the table to the side of the room. Then I sat down to take off my shoes and socks, then stood up again, spinning it all out. I looked straight at Ann and carefully unbuttoned my shirt, slipped it off and tossed it on to the arm of the settee next to her. That made her jump a little but she said nothing, just

166

took a sip of her wine and watched me. I walked over to the table and took another drink.

'OK,' I said, 'I think that will be enough for one day.'

As I expected, they both immediately protested at this. I moved across to Linda.

'Do you want some more then?'

'Yes!'

'What do you want to see?'

She giggled. 'The rest, come on!'

'What rest?'

'You know, your bits!'

I turned to Ann. 'You as well?'

'Yes!'

I grabbed her wrist and pressed her open palm against my crotch and, as I was already beginning to get an erection, there was a good bulge to feel through my jeans.

'That? Is that what you want to see?'

Her face was bright red, but she nodded and laughed a little nervously. She was trying to appear light and casual but in fact I think she was a good deal more aroused than she wanted me to know. I went back to Linda.

'Come on, then, greedy, undo my belt.'

She put down her glass, leant forward and, after a bit of fumbling, managed to unbuckle it. No doubt she would have gone further but I pulled back and returned to take another sip of wine. I looked at both of them as if undecided but in fact I had planned exactly who was to do what. I put down the glass again and went back to Ann. I stood very close in front of her so that she looked up at me apprehensively, still trying to pretend she was used to it all.

'Your turn, Ann. Why don't you unzip my jeans then you can tell Linda what colour pants I'm wearing?'

She swallowed and then, hesitantly, stretched forward her hand to unzip me. She pulled open the zip.

'Oh my God, he isn't wearing any!' she shrieked and then she really sat back and laughed straight out. Linda was most put out.

'Here, let me see, let me see!' she cried.

But I stayed with Ann. I leant forward and kissed her, hard, and ran my hands over her breasts. I squatted down in front of her and unbuttoned her blouse, opened the sides, then stood up and pulled it off her. She said nothing, even when I pushed one hand down inside her bra; her nipple was long and full and hard. Looking over my shoulder at Linda, she was beginning to squirm a little in her chair so I went over and behind her chair, rezipping my jeans as I went, then leant over the back and kissed her upside down, my tongue flat over hers; she liked that. I reached down and pulled up her T-shirt and only broke the kiss for a moment to pull it over her head. Still kissing her, I reached round and undid her bra and pulled that off. She tried to cover her breasts but I pulled her arms away. I wanted to see her, and I wanted Ann to see her. I rubbed my hands, slow and hard, up the whole of the front of her body and her breath came harder and her nipples, small and tight, darkened and tightened further. Linda was wearing trousers so I moved down to her waist, unfastened the front and pushed down into her panties and between her thighs. She parted them a little to help me, and already she was very wet.

Finally I broke away and moved back into the centre of the room. I picked up the wine bottle and, as casually as I could, topped up all the glasses. They watched me but said nothing. I put down the bottle, took a drink, tucked my belt buckle back and told Linda to come and sit over on the settee. She was obviously embarrassed at being half naked when Ann was not, but I liked that.

I looked at both of them. 'Do you want to see all the rest now?'

They nodded and Ann said, 'Yes,' but it came out as little more than a whisper.

I stood up straight in front of them, undid the stud at the top of my jeans and slowly inched down the zip. I pulled the jeans down and they both giggled nervously when my prick came free; I tugged my jeans right off and laid them over the chair; I was now totally naked. I paused to take another drink from my glass while I slowly rubbed up and down the length of my penis; it was soon fully erect and the gesture was so thoroughly obscene and unambiguous that the two women looked quite shocked, as I wanted them to be. Partly I found it enjoyable but also it kept them sufficiently off balance to ensure I kept control. They still said nothing, simply watched me as I walked back, quite naked and very erect to where they sat. I squatted down and ran my hands straight up the sides of Ann's bare legs without stopping, clear up to her waist, then I took hold of her panties and pulled them straight down and off. They were almost dripping.

I sat in the chair that Linda had been using so that I faced the settee. I lay back in front of them, displaying myself completely and still gently masturbating, although not too much because I was already getting quite aroused and I didn't want to blow the lot too soon.

'Who wants to be first?' There was no reply.

'Ann, come here. Would you like to see Linda being fucked?'

She moved over to me. I sat up and unfastened her bra then unzipped her skirt and helped her out of it. She kicked off her shoes and stood, a little shyly, naked. Her pubic hair was quite thick and bushy but the crease was just visible, and it glistened. I had her sit on the arm next to me then told Linda to take off the rest of her clothes. Linda was obviously more used to this; her hair was neatly trimmed and showed a warm plump mound through which her inner lips pushed out cheekily. She stood now with her hands on her hips, legs a little parted and said nothing, but she knew she looked good. I looked her full in the eye and, pushing her legs further apart, reached between them and rolled her clitoris between thumb and forefinger then pushed my middle finger well up inside her. Her lips parted and she pushed forward against me; when I offered her up my finger, she licked it clean without hesitation. Next I parted Ann's legs and ran my open palm over her pussy, digging the heel of my palm hard between her legs before slipping my forefinger and middle finger deep inside her. As soon as I withdrew it, I did just the same to Linda standing in front of me.

I made Ann lie straight out on the floor; next I got Linda to kneel over her, one leg either side of her head and facing down towards Ann's feet. I squatted behind her and reached round to pull her lips even further open so that Ann, lying beneath, could not help but stare right into her friend's pussy.

'She looks nice and wet, doesn't she?' I said, but Ann said nothing.

I pushed Linda forward and pressed my prick against Ann's mouth and, although she readily let me in, I didn't wait long but withdrew once I was thoroughly wet. Then I pulled Linda's hips back against me, keeping her back flat and level with the floor, placed the head of my erection against her, and very slowly pushed forward until it was buried in deep. She sighed and I thrust into her again some half-dozen times before pulling out again and offering myself instead to Ann's mouth. This time she hesitated, knowing whose flavour she would be finding, but I was not going to let her off, and pushed in between her lips and well into her mouth for a few seconds before pulling back out again.

I moved round to a position level with Ann's hips, parted her legs and pulled her knees well open to expose her as well; her lips were dark and swollen and very moist. She too I caressed as she started to twist and squirm; Linda watched it all happening directly in front of her. After a couple of minutes I took hold of Linda's wrist and brought her hand round to replace mine. She hesitated for a moment, but then carried on enthusiastically while I just sat back and watched. I assume Linda had done this before because she was very assured and smooth. At the beginning, Ann didn't even notice the change but, when she did, she half sat up as if to see more clearly what was happening. I thought at first she was going to object, but then she thought better of it and settled back to enjoy the sensation. And clearly she did enjoy it although I didn't want to let it go too far; I wanted their inhibitions, which the wine had already loosened, to be released entirely by excitement and frustration.

There was one other thing that I particularly wanted to do. I pressed down on Linda's head so that, to stop herself falling over, she had to put both hands on the floor. Still I pressed down, until at last her face was entirely lost between Ann's thighs. This was something I had long wanted to see and I loved to watch the pleasure spreading over Ann's face as she reached up to fondle and penetrate Linda's exposed cunt, at first wanting to share the sensations that she was herself receiving, but soon she became selfish, concentrating only on her own feelings. She rubbed her hands harshly up and down Linda's back and buttocks, leaving vivid red streaks from her clawing fingers as she fought to intensify the power of the orgasm building up. I pulled Linda up before Ann could reach her peak.

To even it out, I brought Linda back almost upright, almost squatting over Ann's head, and pushed her gently down so that Ann could return the pleasure. Linda was really quite uninhibited and squatted there with her eyes shut, her head back and caressed her own breasts, sometimes also her own clitoris and, from time to time, she leant forward to pull at Ann's breasts and to dig deep between Ann's well-parted thighs.

I think by this time I was all but forgotten, and I was quite content with that. Oh, I fully intended to have them both, but we had plenty of time, and no doubt plenty more opportunities, for that. This display of pure pleasure was something quite special that does not often come anybody's way, and I did not want to interrupt its flow. I sat back down, and sipped some wine, and just watched. The girls settled down on their sides, totally engrossed in the feelings they were each giving and receiving; very quickly their hands and tongues had brought each other to orgasm several times.

Then, quite suddenly, Linda rolled over almost screaming in a climax of far greater intensity; with both hands she clamped Ann's head hard into her pussy and gripped her tight as she pumped her hips aggressively against her friend's face. I don't know whether Ann was trying to get away or was pushed into a similarly explosive orgasm by Linda's obvious ecstasy; at any rate she was soon grunting almost as loudly herself. When they finally quietened down, Linda sprawled back totally exhausted; Ann too sat back looking spent, panting, her whole face glistening with sweat, saliva and Linda's juices. I fell forward, kissing and sucking and licking at her face and I pushed her down on to her back, pulled her ankles up over her head and as wide apart as they would go and just rammed into her. In less than a dozen strokes I could hold back no longer and I know I roared out as I pumped into her in the most incredible orgasm of my life. I cannot claim to be any super-stud but on this occasion I just kept coming and coming until finally I had nothing left to give.

And that was that; we were all far too spent for anything further that night and then, for a variety of reasons, we never got around to a repeat. I don't think it was because the girls were unduly embarrassed. They certainly didn't seem to be so the next day, a fact that has since led me to wonder whether this was indeed the first time that they had made love together, either the two of them together or perhaps with one man. In any case, a repeat just never happened. I suppose there were summer holidays when one or other of us was away and then, by autumn, well, many seeds that flourish in summer will die when the autumn comes.

I never did make love to Linda (although I once made her masturbate for me to watch, but that's another story), and then I left the company a few months afterwards. Looking back, I remember that night as probably the most intense of my whole life. We, all three of us, had been anticipating the event for several days and were all geared up for it when it finally happened. We were all mentally at an erotic high pitch before we even entered the house that night, and then it all just happened right. Probably it's just as well we never did aim for a repeat; it could not have been so good.

10

Beth's Tale – Triple Calling

There has always been a strange magic attached to the number three, whether in ancient rituals or religions or superstitions. I'd never before encountered it in relation to punishments, yet a triple punishment is a punishment more than trebled, because, whether it's three humiliating displays or three strokes of the cane, it's the repetition that makes it so unbearable.

The first sequence is barely comprehensible; the shock outweighs the agony.

The second time there is just the agony.

The third time the agony is lifted higher by the anticipation, by the knowledge of just how agonising it's all going to be.

In the outpost of the Civil Service that I joined after leaving college, all new recruits attend an introductory training course, held in one of the fading Victorian seaside resorts whose permanent population consists almost entirely of pensioners who have sold their homes and moved to the south coast. The courses are held out of season once the town is safely free of its summer swarm of language students, when whatever entertainments it might then have offered are firmly closed, and when cheap block bookings are available to the training course organisers. This gives the ageing hotel a chance to cover its running costs over the miserable wet winter while allowing the equally aged staff a chance to hone their skills of sullen apathy in preparation for the coming season. Occasionally the chef may take the opportunity of a captive clientele to experiment with a new brand of pre-packaged catering meals, but, if he does, his daring passes entirely unnoticed.

The course lasts four days. We arrived on a bleak and windy Monday evening in time for a 'welcome' dinner, and would leave on Friday after a 'plenary' lunch. On the Wednesday evening, one of the great and good would descend from head office to show how egalitarian he is; how concerned over the well-being of the minions, and how he's just like one of us.

Most of the first evening was spent in the hotel, mutual introductions, brief life histories and 'You must know old ...' When the boredom quotient hit the embarrassment line, we all changed into casual clothes and moved off to a local pub, where at least we were more at ease in steadily getting drunk and telling each other lies. The course tutor, Simon Hackett, came with us, and I made sure that I ended up next to him at the bar. He was tall and serious-looking, but with an attractive confidence and a lovely deep voice. But he was five or so years older than me and, although he said nothing to suggest that he was already attached, he made little response to my discreet offers.

I was still living at home, so this opportunity to let my hair down was like being a teenager again and I made the most of it. The result was that I drank too much, overslept the next morning, and was finally woken by a phone call from Simon himself after I had missed breakfast and half an hour of the first lecture.

'Hello, Beth? This is Simon Hackett. You're running a little late, you know. It is half past nine.'

I mumbled abject and probably incoherent apologies into the receiver, scrambled out of bed and through into the tiny closet of a bathroom. There I stood staring at my groggy reflection in the mirror and splashed water over my blurred eyes, while his words burned into me.

Partly it was shame at seeing no more than a naughty little girl, when I desperately wanted to appear as bright and sophisticated. Mostly it was something much more than that, something that gnawed at me. They had been such mild words, so gentle a rebuke, yet a strength still lurked there that melted me. It was not the words themselves so much as the tone, the timbre, that carried such absolute authority and demanded total obedience. His voice had a superficial softness like the pretty wrapping on the outside of a present, but, underneath, and detectable through the wrapping, was a hardness, a promise, or perhaps it was a threat, of complete authority.

Even in that dim, hung-over scramble to get dressed for the day, the promise hovered just out of my sight, like a spirit on my shoulder, but I knew it was there. I felt it watching, waiting for me to stumble again.

Eventually, still only half dressed, I surrendered to the demands his voice had placed on me and lay back on my bed. I eased my knickers back down my legs, and dipped my fingers between the dampening folds where the promise of his words had lodged. I could only see these images of the control and domination that his voice had implied, but which was so alluring, so overwhelming. As I held his voice in my mind, it felt like having him there in my room. In the face of such power, my shameful disobedience was rendered doubly intoxicating; not only was I late, but I was no longer even trying to make amends. Instead, I was stretched out half-naked on my bed, with my knickers round my ankles and my legs stretching open towards the door – the door through which he could enter, if only he would – and masturbating.

I joined the class just in time for the morning break, horribly embarrassed, and spent the rest of the day avoiding him.

Tuesday, the second night, saw a few changes in our routine: firstly, nobody delayed before changing out of office clothes, secondly, we went to a different pub, and thirdly, having started drinking, we told each other different lies. I'd decided to stay for no more than half an hour, and in the event, after being thrown out of the pub at eleven, continued playing snooker in the hotel games-room until half past two.

One of the other women on the course woke me just before nine and, although I missed breakfast, I arrived just in time for the lecture. I cannot have been looking quite as bad as I felt, nobody could look that awful, but I had not had time for a shower or to put on any make-up, and Simon called me to one side at coffee time.

'Look, Beth, we don't have a curfew or anything and we like those attending our courses to enjoy themselves. Within limits. As course tutor, I do have to try to make sure that people are in a fit state to benefit from the course we provide.'

I muttered more apologies and hid away with the rest.

That evening, being the midpoint of the course, was the formal dinner. Everyone assembled nervously in the bar, falling into a hushed silence when the head office representative rode in on a wave of artificial good humour and declared loudly that he wanted to go out after dinner and drink, 'like the good old days'. I was still desperately trying to avoid Simon, so stayed well to the back as he led the way when we all trooped in the instant that dinner was called. The consequence of this was that the tables filled up quickly, and by the time I got in, the only places left were at the end table with the head office VIP and, in his role as host, Simon. I had no choice but to join them.

In that company, dinner conversation was not just strained, it frequently broke down altogether. Even when running, it relied on the 'Which part of the country do you come from?' and 'Where are you going for your holidays?' classics. The VIP said he was going to Dorset for a long weekend; did I know Dorset at all?

'Well, yes,' I admitted. I did. I had actually gone to school there.

'Oh yes. Where?' It was a commendably convincing attempt at interest.

'A small town in the middle: Sherborne.'

Then Simon joined in. 'I was at school in Sherborne as well, as it happens. Which school did you go to?'

I was offhand in my reply. 'There's one up on the hill on the edge of town. What about you?'

Simon smiled knowingly at me. 'One near the big church in the middle.'

Thus we each revealed our secrets: both gown not town. He knew exactly what I'd meant, and his reply disclosed similar feelings about his own fine education at one of England's lesser public schools. Meanwhile nobody else on the table had the faintest idea what we were talking about. We exchanged details about when we had each been there; he would have left some three years before I arrived, and thus also disclosed, to each other only, our ages, our backgrounds and our views on them.

There was one thing that I had to ask – a rumour that had regularly circulated through the girls' school but nobody had ever been able to substantiate.

'Is it true what I've heard about the early-morning punishments?'

'You mean triple calling? I don't know what you've heard, but I expect so.'

'Pyjamas? Then a cold bath? Then get dressed? Then . . .?' I was not sure how to put it without letting others on our table into the conversation.

Simon carried on. 'Not quite. The cane came after the bath, but you have the basic idea.'

'Three times in fifteen minutes?'

He nodded. 'Three times in fifteen minutes. Normally for three days.'

I was awed, as all of us had been all those years ago when it was talked of in hushed whispers in the girls' school, when we pictured the lines of gloriously naked youths running through the frosty stone cloisters. The deliciously vicious barbarity of such an ancient rite thrilled our excited young hearts. I desperately wanted to know if he had ever had to do it, but he simply looked at me with a smug smile on his face and said nothing, knowing full well what it was that I was dying to ask, and he was not going to tell me.

The conversation moved on and our VIP guest was as good as his word. As soon as coffee was finished, he reappeared from his room in a sweater and jacket and led the way to the pub. The session settled down and none of us left before closing time. I had started playing table football with a group from Birmingham. We were playing for pints, and by closing time, I could barely walk, and was half supported as we stumbled back, blinking blindly through the driving rain.

The following morning, one of the other girls woke me on her way down to breakfast, but I fell asleep again, and so I was still half an hour late for the VIP's early-morning lecture. I managed to sneak in at the back, and to sneak out again at the end, but Simon caught up with me as we were all going in to lunch.

'Beth, just a moment, please. You were late again this morning. That's the third time in a row, and after a warning.'

'Yes, I'm sorry.'

'You've always been sorry, but never quite sorry enough, have you? Well, let's see if this helps. Rather than go out drinking after dinner tonight, we'll try a spot of triple calling. Do you know the drill?'

'No, not exactly.'

'Present yourself at my room at nine sharp in pyjamas. I'll explain the rest then.'

He swept out without another word, and I watched his back disappearing down the long corridor to the dining room. As I faced the reality of assuming the role of victim myself, the ritual suddenly assumed a dreadful tangibility that it had never held as an idle adolescent fantasy which put someone else squarely in that place.

After dinner that night, the Birmingham crowd asked me to repeat the football and I pulled back. Instead, I waited around trying to look busy as everyone prepared to go, but they took ages, and it was almost five to nine before the heavy wood-framed doors closed on another wet evening and I was at last alone in the great bleak hotel reception.

I had gone earlier to find Simon's room. It was on the first floor, in the middle of the hotel, while my own was on the second floor and right out at one end. I quickly hurried to my room and changed into my pyjamas. Fortunately, I had packed sensible thick pyjamas to keep out the cold, although I had found no use for the new lacy nightdress that I had also brought in case I managed any entertaining. I buttoned up my pyjamas to the neck, knotted my dressing gown, brushed my hair and, at exactly nine o'clock, crept out of my room, down one flight of stairs and along the corridor to room 37. I knocked.

'Come!'

I pushed open the heavy door and shuffled in. The room was much bigger than mine, much better furnished and with huge embroidered curtains across the window. Clearly this was one of the original rooms which, on my floor, had all been split into two, to create the little hutches in which I and the other minions had been packed. His would have a view of the sea, and I could see a second door leading to a proper bathroom with its own window, where mine had a small dark cubby hole containing no more than a toilet and a cramped shower.

I waited as he sat writing at a round table in the window bay, still wearing the polo-necked sweater and jacket he'd been wearing all day.

'Well?' He didn't even look up as he spoke.

'I've come to "call" you.' Then I added as an afterthought: 'Sir.' Finally he did look up.

'Ah. Yes. So you have. Repeated lateness.' Then he frowned at me. 'What's that dressing gown for? You don't need that. Put it over the chair there.'

I quickly untied it and laid it over the faded chair back, before returning to stand to attention.

'Right. Now the procedure is quite straightforward. You will have a bath here, it is already filled, then present yourself for three strokes. Normally that would be with a cane but, in deference to your sex, it will be my hand instead. Then go back to get dressed and get back down here again for inspection. The whole circuit is to be completed three times within fifteen minutes. If you are over time, you start again. Clear?'

I swallowed, and felt my stomach knotting and my nipples tightening as I tried to comprehend the full scale of this utterly unknown territory. Finally I nodded.

'Yes.' He raised his eyebrows. 'Yes, sir.'

'Good.' He took off his watch and laid it carefully on the table, then walked over to push the bathroom door wide open. This revealed a huge old-fashioned iron bath tub, full almost to the brim with still bright clear water. No bubble bath was neatly laid out on the side; no comforting wisp of steam was rising from the surface; indeed, from where I was standing, the water looked almost blue in its steely frigid stillness.

Simon took up his wristwatch again, and stood in the bathroom doorway.

'It is now 9.03. Start!'

Without thinking, I ran over to the bathroom and started to close the door, but he didn't move.

'Come on, Simon, I mean sir. Let me have the bath.'

'Oh no. I stay right here and make sure you get in properly, shoulders under the water or it doesn't count.'

'What? I can't do that! I'm not having a bath with you watching.'

He shrugged. 'You're wasting time. 9.04.'

So I obeyed. Turning my back to him, I stripped off my pyjama top and threw it on the floor and then pulled down the trousers and quickly jumped into the bath for some covering. The instant my feet hit the water, I stopped. I have never known water so cold; it came less than halfway up to my knees and it already numbed me. I would never be able to immerse myself in that. I looked over my shoulder at Simon, standing grinning by the door, and, although only my bottom was visible to him from that angle, he made no secret of looking up and down my nakedness.

'It's freezing!' It was all I could think of to say. 'I can't lie down in this.'

He looked at me, and for a moment he softened, and lowered the watch.

'Step out again.'

I stepped out carefully, but I couldn't continue to keep my back turned to him, although my nipples were already erect and I could feel goose pimples all over. I turned with my arms clasped in front of my chest for some warmth. I know I should have been modestly covering my sex and my breasts, but modesty took second place to trying to regain some warmth. He had the decency to glance down only once before focusing on my face.

'Beth, you will do this, because otherwise you will simply be standing naked and shivering in this bathroom for the whole night. However, I will tell you how to do it and, take my word for it, it is the only way. You take a deep breath, then get in, sit down, lie back, sit up, get out. Do the whole thing in one smooth movement, as quickly as I said it and it will work. Now, we'll start again. It's 9.05. Go!'

I hesitated for an instant but inside I knew he was right. Without pausing to think, I stepped in, sat down, lay back and the numbing cold only hit me as a wave of icy water sluiced up over my shoulders and down over my breasts. By then I was already half out of the bath again, and the instant that my feet touched the floor, I grabbed a towel and wrapped it round myself, standing dripping and shivering on the little pale mat.

Simon moved back into his room.

'Come along. You haven't got time to wait around.'

I still felt so numbed, almost bruised, by the bitterly cold water that I was barely thinking what was next, except that I knew I wanted to get back to my room, get dry and put some warm clothes on. Yet as I shuffled along across the rough carpet after him, he pointed to a clear space in front of him.

'Stand here. Face the window. Legs apart and touch your toes. And for heaven's sake, get rid of that dreadful towel. My hand will warm you up much quicker than that will.'

I was shivering: cold, mixed with fear, mixed with anticipation as I clutched the thick white towel tighter round me and tried to work out what I had got myself into. The ends of my hair hung wet and cold on my shoulders, dripping down my back and I trembled again. Already I had stripped naked in front of this man, and stood quaking and wet before his eyes, yet still he wanted more. I was barely able to take in what had happened so far and here he was already pushing me on to the next stage, a stage of the punishment that I had not fully considered. Worse, he said he wanted me to take off the towel. I had already been naked, he had seen me once, but that was just circumstantial. Now he wanted me here right in front of him, bent over and displayed within arm's reach. His voice dropped down a pitch.

'Come along, girl. Do as you're told.'

That voice again, that tone of absolute authority, ruled me. I simply untucked the towel from over my breasts and tossed it down on to the chair. Then I stood in front of him so he could see me, could see my small breasts heaving with every breath, my nipples puckered against the cold and the exposure, and my sparse pubic hair, flattened by the water and matted flat against my skin. I waited a moment to let him look at me, hoping he would appreciate and desire what he saw, but his eyes skimmed over me too quickly and then he gestured again to the space arranged for my punishment.

I took a step forward and bent down, my hands resting on my knees, and waited. I had been spanked before, not recently, admittedly – not since I had been quite young – but even so I knew there was nothing here I could not withstand. He stepped up beside me and I pushed my bottom out further. For a brief instant his hand rested on the small of my back, then skimmed ever so lightly over the skin and down to my buttocks.

'Lower than that, girl. Feet apart and touch your toes.'

I shuffled my feet further apart and reached down to my toes. I wanted to ignore the heightened exposure this caused, but I couldn't wash it out of my mind, and I shivered again at the knowledge. There was a glorious humiliation in so abject, so degrading, a posture of utter obedience, and for a moment I savoured the realisation of how fully I was displayed, how my breasts would hang down beneath me, how the cheeks of my bottom would be stretched apart and even my sex, the crease between my thick lips, would be visible if he should happen to move round and stand behind me.

He moved round and stood behind me. I tried to picture it all as he would be seeing me and what reaction it might have.

However, Simon was not to be distracted at all. He

185

came round the other side of me and again lightly rested his left hand on my back as I sensed the swinging movement of his body and his hand came down across my bottom with a loud smack. The sting and the pain were certainly greater than I had remembered from my childhood, but it was not unbearable, and in fact the shock and the noise were far greater than any real pain.

The second blow followed quickly, and although this stung much more, and I yelped, it was more for his benefit than from any real hurt. The third landed on exactly the same spot, and I cried out again. My bottom really was sore now, and I was glad that he quickly let me up.

'Right, off you go. Get back here, quick as you can, fully dressed.'

I gathered up the pyjamas and started to pull them on, but he stopped me.

'You haven't got time for that, you know. You really will need to get a move on if you are going to get the three laps finished before the deadline.'

So I gave up on the pyjama trousers and just scooped everything up together with the towel. Clutching the bundle to my chest, I ran out of his door and along the corridor. The hotel was still empty, which I know should have been a relief, but it was not my choice that I was being made to run naked around the corridors. So if someone had chanced to see me, had seen my red marked bottom as I flew down the hall and up the stairs, I could hardly have been held responsible, and could hardly have been blamed.

Back in my room, I hesitated about what clothes I should put on. Presumably when this was being done at school, the victim would simply have worn school uniform. I had no such easy choice, so instead I selected the clothes I had been wearing during the day: sweater and skirt with tights and good sensible shoes.

I ran back down to his room. He looked me up and down then nodded.

'All right. Now pyjamas again, but you must be a good deal quicker this time.'

Back through the empty corridors again to my room, and I was half pulling off my sweater even as I reached it. I threw all my clothes on to the bed and quickly dragged my pyjamas back on. They were damp from where they had been tangled up with the towel, but I snatched this up and ran back to Simon's room.

I felt an utter mess standing in front of him, with my hair damp, bedraggled and unbrushed, my pyjamas twisted, and a ragged towel clutched in front of me. His wry amusement reflected what I felt, but did not offer any consolation.

'Bath!'

I stripped off the pyjamas again. It was a little bit easier to undress in front of him this time than it had been the last, although it was still humiliating how little notice he seemed to take. I was additionally intimidated by the much grander surroundings of his room compared with my own little cubicle, and the way he sat there, fully dressed in dark-grey trousers and a heavy jacket, seemed to emphasise my own condition. My being made to strip made me even more fragile.

As I dropped my clothes on to the floor of the bedroom and turned naked to go into the bathroom he called me back.

'Beth, just a minute.'

I hobbled back, naked, my hands trying ineffectively to cover my breasts and pubic bush.

'Haven't you forgotten something?'

I racked my brain for what part of this torturous medieval ritual I could have forgotten but could think of nothing. I realised that my hands were a very poor cover for my nakedness and that Simon was examining me carefully as I stood in front of him, so that I reached down and clutched myself tighter for protection.

187

'No, I don't think so.'

'All right, then. Carry on.' His tone was entirely light and uncaring as he smiled at me, and continued watching as I turned away and stumbled back into the bathroom.

This time I hesitated only briefly before stepping into the icy water. Supporting myself with my hands on the solid sides of the ancient iron bath, I lowered myself slowly down to the icy water again. I did pull back as the tender lips of my sex hit the freezing surface, but then I took a breath and carried on, pushing myself back in one quick movement that washed a wave of water up the bath and back over my chest and breasts.

This time I didn't reach for a towel but padded through to Simon's room and immediately took up the position as before. My breasts hung tight and puckered beneath me as I bent down to grip my ankles, bent right over with my bottom pushed out. He was already waiting for me and, once I was sufficiently bent over for him, he came round behind me and half squatted down to inspect my bottom, his slim fingers feeling warm as they slid across my cold wet skin. It all seemed so intimate that I should let this man, little more than a stranger, examine my bottom, staring and feeling at the soft round cheeks to see the effects where he had spanked me before and consider how best he wanted to spank me again.

'That's no good at all. There isn't a single mark on you. I will have to use a slipper.'

I stood up to protest, but he roared out at me.

'Stay down!'

I returned to my position, my teeth chattering as he kept me bent over in an almost feudal attitude of penitence while he searched about and returned with a faded grey leather slipper.

He smacked it across his hand, grinning, as he approached. The heavy slap on his palm sent a

188

sickening jolt tumbling down through my body to fetch up in a surge of inexplicable pressure between my legs.

'This will be more effective, I think you'll find.'

Again his palm rested on my back to steady himself, or maybe it was to steady me, and then the first stroke of the slipper landed. This was utterly different from a hand. I almost screamed out as the sudden raw shock of pain seared across my bottom. It cascaded over and through me like nothing I had ever experienced, and I was still drawing breath when the second stroke came in exactly the same place, just as unbearable, just as agonising, and so loud and concentrated a force that I screamed out again. The whole intensity and ferocity of the blow concentrated all my attention on that one raging part of me as I waited for the third blow. When that was delivered, right on the same spot as the first two, I almost crumpled to the floor, and it was only my determination that Simon should not think he had bettered me that held me up.

I kept my face turned away as I scrabbled down to gather up my things and stumbled back as fast as I could to the refuge of my own room again, with the knot of my pyjamas and the sodden towel again clutched to my breasts. I was blinking back tears, not only of pain, but also anger at the treatment and the way I was ignored. I had expected some price to pay for this opportunity to show Simon my strength, but this was too much. He treated me as nothing and yet expected me to bear so much.

Worse, I knew that time was running out, so, when I dressed this time, I didn't bother with tights and underclothes. After all, he would never know and it would speed up both the dressing and undressing afterwards.

He barely looked up as I presented myself next for his inspection, but, as I turned to leave, he stopped me again.

'This time you have forgotten something, haven't you?'

I frowned, and tried to look puzzled. 'I don't know what you mean.'

He shook his head. 'Oh, yes you do. You know just what I mean. Lift up your skirt.'

'What?' He may have seen me standing naked twice already, but that was no reason for him to think he could demand additional displays like this.

'You heard me. Lift up your skirt. For heaven's sake, girl, there's no need to be coy. There's nothing under there that I have not seen already and I just want to check you've not forgotten any underwear.'

I lifted the hem slowly and he smiled triumphantly across the room when the hem reached the point where I was exposed again and he was proved right. Then he grinned, raising his eyebrows and staring at my bare stomach. I just stood in humiliation, my skirt still held up to my waist, revealing my shame.

'I thought so. Go and put them on and come back. And you really must hurry up, or you'll run out of time.'

I ran back through the still-deserted corridors to my room, quickly put on my knickers and tights and returned down a floor to his room. As I opened the door, he was sitting hunched over the table again with his back to me. He didn't even look round as I stood in the middle of the floor, waiting to be humiliated again by being made to lift up my skirt. Instead he shamed me even further, because he didn't even bother turning round.

'OK. Now pyjamas. Last time, and you had better get a move on; you've only three minutes left.'

It was just a whirl as I raced back to my room, pulling at my clothes as I went, throwing them on to the bed and dragging on my pyjamas in their place. I didn't even bother snatching up the towel. I was given no chance to dry myself and no time to wrap it round to cover me.

Back in his room, Simon glanced up, nodded and gestured towards the bathroom. Again, I peeled off the pyjamas and ran through into the other room, then stopped. The water was standing as still as an ice pond in the ornate iron bath, and the sight alone reminded me of how paralysingly cold it would be when I sank myself into it. I could still feel the numbing ache where my tender nipples and the delicate lips of my sex had been immersed before, and I shuddered as I tried to bring myself to face it again. It was then that I felt the full weight of this third circuit and understood the devious cruelty of the repetitions. The first circuit had all been a shock, a whirl that I could not begin to take in. The second had been dreadful, humiliating and twice as painful. Now I faced it all again, with the memory of the last run still fresh in my mind. I knew how dreadful would be the third submersion in the freezing water, the third display of my naked body, the third obscene ritual of my bending over for his pleasure, the third set of three excruciating strokes with his horrible leather slipper.

I pushed myself forward, for even if this were the third, it was also the last, and stepped into the bath. The shock of the cold was if anything worse than before, and I glanced round over my shoulder. He was not looking. I hesitated, then made up my mind. Noisily I sat down, and splashed water around the bath before I leaped out again, ran through into the bedroom and stopped dead. He was looking straight at me, with that same look of amused disapproval on his face. He shook his head.

'In again, I'm afraid, Beth. Shoulders under, and this time, wait until I have given you permission to get out.'

'But Simon, I –'

'Again!' His voice roared out and quelled any possible argument.

I stumbled back to the bathroom, where the body of water was still swaying silently up and down the cruel white tub. I hesitated only for a moment before I stepped in, then lowered myself down again and finally lay back against the hard cold end, trying to hold back a cry as the water ran up over my shoulders and down my breasts. The aching cold grabbed at me and when no sound came from the other room, I called out.

'Please, can I get out now?'

'Just a minute.'

Simon came ambling in and walked right up to the end of the bath. Like any bath, the only one way that I could lie back far enough to get my shoulders under the water was by bending my legs up, so that my knees were sticking up on either side of the tub. And this meant that my sex was displayed open for him, contracted by the cold, no doubt, but still displayed, still with the lips peeled apart for him to enjoy. And he did enjoy it. He stood there at the end of the bath, smiling down at me, and running his eyes over my face as I fought against his intrusion and tried to hold back the sobs. He tapped his chin casually with a pencil as he stood gazing down at my nipples, tight and puckered and just breaking the icy surface, and then down to my parted thighs and open lips, my privacy exhibited at his command.

'That's better. You can get out now.'

I leapt out immediately, and pushed past him straight through to the bedroom, to the place where a scattering of dark spots on the pale carpet showed where I had stood and dripped before.

I immediately took up the position, and was aware of Simon following me in. I had my back to him so, as I bent forward, my bottom cheeks were stretched open, and I must have been presenting him as exposed a view, not just of my bottom, but probably of the open lips of my sex and even my anus itself, as it was possible to present. He came up directly behind me, so that as my head hung down I could see him between my pointed dripping breasts as he squatted down. He rested his hands on my cheeks, pulling them even further apart and then ran his fingers the length of the crease in what could only be described as a caress.

'That's much better. Now you're reddening up nicely. It's only a pity that I do not have a cane, because I am sure you would take that very well. Pity, too, there is only this one day. Even with the slipper, the full three days would have produced a more suitable result.'

His hand was continuing its steady caress over my bottom and, although he was ostensibly examining the marks of the slipper, I felt it steadily dropping down towards my sex. Finally, there was no doubt. His fingertips were definitely running lightly over my puffed-out lips and pressing gently at the folded crease. The worst of it was that I could feel the growing dampening response to it all and that must have been evident to him as well. Yet the response was not just to his caress, it was a response to the cold and to the humiliation and the pain that I knew was still to come, and I think he knew that too. Briefly, and only once, his fingertips reached far enough round to nudge lightly at my clitoris, but that would have been enough for him to discover its hard erect state. As soon as he had touched it, had stroked it lightly a couple of times, he pulled back and took away his hand.

'Yes, a great pity. You obviously respond well to the right treatment.' It was wistful, until he pulled himself together and an unnatural, unjustifiable jollity returned to his tone. 'Now. Last three.'

Almost immediately, the first stroke of the slipper landed on me, much lower than before, almost across the tops of my thighs, and I sobbed out a wail of pain as the full effect of the stroke spread through my body. It was unbearable and I think I would have stood up, but his hand returned to my back and held me still again just as the second stroke landed. Again I screamed out, and felt the tears rising in my eyes at the terrible sting

193

burning across so tender a band of flesh. I begged him to stop and, although I was given a moment's rest, the next thing was his hand in the small of my back, pushing me down even lower. I knew immediately that this would have the effect of pushing my sex back and out even more. So far down was I bent now that even the lips themselves would be exposed beyond my thighs, and I realised he intended them to receive this final stroke. Again there was a pause as his hand lifted away, allowing me, if I wanted, to pull myself back up again. I swallowed down my sobs, shifted my feet still further apart and sagged down lower as I waited for this final awful stroke.

It landed across the backs of my thighs and straight across my swollen lips in an arc of biting fire that seemed to burrow into me and forced a final excruciating cry of pain from me. As Simon released me, I couldn't even stand up, but reached down between my trembling thighs to cradle my wounded sex in my hands, and hold myself in a gentle sobbing rocking embrace of relief and comfort.

I think I would have stayed there all night if Simon had not interrupted me.

'Well done, Beth. Home straight now. Get dressed and back here. Quick as you can.' He sounded almost kind, as if he were not the man that had put me through all this, stripped me, humiliated me and beaten me.

For the last time I picked up my things and set off back to my own room. Moving practically automatically and blinking back tears as I did, I threw the bundle down on the floor, pulled on my ordinary clothes and ran wildly back down the stairs through the long straight passageway towards his room. As I ran, I realised that I was passing someone else in the corridor, someone whose face had not registered, but who my subconscious dimly recognised as from the course. I cannot imagine what they made of my bedraggled hair, tear-stained face and dishevelled clothes, but I had passed before I even acknowledged their greeting. Although I was ashamed at being found at all, it brought home the risk I had been running during all those earlier trips when I had been dressed only in my pyjamas, or, on three occasions, entirely naked but for a few clothes clutched in front of me, concealing nothing.

As I pushed open the door, Simon was once more sitting at his little table. His watch was in his hand, and as I stopped, panting in front of him, he glanced down at it and shook his head.

'9.24; a clear four minutes over the permitted time. You will have to try all over again, I'm afraid, and no dawdling this time. Your course ends tomorrow at twelve, but another one starts next week so the rooms are booked through for the whole month. Call me tomorrow at 1.00 p.m.'

I tottered back to my own room and slumped down on the bed, surveying the scattering of pyjamas and towels and dressing gown strewn across the floor. Then I burst into tears; tears of humiliation at the way I was ignored, of anger at failing to achieve what I wanted, and of frustration.

Until another course occurred to me. I jumped up and changed my clothes again, washed my face, brushed my hair and scuttled back to Simon's room, much more careful this time that no one should see me.

I found him exactly where I had left him at the silly little table, but he looked up in some surprise as I strode into his room. I let him look for a few moments, time enough to take in the neater appearance, the repaired make-up, and properly arranged hair. However, mostly he was looking at the long, sheer nightdress that did nothing to conceal my nakedness, and through which the eager erection of my nipples was plainly visible. I started slowly inching it up my legs. Even though the man had seen me entirely naked and utterly exposed already, what man can ever resist the slow revelation as the hem is lifted, inch by inch, up a body that he knows is not being merely revealed but also offered? I pulled it over my head and tossed it over on to the chair where I had so recently been made to lay down my dressing gown. I padded naked across the room to his bed.

He smiled as he watched me climb in, then put down his pen and glanced at his watch as he stood up and started to remove his jacket.

'9.32. Eight minutes. Not bad. And I suppose you think that after this I'll let you off tomorrow's calling.' He unfastened his tie. 'Well, I won't.'

I couldn't keep in the smile. 'No, sir. Thank you, sir.'

11

Irene's Tale – An Examination

Irene had always known that this would not be like
other applications although when, after many anxious
days, the phone call had come which asked her to attend
for a 'new entrants' check-up', the woman who had
called was efficient and business-like. She had introduced herself with her first name, Margaret, Margaret
Brewer, carefully explained where it was to be held, how
best to get there, and then added, as no more than an
afterthought, that there would also be a sort of medical,
but presumably Irene had no objection.

'No, I don't mind.' In fact Irene did mind, but she
could think of no good reason to hide her objections
behind.

'Good. It will be a full medical, I'm afraid, including
a bladder control test. I just thought I should let you
know because I know how awful it can be when you are
asked for a sample and cannot manage to produce
anything.' She had laughed lightly. 'I know these things
can be dreadfully embarrassing, but I'll stay with you if
you like. Please come at ten for the appointment, and
don't be late.'

The woman had laughed again, a well-rehearsed
sound that did nothing to make the idea sound any
more appealing, and quickly rang off before Irene had
time to say that she would not need her to stay.

On the day, Irene arrived early, having taken note of

the warning and drunk an extra cup of tea, which she could feel sloshing about inside her as she followed the receptionist down the corridor of a modern extension projecting out of the back of the building. One side was all offices, the other all windows, and she could see the last few daffodils in bedraggled bunches under the trees.

The end room proudly carried a plastic red cross symbol, and in case that was too vague, the words First Aid Room underneath it. Three small plastic chairs stood guard against the wall outside and Irene was given another bundle of forms to fill in, to confirm that she had no previous convictions for murder or arson, and was not an active member of any terrorist organisation.

Muffled sounds trickled down to her, evidence of other lives far off in the building, but the passageway remained entirely deserted for more than ten minutes until finally the door at the far end opened again and a woman about ten years older than Irene came bustling down the corridor.

'Hello, Irene, so sorry I'm late. I'm Margaret Brewer, from personnel. We spoke last week. What a lovely sweater! That colour really suits you. Shall we go on in? We generally use the First Aid room.'

She pushed open the door and led her into a box much like all First Aid rooms: an undisturbed white paint on the walls and ceiling, sparsely furnished with a utilitarian wooden desk and chair, a couch and two other straight-backed chairs. A small washbasin lurked in the corner alongside various cupboards, all white and scrubbed and looking healthy and hygienic. Irene was directed to take the chair in front of the desk, and was about to say that she didn't think the other woman needed to stay, but somehow the words wouldn't come and then the moment seemed to have passed and it was too late. Margaret settled into the other chair in the corner and put on her smile again.

They waited for several silent minutes until, to soften the silence, Irene tried to make conversation.

'Will the doctor be long, do you know?'

Margaret looked away a little nervously. 'Oh, Mr Weston is not a doctor; he is the personnel manager, but he always does these checks.'

Mr Weston duly arrived, a man of about forty-five or fifty, greying a little at the temples, respectably heavy without being fat, and dressed for business in a shirt with the sleeves rolled up and no jacket. He barely glanced at them as he came in, but settled down behind the desk, gathering up the papers there.

'Good morning. I'm Brian Weston. I deal with all the new recruits here. There are just a few questions and so forth.'

He studied the papers again and started on the usual questions about age, height and weight, whether Irene had any major illnesses and whether she smoked. All the answers were duly ticked, crossed or noted, much like many other interrogations of this sort.

He turned over the page, and shifted in his seat.

'Now, section two. Are your periods regular? What contraception do you use? Have you had any incidence of venereal complaints or infections? How many partners have you had in the last twelve months? At what age did you become sexually active? Are you heterosexual, homosexual or bisexual?'

All the answers were again carefully recorded.

Finally he put down the folder and came round to her side of the table, where he took her pulse, felt the glands under her neck and finally asked her to take her sweater off, and her blouse.

In the silence, Irene felt the eyes of the other two following her as she carefully pulled off these outer clothes and laid them over the back of her chair. When she was sitting back down again, feeling cold and exposed in her bra, he asked her to raise her arms so he could feel into her armpits and, taking a stethoscope from the drawer of his desk, he listened first to her chest and then her back. The results of these investigations joined all the others on the file spread open in front of them.

'Now, please take off your bra. Had a breast examination recently?' He watched closely as Irene fumbled with the catch – it was a new bra, white, strong and sensible, that she had bought specially for today – and suddenly she became aware of the other woman bustling up close behind her.

'Here,' she said, 'let me help.' She unhooked it, then helped Irene ease the cups off her breasts and slide the straps down her arms.

'There we go. That's it.' She seemed very keen to help and kept hold of the white lace as Irene sat down again.

Mr Weston perched on the edge of the desk, still watching carefully.

'Well, my dear, have you had a breast examination recently?'

'Er, no,' Irene answered, 'not really.' Thinking back, it had been several months, if not a year, since she last attended the clinic and was prodded, poked and patronised.

'Right, well, stand up, please.'

When she stood in front of him, he took hold of her wrist and, raising it high above her head, carefully watched the way it caused her breast to lift. Then his free hand ran down from her shoulder, squashing her breast down as it went, and his fingers traced almost down to her waist before returning back up, raising but pressing the swelling of her breast again. Having done the same with the other arm and the other breast, he invited her to sit down again and then, positioning himself back on the edge of the desk in front of her, he smiled mechanically, reached forward to encircle one breast in both his hands, and gently kneaded it like bread. His thumbs were poised either side and, as he squeezed and rolled her between his hands, her nipple erected of its own accord until she felt his thumbs slide in together and pinch her nipple cautiously. His thumbs continued to flick lightly at her nipple, before he moved on to the other breast, where he repeated the procedure.

It was only then that she looked up and found that Margaret had moved round from her seat at the back of the room to take up a position beside the desk where she could see better everything that was happening. She appeared almost mesmerised as she stood sucking at her bottom lip, still clutching Irene's bra to her chest, and gazing fixedly at the man's big dark hands moving across the pale skin.

'Fine,' Mr Weston finally pronounced. 'That all seems fine. Now, could you slip off your skirt and tights, please.' He returned to the notes on the desk and continued filling in details on the form, while Irene glanced at the other woman for some guidance, but she just smiled cheerfully and waited.

So Irene unzipped the skirt and slid it down her legs under Margaret's continuing gaze, although Mr Weston appeared to be taking little interest. She laid it smoothly over the chair and kicked off her shoes, then pushed down her tights as well. As soon as she slid out of them, Margaret reached out to snatch them from her and they joined the bra clasped in her hand against her own breasts. Still Margaret said nothing but she glanced from Irene's face down at her panties and then back again, smiling still, so Irene addressed her question to Mr Weston.

'And my panties?'

He looked up, frowning at the interruption. 'What? No, that's not necessary. Keep your knickers on.'

When he returned to his writing and appeared to be ignoring her completely, she asked again.

'Should I do the sample now?'

This time he was thoroughly irritated at the interruption.

'Sample? What sample?'

'I was told you would want a urine sample. Only I wonder if I could do that now, because I'm not sure that I can hold on too long.'

'No, that comes last.' He caught her sudden look of distress and tried a smile. 'Don't worry; we won't be much longer. Now, could you get up on the couch?'

She carefully lay down on her back, her hands neatly clasped over her stomach but, when Mr Weston came over, he wanted her to put them up behind her head, and she saw Margaret sidling over to lean against the wall by the foot of the couch, smiling serenely again.

Mr Weston peered down at her and ran his hands over and around her breasts again in a movement that was even less of an examination than the previous one had been and even more of a caress. It was not long before he had focused in on the dark peaks of her nipples, fondling and squeezing her, plucking at the nipples until they were thoroughly erect. Whenever she glanced farther down, beyond his hands, she met Margaret's rapt stare, still taking in every move.

'Now, my dear –' Mr Weston loomed over her again '– are your breasts sensitive?'

It was a strange question from a man who had been fondling them for several minutes and who still held firmly between his fingertips the evidence of their reaction and the unambiguous answer to his enquiry.

'Well, fairly, I suppose. I mean, I know they are often erect.'

'And to pain?'

'How do you mean?'

While she was still trying to work out what he meant, there materialised in his hands a pair of silver clamps. In one swift movement, he had taken hold of her nipple, stretched it out longer than she could bear and attached the cruel jaws of the small clip. The other nipple was treated the same.

'Let's see how you get on with those.' He turned away, leaving her sucking in her breath at the sudden shaft of pressure that was certainly not pleasure and yet was not exactly pain. It was almost like being hugged far too tight and she immediately tried to pull them off, but pulling was even worse than leaving them, in fact moving them was even worse than leaving them – and panting.

He moved down her then, down to her legs, where he rolled the muscles of her thighs and her calves carefully in his hands, like a masseur, and raised each leg in turn, to test or weigh or check whatever it was he was seeking. His hands steadily moved up the inside of her thighs until they reached the top, but nothing in his expression suggested he had noticed that his examination of her thighs was now causing his hands to rub firmly through the thin protection of her panties against her lips.

Still, whenever Irene looked down the length of her body, laid out along the clean white couch, she found Margaret closely studying the procedure and the reaction, still with Irene's underclothes clutched against her own breasts.

It was only after Mr Weston had finished an extended prodding and squeezing of the very tops of her inner thighs that he spoke again.

'You might at least have put on clean knickers this morning.'

Irene felt herself blush to the roots of her hair. 'I did.'

He glanced dismissively down again at what he obviously found to be the offending area and sniffed.

He returned to her breasts. 'Now, how was that?'

He brusquely unclipped the two clamps and immediately leant down to examine where the jaws had made a clear indentation in her delicate skin. Again he pinched at the nipples and she winced at the sudden return of the circulation.

'Painful, is it? Well they seem to have responded pretty well, in the circumstances.'

He added this finding to the notes.

'Turn over on to all fours, please, and go down on your elbows.'

Irene shuffled over, her face almost squashed against the antiseptic smell of the firm foam pillow, and her bottom stuck up in the air like a flag. His hand ran once up and then down the length of her spine but then almost immediately she felt fingers hook into the waistband of her knickers and pull them down below her buttocks, where some fumbling gathered them into a neat band at the top of her thighs. The fingers returned and started pressing into the soft full contours of her bottom, testing the resilience in a variety of places, prodding her from side to side and pinching – pinching quite hard as she squirmed under the attack. Finally satisfied with that, the fingers eased her cheeks apart and she became aware of him peering closely at her terrified puckered rose.

He sniffed again. 'Relax, please, I need to investigate this more.' He went back to his desk and, when he returned, she saw he was holding a smooth round plastic rod, six inches long and pale and intrusive. In the other hand he had a jar of Vaseline into which he pushed the rod as she watched and withdrew it, gleaming. She was already expecting the invasion when she felt it pressed against the tightly defensive muscles of her anus and firmly, coldly, unstoppably pushed deep within her. After a few gyrations, it was part withdrawn and then pushed even deeper home so she could feel it cold and alien far up within her. He walked away, leaving it sticking out of her bottom as he returned to his desk and read through some notes. Glancing over her shoulder, Irene could still see Margaret, her eyes

204

gleaming and focused as she swayed with emotion at the foot of the couch.

When Mr Weston at last turned back to his victim on the couch, he casually withdrew his anal probe and made her lie down again on her back, but he did not bother replacing her knickers. He just let her lie there with them stretched in a tight band across her thighs, covering nothing but underlining her naked curls as he read through the notes on his clipboard.

Finally he passed the board down to Margaret – the first time he had acknowledged the other woman's presence – and reached out to tug Irene's knickers right off her. He again peered into them critically and, for a dreadful moment, Irene was afraid he would repeat his criticism. Instead he merely shook his head and said nothing, but simply handed the offensive item into Margaret's eagerly clutching hand.

She was finally entirely naked, spread out before the man, before both of them in fact, but they made no overt recognition of this. He disdainfully pushed her legs apart until her knees reached the edge of the couch and her legs dangled over the sides; she watched him do it. Casually he smoothed her pubic hair away from her vulva in order to clear his view, and then retrieved his clipboard, which he consulted carefully.

Again he peered at her vagina, splayed the outer lips open and revealed the smaller lips concealed inside. He started to examine her vulva, massaging, gauging, probing, roughly pulling open the inner lips to peer inside, peeling back her skin to expose her clitoris, all the time massaging and circling and arousing. After some moments he withdrew his fingers, wiped them disdainfully on a tissue, and made another series of notes.

'You appear to lubricate extremely freely.' The comment was to himself more than her and she could think of no appropriate response.

He returned to his exploration and, with the fingers of one hand holding her lips open, flicked at her clitoris while his other fingers dug deep inside her. Then he turned to Margaret for the second time.

'Here, hold these lips open for me, will you. I'm afraid they're dreadfully slippery.'

Margaret jumped eagerly to his aid, her face already flushed, her eyes dilated and searching as she came to lean over the subject and peer closely between Irene's wide-spread thighs. Both Margaret's hands were down there now, the fingertips on each side holding open her plump succulent vulva while her thumbs caressed the length ever so lightly, just occasionally, just tantalisingly irregularly, reaching up as far as Irene's clitoris.

Mr Weston returned to his desk and retrieved another of his pale intrusive rods, even longer and much fatter this time, although certainly, Irene realised, as big as the handle of her hairbrush. While he had been absent, Margaret's caresses had become more blatant and he brushed her hands aside with a slight expression of disapproval, but Margaret did not return to her station at the foot of the couch. Instead she stayed standing close by, and, when her hands dropped down by her sides, they seemed of their own accord to come into contact with Irene's breasts, where the backs of her fingers caressed gently the soft ample swelling as it lolled off her chest.

It must have been perfectly clear to Mr Weston that the natural reaction to so much attention had made any artificial lubricant quite unnecessary. Even so, the second, thicker, white rod was generously stirred round in the same jar of cold Vaseline before he leant over to slip it up and down her crease and then slide it slowly, twisting as it went, deeper and deeper within her. The shock of its pushing against her cervix made her suck in her breath, and he glanced down to read a measurement off the side of his probe, noting it carefully.

He did not withdraw the rod but turned it carelessly in his fingers as he studied the notes.

'When did you last have intercourse?'

Irene could not think for a minute; it had been quite a while, when Paul had been down.

'About three weeks ago.'

'And when did you last masturbate?'

Irene blushed deeply and glanced first at the woman on one side and then the man on the other. Margaret was twisting her legs together, squeezing her thighs, her fingers still lightly stroking the side of Irene's breast.

Eventually the man broke the silence. 'Come on, it won't affect your application.'

'Yesterday.'

'You mean last night?'

'Er, no. In the afternoon.'

He noted that without comment.

'And what technique do you use?'

'Sorry? What do you mean?'

'Do you use a vibrator, or your hand? Is it fingertip on the clitoris, three fingers in the groove or palm all over?'

'Well, it depends. Mostly three fingers, I suppose.'

'You'll have to show me.' At last he removed the rod, checked his watch and noted the time on his pad.

'Now? Here?'

His irritation started to overboil. 'Yes, of course here. Where else do you think I mean?'

This seemed too much, and Irene searched round in despair for a way out. There was none, but she caught Margaret's eye: she smiled at her and gently, kindly, stroked her cheek and then her nipple.

'Don't be shy, Irene, dear. Everybody has to do it.'

So Irene closed her eyes and let her mind wander to other places, other people, other lovers long ago both real and imagined. Her hand homed in on her willing lips and eager clitoris as she gently massaged up and down. Her middle finger just grazed the entrance to her vagina and lifted at the top to allow her third and forefinger to meet and pinch her clitoris on each stroke.

Even with her eyes closed, she knew what she looked like. She had watched herself in the mirror many times before and could visualise the progression as the feelings intensified and that middle finger stopped lifting and instead pressed in as each stroke dawdled at the top of her gaping crease. She could feel her lips swelling yet more, seeping even more profusely.

Still without looking, she knew that the man was gauging her carefully, watching the increasing involuntary squirms of her legs and body, the little gasps and sighs, and when she abandoned any attempt at modesty and allowed her free hand to reach up and maul at her swollen breasts, he merely checked his watch and noted the event on his pad. She did not cut out the knowledge of the two others in the room with her, but she started to turn the shame of their presence into stimulation and fed on their avid attention, growing more wanton and uninhibited with every long pant.

It was when she was almost there, a few tiny seconds from the tantalising gorgeous precipice, that he grabbed hold of her wrist and hauled it away from her swollen clitoris.

'That will do. You can stop now.'

Of course he knew that now she didn't want to stop, but he held her hand away still and denied her the last release. Instead he leant down to examine her vulva closely and to inhale the powerful scent that, even over the antiseptic smell of the room, Irene could smell herself.

'Quite an impressive degree of engorgement here,' he said, and he prodded almost painfully at her clitoris with the end of his pencil. Margaret stooped down to see as well, and when the pencil was withdrawn, her fingers took over, pushing and probing.

'Now the bladder test. Sit up on the couch over this bottle.'

He held out a bottle, wide-necked like a wine carafe, and when she had managed to manoeuvre herself into a squat on the couch in front of him, he pushed it under her bottom, pressing its cold hard rim against her hot, overstimulated flesh. She closed her eyes and tried to relax, but it was no use; she could not let go.

He was getting impatient and checked his watch, screwing the neck of the flask against her tender skin.

'Come along, I haven't got all day.'

So she reached her fingers down between her thighs and, opening her legs even further in front of him, she swiftly and shamelessly manipulated her body to the glorious juddering climax that at last relaxed her clamped-up muscles sufficiently for her to shoot streams of hot golden piss into the bottle. When the stream died away and she was finally finished he took the bottle back and held it up in front of him. He sniffed.

'Barely quarter of a litre. You'll have to come back next week and try to do better than that,' and he turned away to note her performance on his sheet. Before she had time to register his comment, he had gone, the door banging loudly behind him.

It was so fast, so unexpected, that Irene barely noticed Margaret pull a delicate fresh lace handkerchief out from the pocket of her own skirt and use it to wipe carefully and lingeringly at the last droplets on Irene's warm moist crease. However, she could not continue to ignore it for long. Margaret was still smiling at her, and the wiping was continuing, gently, insistently and entirely ineffectively. Irene knew it would need a thick towel to absorb all the juice that she was still producing; knew that Margaret's attentions were increasing the flow, and knew that although her legs felt barely strong enough to continue to support her, her body was teetering on the edge of another shaking shattering climax and that this woman was determined to shame her into releasing it.

Irene gave in. She reached over to hold both Margaret's shoulders for support, and sobbed with joy when Margaret raised her other hand to Irene's eager breast and squeezed encouragingly at her ripe nipple.

It was enough; Irene grunted, blindly shoved her pelvis forward into Margaret's hand, and then opened wide her eyes to stare unseeing into Margaret's face as she thrust hard and then harder against the probing fingers and they in turn rasped ecstatically painfully over the head of her exposed clitoris with every lunge.

Finally satiated, Irene stopped, swallowed, and pulled away. From the wide stare in Margaret's eyes, the panting open mouth and bright red colouring, Irene guessed that Margaret too had climaxed, but with much more restraint. She was suddenly washed with shame at her own obscene exhibition, and climbed stiffly down from the couch to gather up her clothes. She could not bring herself to speak, could not guess what her examiner would report, and was hugely relieved when she heard the door slam a second time and looked round to find herself standing still naked, but at last alone, in the sparse little room.

12

Sally's Tale – Taken Over

How can I pinpoint when the whole affair really began?
I suppose the number of incidents slowly grew more
frequent and less ambiguous until the situation was fully
developed. Even now I'm not sure when I should have
called the halt, if I should and if I could. Was it really
my responsibility to make that decision? I certainly
didn't instigate any of it, and I honestly do not think I
actively encouraged it, but then I didn't put up much of
a resistance either, and maybe passive acquiescence is as
culpable as direct incitement in situations like this. In
any case, the situation as it finally crystallised was not
of my making but that doesn't mean it was not to my
liking, and I definitely feel no guilt for it now. Maybe
the freedom from the responsibility (which for me was
something of a novelty) was all that I needed to allow
me to relax into a deeper pleasure and a more fulfilling
enjoyment.

First things first. I love Graham, my husband. He is
warm and very kind and sensitive. He looks after me
attentively and anticipates what I may want. He has
worked hard and is now financial director of a company
that makes lots of the small electrical components in
cars, the central locking systems, electric windows and
so forth. Although the company is not an international
concern, it has a good reputation and supplies most of
the main car manufacturers. One day he came home to

say that his company was going to be taken over by a large American corporation, and our immediate concern, naturally enough, was for his job. I expect I'm just like many people whose opinion of America and Americans is shaped more by television and films than personal knowledge. We expected a brash, insensitive and aggressive concern that would run straight over the local company and its people, would pick out the parts it wanted, mould them to its own whims and throw away the rest. However, it soon became clear that we were entirely wrong. The intention was not to close down the company at all; indeed, once the takeover was complete, the new owner planned to build it up as a base for expansion into the whole of Europe. They would be looking to promote several of the existing staff and Graham was given to understand that he was in the running.

The American firm sent over its financial vice-president, a man of considerable authority, who was to complete the details on the merger and take over the running of the UK section. Graham was working closely with him in agreeing the details and was also explaining the way the company functioned and showing him around its operations. I met him one morning outside Graham's office. He was a very tall man, broad and big in all respects, and good-looking in a rather old-fashioned way. I do not know who I can really compare him with; Gregory Peck is perhaps the best, but more for his style than his looks. Anyway, he was easy to be with, was clearly comfortable with other people, even people he had only just met, and had the gift (superficially at least) of spreading that feeling of calm and relaxation. He was the kind of man who could never be mistaken for anything but American; his style of dress was smart but totally unimaginative; his bearing assured but responsive; he was well-mannered but self-centred. He was clearly the boss, but did not make me feel at all shy in his presence. He shook hands firmly but warmly, insisted on using first names straight away and expected to be called by his first name, Stewart, by all the company staff and their wives. He really did seem to be pleased to meet me and to talk, and I do not think that was only because he had been sent over by his company without his family.

Well, all that is really nothing to do with it; I met him one day and he seemed quite pleasant. Graham was getting to know him well because they were working together most of the time, and frequently away for a couple of days when they were visiting other factories. They quickly became very friendly.

Later, the firm held a cocktail-party reception in the hotel at which Stewart was staying when he was officially introduced to the staff of Graham's firm; all the staff and wives were invited. Graham was acting as the host, had helped to arrange it all and was needed to introduce Stewart to the employees that he did not know, so we went along early and up to his room to collect him. When we knocked, the deep voice called out to us to come on in but, as we pushed open the door, he emerged from the bathroom with only a towel wrapped around his waist. He was unabashed, came up and shook Graham's hand and kissed me on the cheek. I didn't like it, not so soon after meeting him, not with him so barely dressed. I didn't say anything at the time, but I caught him studying me a few times before we went down and I was unsure what opinion he was forming.

Generally the reception was as dreadful an affair as any other office party. Stewart gave a speech, which I took to be the usual lecture to staff of a takeover target: 'We will all be a team, one happy family to share each other's fortunes and setbacks.' Although sitting there it all sounded reassuring and as if he really meant it, I wasn't convinced. When I concentrated on the words themselves rather than taking the entire speech, delivery and gestures included, as a whole, the speech was quite impersonal. He could have written and used it many times before this; he could have learnt it at business school for all I know. I let it all in one ear and out of the other.

However, while I was standing at the buffet later, Stewart came up and stood behind me, I mean very close behind me, so that we were virtually touching, and put his arms round my waist to pull me close against him. 'Graham is a really lucky man,' he said. 'You're the best wife that he could hope for with a job like his.' I pulled away and thanked him politely but quickly moved away to join a group of wives in a corner. When I told Graham about it later, he said he thought I was over-sensitive and this was just Stewart's normal way.

'Well, it may be but I don't like it. He is pleasant enough without having to overdo it.'

'Come on, love, he always behaves like that. Don't worry and please don't antagonise him. Lots of opportunities are coming up and I want to keep on the right side of him. Look, here he comes again. Please be friendly for my sake. It will be worth it in the long run. You'll see. Hello, Stewart. I think it's all going pretty well. People seem very happy. What time do you want to wrap it up?'

So the conversation drifted away without my following it. I was vaguely aware that they were discussing the company's future expansion plans, and also Graham's future role and prospects, but at the same time I was conscious that Stewart was glancing at me frequently. It was clear, and may even have been specifically stated, as I say I was not paying all that much attention, that if Graham played his cards right, he could expect great things. Yet, just as he left, Stewart turned and put his arm round my waist, breathing whisky into my hair and said. 'You really are the most beautiful lady; and you have to believe that I know what I am talking about, don't I, Graham, huh?' And he patted my bottom as he moved away. I was quite deeply shocked, and would have taken it as a clumsy attempt at a 'pick-up', but it had been done right in front of my husband, so could hardly be that. Graham had just smiled, but he also blushed a little.

I asked him what he thought Stewart could have meant.

'I have no idea,' he said, and he tried to laugh, but it was hollow.

'I rather get the impression you do, Graham. Tell me.'

'I don't! Not really.'

'Graham, come on.'

'Oh, lord, well he saw those pictures of you that I took last summer.'

'You don't mean the holiday ones?'

Graham nodded.

'Which ones? All of them?'

'No, not all of them, just some.'

'For Christ's sake, Graham, they were not for passing around, I told you that! You agreed! How did he come to see them? Which ones exactly did he see?'

'Just a few.'

'Which ones, Graham? I want to know.'

'Well, on the beach, and on the hotel balcony.'

'What about in the bedroom and the bathroom?'

'Just the one with you sitting in the chair.'

'No others?'

'No, certainly not.'

'Are you sure?'

'Yes.'

'Well, that's something, I suppose. But why did you let him see any of them?'

'He asked.'

'Oh, come off it, Graham, you mean he just walked in one day and said, "Hello, Graham, why don't you

215

show me those pictures that you took of your wife naked when you were on holiday. You know, the ones you promised her you would not pass all round the office". Is that it?'

'No, of course not. We were talking about cameras, because he's quite keen as well, and he asked if he could see some of my photographs. I agreed to that, but then the subject moved on to nudes and he asked if I'd ever taken any of you. I couldn't very well just lie.'

'Why not?'

'Well, he wouldn't have believed me for one thing. Everyone takes nude pictures of their girlfriends and wives; everyone knows that. And with you in particular, there's no way he would have believed me if I had said no. Anyway, I don't see that admitting I'd taken them did any harm, but then when I showed him some of my landscapes, he wanted to see some of the ones of you as well, and I couldn't refuse. Really, I don't know what you are so upset about. When I was taking them, and you were sitting on the beach and the balcony, you weren't worried about people seeing you in the nude; why does it matter now? You were happy to show them to Maureen and Richard.'

'That was different, you know that. They're our friends, not just people in your office. I told you I didn't want everybody to see them.'

'Well, it wasn't everybody, only Stewart.'

'You still should have refused.'

'I couldn't!'

'Why ever not?'

'He's very persuasive; you know that. And I really do want to keep in his good books.'

'Well, for goodness sake, Graham, why can't you stand up to him?'

'It's difficult,' he said limply.

Graham and I had to stay on right until the reception wound down, after Stewart had seen all the other staff off. Eventually, at the end of an interminable line of handshakes and goodnights and when only the three of us were left, he invited us to join him for dinner in the hotel. I wasn't very keen, but Stewart was most insistent, complaining that he would be left all alone while Graham took away the beautiful female company. It was clumsy and patronising but I believe that was unintentional – he just had no idea how else to behave. In the end I could find no convincing excuse to get us out of it, and Graham wanted to go, so I prepared myself for what I expected to be a difficult evening. I certainly didn't want to say or do anything that would prejudice Graham's chances of getting the good jobs coming up, but neither did I want to encourage, nor even expose myself to the dangers from, Stewart's roving hands.

In fact, the dinner went very well and Stewart was a great deal more relaxed and amusing when only the three of us were there. Although he was still very much the senior party, he and Graham had a good rapport and I found him to be more agreeable company than I had previously thought. Certainly he was very forward and confident, but then he has done a lot with his life, so maybe he can be allowed some lack of modesty. He has travelled to a vast number of countries, worked his way up from the bottom, and he started with no advantages in life at all – precious little education, and certainly no family backing or capital. I found him to be easy to talk to, and he wasn't limited to discussing business, but talked of a wide range of things without seeming to monopolise the conversation.

Anyway, between the pleasant conversation and having drunk all my share of two bottles of wine with the meal (very good wine, I should say), I was feeling much more kindly disposed towards him. Graham invited him to our house for a nightcap afterwards and, while I was in the kitchen making coffee, Stewart came out. He thanked me (rather over-generously) for the coffee and the 'enormous help' with the arrangements for the reception, which we both knew to have been catered entirely by the hotel staff. Even so, he was so direct and open that I couldn't be surprised and wasn't even upset when he came right up and kissed me. But it was a longer kiss than it had any right to be, and it ended with his hand, over the top of my dress, cupping my breast just as Graham came in. Obviously he saw what was happening, and yet I was the one that acted and felt guilty when really it was Stewart who was to blame. He had started it. I tried to pull away quickly, but Stewart would not release me; he just gave my breast a little squeeze and smiled at Graham.

'She's a real beauty, Graham, you know that?'

Graham looked at me, at Stewart, then at me again, but he wasn't angry. In fact, my immediate impression was that he was more excited than anything else. We all went back to the living room and, other than a perfectly respectable peck on the cheek as he left, Stewart didn't touch me any more. Nor did he make any reference to what had happened.

While we were getting ready for bed, I wanted to apologise to Graham for the business in the kitchen, but I didn't know how to do it without appearing to be trying to excuse my own wrongdoing. I explained that Stewart had started it, and I had not encouraged him at all. Graham said I shouldn't worry, that it was just Stewart's way and he really didn't mind. He then asked if I liked Stewart any more as a result of knowing him better.

'I never said I disliked him. He's perfectly pleasant and easy-going. I just find him, I don't know, a little bit too much, that's all. He's too forward, and I don't know where I am. I don't feel entirely safe with him.'

'You're sounding just like your mother; you always say she only likes wimps and you like a man to be more assertive.'

'Well, I do.'

'Well then, isn't that what Stewart is? Just assertive?'

'Yes, I suppose so.'

Graham seemed unreasonably pleased with this reappraisal and I suppose I should have been on my guard, but we were lying in bed, he had lifted my nightdress up to my neck, and his hands were distracting me, so I was only half concentrating on what he was saying.

'He mentioned the photographs again the other day, and he asked, you know, if he could, well, if you would model for him.'

'What did you say?'

'Nothing really. I just said I would have to ask you. See if you wanted to.'

I thought about it for a while and Graham's fingers continued digging and rubbing and that began to affect the way the proposal appeared. 'What sort of modelling?'

'Well, he didn't say.'

'Nude? Does he mean that?'

'I don't know, Sal, he didn't say.'

There was a silence, and maybe Graham was deliberately allowing time for his hands to excite me further.

'Of course he's seen those ones I took, so he could well be thinking of that.'

'I couldn't do that. I mean I wouldn't mind a bikini or something, perhaps even topless, but I won't go nude.'

'OK, that's fine. Don't do anything you don't want to. Don't do it at all if you don't like the idea.'

'What do you think, Graham? Should I?'

'It's up to you, love. If you want to. I mean, I don't mind.'

'What else did he say?'

'Nothing, really; we were just talking about

219

photography and things. He asked if I had a video camera.'

'Well, all right, I suppose. I don't mind the modelling, just so long as he understands. You would have to stay there with me.'

'Yes, that would be fine.'

It had emerged during the conversation over dinner that Stewart's birthday was only a few days after mine, and they were both just coming up. Although he had said nothing then, he came round to the house again a few evenings later, on the day before my birthday, bringing a big box that he presented to me. I muttered something about waiting for the next day but he said I could unwrap it then and there, which I am impatient enough not to object to. It contained a fabulous red dress, from an exclusive shop that I can never afford to shop in. It really was quite stunning, in my size and my style, and a colour that I never wear but wish I had the nerve for. Certainly a very much better choice than Graham would ever have made.

It was very well cut: long and full in the skirt, but cut away at the top into a very low, daring front; the straps were just steadily narrowing extensions of the bodice and it had virtually no back at all. Stewart encouraged me to try it on and Graham joined in the urging. So I went up to our bedroom and took off the casual skirt and sweater that I'd been wearing. The dress was definitely cut too low to be worn with a bra, so that had to come off, along with my slip. Turning around in front of the mirror, I couldn't help smirking; I had to admit that it looked good, very good. To help the overall effect, I changed into some white high-heeled shoes and then, I'm not at all sure why, I took off my tights and put on stockings and a suspender belt. I felt really good, quite special, attractive and desirable. I touched up my make-up before going back down to the men.

When I did go back downstairs again, I found that they (who? I wondered later) had dimmed the lights and put some music on, although the television was still flickering dimly but silently in the corner. I felt seductive, magnificent even, entering the room, almost as if I were a glamorous model on a cat-walk.

Graham was in a chair opposite the television with Stewart on the other side on the couch, so that I had to walk down between them. I twirled at the end, and they were both very appreciative, Graham was even more taken aback than Stewart; he wasn't used to seeing his good little wife in dresses like this.

The fabric was thin and very clinging, so that as I walked my thighs were quite clearly outlined and, as I said, the neckline came very low at the front. They could see I was not wearing a bra and in fact I could feel my nipples hardening and pushing out. I paused at the end and thanked Stewart profusely for the dress, apologising that I had no gift for him.

'Don't worry about that. I will happily settle for a birthday kiss instead!' And he stood up and advanced towards me.

I was hesitant, but Graham was not. 'Yes, go on, Sal, I think Stewart definitely deserves a kiss for that!'

So I stood up in the middle of the room, with Stewart's great arms enfolding me, and he kissed me and then, with one arm holding me tight, the other hand ran down from my neck, snaked inside my dress and wrapped around my breast. I was shocked, but I honestly cannot remember now whether I was so shocked that I didn't resist much. I suppose I was expecting Graham to leap to my defence. He didn't, although, as we were facing him, he could clearly see what was going on. I had looked at him, my face still squashed against Stewart's chest and there he sat, my husband, watching. He looked tense, but there was also something of excitement in his eye. What the hell was going on? Surely he wasn't going to allow this? Was he nervous because he was not sure how to interrupt? I was totally bewildered, and found I was still standing there in the man's arms; he still had his hand caressing my nipple and his tongue was now probing between my lips. That really was going too far and I pulled away, hauling his hand out of my dress and straightening the top.

'I, er, I think I should get some more coffee.' I wanted out, time to think, time to let Graham have a word with our guest. But Stewart said:

'That would be great.' Cool bastard, wasn't he even ashamed of himself?

From the kitchen I could hear the voices but not the words. They were not angry; there was even a low laugh at one point. What the hell was going on? Why didn't Graham do anything? I mean, he may be anxious not to upset his new boss but that doesn't mean you have to let him fuck your wife. For Heaven's sake, had he set this up? Agreed to it in advance? Was his fear in case I rejected Stewart? Was I perhaps the price to be paid for his promotion? What was I supposed to do? When Graham had pressed me for my opinion of Stewart after the dinner the previous week, was this what he had in mind? Had he been referring to Stewart's kissing me? And if he did, what had I meant? Graham knew what kind of man I liked and Stewart was certainly attractive. I had been on at him often about being more positive and assertive. Was this what he thought I wanted? To be honest, it was in a way. Would my accepting Stewart's approach show my husband a little more of the way he should behave? It could be worth a try. At least if it failed, it would have done no harm, and might have done Graham's career some good.

As I returned with the coffee tray, I heard some music starting in the living room.

Graham said: 'This is one of Stewart's favourites too,

love. He has all the records but he has not brought them over yet.'

Stewart was sprawled along the couch. 'Why don't you two young lovers dance, eh? I bet you never get to dance together these days and I do like to see a couple enjoying themselves.'

I accepted the offer and, feeling much safer in Graham's arms, I showed off, twirling my skirt to show my legs, and when the next song was slow, pulling in close to him. Graham was, surprisingly for him, very forward, and dropped his hands down on to my bottom, pulling me in tight. He was evidently physically aroused, I could feel his erection squashed between us, and at the end he kissed me, quite affectionately, on the lips.

'Hell, that's no way to kiss a gorgeous girl like that, Graham. What the hell's the matter with you? Give her a proper kiss, for Chris'sake!'

Graham kissed me again, much more passionately, but still it was not enough for his boss.

'Go on, boy, that's not how I kiss a girl, is it, Sal, eh? Do you need me to show you how, Graham?'

I think we both giggled at that, at his totally unashamed candour. So Graham kissed me a third time. It was long and wet and his hand followed the same path that Stewart's had done, up outside the front of my dress and over my breast before slipping inside the material and around the nipple. It certainly did excite me, not just the kiss, but also the caress and particularly the knowing that Stewart was watching. When Graham eventually pulled back, Stewart stood up and came over to me. One of his huge hands hooked into the front of my dress and pulled it out. Quite unashamedly he peered down, saw my long, dark-red nipple and winked at me then smiled at Graham.

'That's the way, boy! She obviously liked that.'

And again we both laughed. I mean, looking back, I cannot understand why I wasn't embarrassed, ashamed and angry, but then Stewart was so calm, collected and comfortable that it was difficult not to follow his lead.

When we were all sitting down again, Stewart went on: 'I gather you do a bit of modelling, Sal. Graham tells me you used to do a lot at one time. I expect he told you that I'm a bit of a photographer, like he is, and I saw some shots he'd taken of you. They looked really good. You are quite a girl! Would you care to let me take some one day?'

He didn't seem to know that Graham had already asked me about this and so I didn't let on either. I shrugged. 'Maybe. What kind of shots?'

'Well, the usual sort of thing, I suppose. Something a little bit glamorous. Frills and lace, you know the kind of thing.'

'You mean lingerie?'

'That's it. I'll bet you have one hell of a collection.'

I giggled. 'Some, I suppose.'

'Real old-fashioned stockings and garters and that?'

I didn't say anything, just pulled the hem of my dress up far enough so that he could see the stocking tops, just for a second before I let it drop down.

'OK, Sal, I'll do you dressed just as you are now! You'll do great like that, except maybe we'll lose the dress.'

'I don't know if my husband would approve of me parading around in front of other men dressed only in my underclothes.'

'I'm sure he wouldn't, but if it were only me, I'll bet he wouldn't care at all.'

I glanced across. 'Well, Graham?'

'As you like, love, If you would like to, I'm perfectly happy.'

'You wouldn't mind?'

'No, I think it would be fine if you want to. It's entirely up to you.'

'All right then, maybe I will. I'll think about it.'

'Great! Do I get to see the model now?' Stewart asked.

'No, you don't!' I protested.

'Why not? If I can see later, why not now?'

'Yes, go on, Sal, let him see,' said Graham.

'Why now? Besides, I haven't got a bra on now.'

Stewart laughed. 'It's a bit late to tell us that, Sal. We already know that, don't we, Graham?'

'Yes, go on, take the dress off.'

'I don't see why I need to.'

'I think she's just a little bit shy, Graham. Why don't you be a gentleman and give the lady a hand? Help her out a little?'

I suppose I had not sounded very convincing to either of them and so, when Graham came up, I didn't move. He leant forward to kiss me on the top of the head then reached round and unfastened the single button at the back of my dress. He peeled back the top like fruit peel to expose my breasts and I let him. I just sat there looking up at my husband and accepting the hand that he proffered to help me up and then help me step out of the dress. He picked it up while he left me standing there for the other man to see. I was not completely naked, and was wearing a French cut of knickers rather than a bikini, so was very much more covered than I might have been usually. All the same, I felt very exposed. Probably the contrast with the other two being fully dressed made it worse.

Stewart turned me around, ran his fingers lightly down my sides and across my breasts. Then he briskly patted my bottom, bent and kissed both nipples, said goodnight and was gone.

Immediately the door shut, Graham simply grabbed me and we were kissing straight away. He almost ripped the rest of my clothes off me and we ended up on the floor, both of us more excited than we had been in several years, since we had first got married probably.

Why? Well, I had this picture of Stewart still being there and kind of making us do it so that he could watch. But then that was interspersed with a picture of Graham watching while I was forced to do it with Stewart. I had never had any fantasies like that before, but they were both very powerful and wild and I was attracted.

On top of that, there was the business of the photographs. Graham had been right about them earlier; I had been quite open in public when he'd been taking them, first sitting on the hotel balcony in a sheer nightdress, but visible and knowing I was visible to other guests in the hotel. Then I had loosened the nightdress so my breasts were exposed, and finally totally naked both on the balcony and more in the bedroom. By the end, several of them were more than just suggestive. Later we did some more out of doors, me completely naked on a secluded beach. In fact, it wasn't completely secluded, a couple of people had come by and had seen me from the cliff top. I had been glad they were there but had wished they had come nearer and stayed for longer. Our love-making after that had been very heated, although nothing had been explicitly said, we were both excited by my exposure.

It was also true that I had been keen to show the pictures to Richard and Maureen. They're our closest friends and we often go out, and sometimes away for weekends, all together. We never swap partners or anything like that, but there is always joking and teasing about that possibility. At first I thought it might happen, that the talk might be sounding the way and would lead into the event, but now I know that it will not, and the joking has come to replace the reality.

One hot summer some years ago when we were together in their garden, Maureen and I had taken our tops off in front of the men and I had dreamt of that going further, but it never did. I mean, we had both been topless in front of them on beaches before, but then it had all been quite restrained by there being other people around. This time had been a bit different because the men had asked us to take our tops off, and then Maureen and I had done a joint mini-striptease. We were fooling around, throwing ice cubes about or something, and when I tipped some cold water over Richard, he threatened to put me over his knee, pull down my knickers and spank me. I wanted him to do it, not so much the spanking as the being made naked in public. Do your husband and best girlfriend count as public? Probably not, but I had never seen Maureen naked, nor she me and it would have been a little bit public, enough to give it some added spice, if only it had happened. Once I had tried to arrange things so that she saw me 'accidentally' but that hadn't worked either and you cannot stage an accident twice.

On Graham's side, what was getting him so excited? I couldn't tell and I didn't know whether to ask him. On balance I decided that I was not prepared to come out and describe my thoughts, so I didn't really want to bring the conversation around to specifics. Better to leave it, see if anything else happened. What if it didn't? Then I could suggest inviting Stewart round to dinner to return the hospitality.

As it turned out, when Graham came home one night a week or so later he was keyed up, trying to tell me something, trying to work out how to express it. It had to be concerning Stewart, so I gave him an opening.

'How is Stewart? How was his trip to London?'

'Oh, fine, yes he's fine. In fact I was talking to him today. He mentioned the photographs again. You remember we talked the other night about him taking some of you.'

'Yes, but I had rather a lot to drink that night and got carried away. I'm not sure if I still want to.'

'Oh.' A pause. 'I have already told him you would.'

'What? Why?'

'Well you did say, Sal. I really don't think we can back out now.'

'We? What do you mean, 'we'? I'm the one who has to do this! You shouldn't have agreed without consulting me.'

'I did consult you! We talked about it and you agreed! How was I supposed to know you were going to change your mind?'

'When does he want to do it?'

'Well, we thought, that is it was kind of suggested, perhaps next Sunday. If he came round to lunch we could do it afterwards. We aren't doing anything, are we?'

'No.'

'Well then.'

'But you will stay with me, all the time?'

'Yes, I said I would.'

'No matter what Stewart says, you stay.'

'Fine.'

When the day came, I was nervous now that I was facing the imminence of the actual event, but I turned on some heating in the living room and cleared a space at one end by the big bay window where there was good natural light, and plenty of room to set up the camera. We kept a wickerwork chair there which looks very old-fashioned, but comes across well in photographs. Graham had often taken photographs of me there.

Stewart brought a whole load of things in with him, not just a camera but armfuls of other stuff and a suitcase of what he called props.

We drank a fair bit of wine over the lunch, and Stewart kept giving me more. He was relaxed and easy-going and that passed on to me, creating a friendly and intimate atmosphere, so that I gradually started to overcome the nervousness and was even looking forward to what was to follow.

After lunch, and coffee, we started on the photographs. First Stewart took several with me in the clothes I'd been wearing when he arrived, but then he asked me to change into the red dress he had given me for my birthday. I wondered whether this would lead to anything more; logically there was no reason why it should, just that the dress had connotations for me. Anyway, it didn't happen like that and instead he then had me put on a light summery dress and wear a big straw hat he'd brought with him. Then change again into a pair of my old and faded jeans and a checked shirt. I was actually starting to get fed up with going up and down stairs to change. This was not at all what I'd expected. I had envisaged Stewart asking me to change into steadily more revealing clothes and then to remove them one by one (which was what Graham generally did when he took photographs of me). I'd already decided that I was prepared to go down as far as my underclothes and if pressed would remove my bra, but that I would go no further; I had put on some specially attractive underthings for the purpose. Stewart seemed to have other ideas, and the costumes were not getting any more suggestive. Anyway, after a couple of me sitting in the cane chair, he asked me to undo the front of the shirt, so a thin gap of skin showed all the way down. When I complied, he asked if I could take my bra off so that the strap wouldn't show across the middle.

I started to go upstairs but he said, 'Oh, do it here. Turn away and I won't look. Besides, we're all one happy family, aren't we?'

So I stayed where I was, turning my back away from them and, half crouched in the corner, aware of eyes over me, hurriedly slipped off the bra before replacing the shirt.

After a couple of pictures of me alone – in one I was turned sideways and I think I was leaning forward enough for at least part of my breast to be visible – he asked Graham to join me.

At first Graham just stood behind the chair, like in an old Victorian photograph, but then Stewart asked him to sit in the chair while I sat on the floor at his feet. Stewart wanted us kissing, but after one quick peck he told Graham to kiss me, 'like you did before, the way she likes it'. Graham didn't seem to need much encouragement and immediately brought his mouth down to mine while his hand slid deep inside the half-open shirt and found my nipple.

After that bar was crossed, Stewart increased the pace of the directions until it was almost continual, more like directing a film than posing a model, but taking photographs all the time.

'Put your hands over Sal's breasts, Graham; no, inside. That's right. Good. Sal, pull the shirt over a little more, so I can see Graham's hands on you. Good! Very nice! Tip your head back, Sal, look up at Graham. Great! Graham, lean down and kiss her, like that, good. Now open her shirt more, further, off her shoulders, that's fine. Caress her breasts. Yes, they're gorgeous, all around, and now concentrate on her nipples. Rub them around, use just finger and thumb, don't cover them over, pull them up so I can see them, lovely, they are really beautiful.'

Stewart paused to change the film, and it was really only then that it registered exactly what had happened. In fact, as soon as he had been asked to, my husband had exposed my breasts, shown me half naked to his boss. He had not even bothered covering me up again when he stood up. I shivered in fear and anticipation and excitement and pulled the shirt across again.

Stewart then produced from his case of props another box which he presented to me. 'This is a present for you, but I would like to take some shots of you wearing it.'

'What is it?'

'Put it on.'

The box bore the name of the same boutique that the dress had come from, but inside was a cream-coloured silk camisole and matching briefs. It was absolutely beautiful, so elegant and seductive, easily the most beautiful thing like that I have. Again I started to go upstairs to change, again Stewart interposed.

'Come on, Sal, we're all friends here. There's no call for unnecessary modesty.'

'This is different, Stewart. I would prefer to change upstairs.'

'As you like, honey, but I don't really think it's necessary.'

But I went up to my bedroom anyway to put it on. The bikini-style bottom was cut high on both sides, and the little bit of lace around the legs did not go far to cover the hair that was poking through. I tried to tuck it in behind the elastic, but it wouldn't all go. The camisole laced up the front, it was thin and felt like a breeze against my skin, soft, caressing almost kissing me. I mean, I have other camisoles and whatever, because I like wearing them and Graham likes to see me in them, but this was different: an entire class finer than anything else I had. It covered me with a promise that it would reveal me, and really it was that garment more than anything else that finally made me face myself. It showed me what I wanted: that I wanted to show off. Wearing that, anyone would want to. I knew then, before I returned downstairs, that it was going to be very difficult to maintain my previous limit. If they insisted, when they insisted, I would be tempted to take everything off.

Even so, I laced the front up tight, from the waist right up to the neck; they would have to work for it.

When I went back downstairs, they liked the effect. I turned a couple of times to show them, and that seemed to go down well. Stewart had me stand by the chair, one leg up on the seat, then sitting across it, legs over the side, legs drawn up, but then he said, 'Undo the lace, Sal, just a little.'

So I did, just a little, enough to show the beginnings of the tops of my breasts as I followed his orders and curled up in the chair, bent across it, stood behind it. It satisfied him for a few shots but then:

'Undo some more, Sal. You're too beautiful to keep hidden.'

A few more inches of unused lace showing a few more inches of private skin. How much was visible when I leant over the chair now? The silk was sheer enough that I am sure my nipple was no longer hidden; the two men stood in the room watching and I stayed in the bay, posing. In the end it was Graham who said, 'Take the top off, Sal.'

I obeyed: simply stood up and pulled the warm silk up and over my head and laid it across the back of the chair, turning back to face them both, left with only a tiny wisp of almost sheer silk. My hands went up and covered my breasts, covered and then squeezed, pinching my nipples between thumb and forefinger.

The exact sequence after this is not entirely clear, but first he had Graham sitting in the chair, and me sitting on his lap. We were kissing. His arms were around me, and then his hand was over my breast, caressing me. Then I was kneeling in front of Graham, my hands reaching up to undo his shirt, then his shirt off. My head resting in his lap and hands reaching up over his chest; he has a lovely chest. Then my hands as well as my head were in his lap, a hardening lap, hands on his zip, his zip undone, my fingers inside feeling for him, him free and my hands grasping, pulling off the last of his clothes. He is now more naked than I am, although Stewart is still fully dressed. Kissing; tongues touching; his lips on my nipple; his hands on my bottom, squeezing the cheeks; then the hands are reaching inside my knickers; then he leans over me, stretching to push them over my buttocks, down my legs, to show me off. Although I am part hidden, kneeling on the floor and with my back to Stewart and my thighs clamped together, I am now naked. My limit has been reached and passed and I have not tried to resist.

Before I can think, Graham stands me up, and turns me round to make me face Stewart and show him my triangle. Graham is behind me, pushing his leg forward between mine to force my legs apart. His fingers are digging into the warmth, then tugging the hair up and away so that the groove is opened up, my legs pulled further apart, his fingers splay my lips wide and I feel the cool air as he pushes me forward, displaying me obscenely. Stewart smiles and comes forward for a close-up shot of this.

Then I am kneeling again; my head in Graham's lap; my hands encircling his erection; my tongue out and just touching him; my lips opening, first kissing and finally taking more and all of him into my mouth.

Stewart has moved in close by now, to catch my tongue running beneath the rim, careful not to lose the first little drops, the head pushing in past my lips and deep into my mouth.

Then suddenly we are to change places. I'm sitting in the cold wicker chair, my legs spread wide and at first I have to hold open my own lips, pink and slippery and hot, for Stewart to see me. My own fingers are told to pull back the little hood to show it all. Then Graham is back, his lips nipping at me; his fingers at my nipples and his tongue circling down there, pushing and probing, bringing me up higher, near, so near my peak and then away, and always Stewart, watching, leaning in closer, never touching, but always there and photographing.

Then he wants me on my knees, with my breasts swaying beneath me like an animal; full and ripe, and the two men are behind me. I cannot see them but I feel the palms push between my thighs easing them wider, my buttocks being spread; a finger tracing patterns of running juices up and back. There is a pause as my anus is touched, pressed and I clench up, but with a mutter and a laugh they move on. I hear the continuous clicking of the shutter and drop on to my elbows so that my nipples can grab a few gentle caresses from the soft pale fur of the rug. Fingers pulling at my lips, opening me up still further, a finger then two pushing gently inside me and then finally, slowly, the clicking all the time, no longer just fingers – Graham is penetrating me and steadily the pace of his movements is building up. Without warning, all the slow progression is forgotten and after only a half dozen more violent grunts he erupts into me, the fierce final thrusts pushing me over the top, and I think I screamed as the bursts exploded deep in my womb and I collapsed on to the floor.

When I looked up, Stewart was perched against the back of an armchair, still holding his camera. He was still fully dressed and gave no impression of having been in any way affected by the scene which had just been acted out, acted virtually entirely at his direction, just a few feet in front of him. I went upstairs to tidy up and when I returned some fifteen minutes later, Graham, now with his jeans back on, said Stewart had already gone home.

About a week later Stewart took the pictures into Graham's office and he telephoned me during the day to tell me he would bring them round for me to see in the evening. It was odd, knowing that Stewart had already been looking at them all, and Graham too. Had anyone else? Did I want them to have been seen around? In a way I did, some people, anyway, I wouldn't mind, but only if they appreciated me and not if they just gloated.

No, it was too much. They really had been too uninhibited.

Stewart came around, after we had finished supper, making my stomach tighten and my pussy quiver and moisten as I heard the doorbell ring. He barely waited to be invited to come in, nor to sit down, but took that as his due. When Graham brought him a drink, he again made only a token acknowledgement. He laid a fat brown envelope on the table beside him and, although neither of us made any direct reference, my eyes were drawn across to it time and again. He sat with one hand resting casually on the envelope while the other continually rattled the ice cubes around his glass, and he just kept looking at me. Finally he said, 'Take off your clothes.'

His words whipped across my face. Naturally, after what had happened last time, I expected something at some stage during the evening; we could hardly just sit and look at the photographs and pretend it was a normal social occasion, as if we were exchanging holiday snaps. Even so, the order was so direct and so immediate that I was insulted; the complete lack of introduction, the presumption that he would be obeyed without question, demeaned me. I did not move and he did not react. He didn't get angry, didn't even repeat the order. He simply spoke to my husband instead.

'Graham, undress her.'

Graham looked at me, at Stewart, then back at me again. Perhaps he was waiting for me to object but, when I made no move, he carefully put down his glass and crossed over to where I was sitting. I didn't try to stop him, although neither did I do anything to help, but I let him do as Stewart had asked. It felt so different from my obeying the request, so much richer a surrender, a helplessness, of being exposed as each garment was pulled away and more of me was put on display. So I meekly raised my arms while he pulled the sweater over my head, and sat unmoving for long seconds enduring his fumbling with the clasp of my bra. I submissively stood up to allow him to slide the skirt down my legs, but I quickly sat down again partly, in truth, to press my pussy into the chair, but also so that I would be made to stand again. Every time having to show Stewart some more, to have another defence taken down, steadily more exposed. When Graham had finished, had finally laid my damp white knickers on the top of the discarded pile over the chair arm next to me, Stewart just held his empty glass out, but still looking at me, not at Graham. I had to drop my eyes and try to pull my arms and legs further in against myself although, all the time that my husband fiddled about behind me with glasses and bottles, I could feel the pile of clothes mocking me and the man watching me. Stewart acknowledged the new drink with a nod and spoke again.

'Fine, now, show me her cunt. Turn her to face me and open her legs. Wider, come on. Good. Very nice. Open her lips up for me. That's it. Open her up. She looks wet enough for it already.'

Did Stewart know me so well? Could he read me? I could not have undressed like that, displayed myself so totally, but if Graham did it to me, if I were simply unresisting, acquiescent but passive, I was not culpable. I was simply powerless. As Graham's fingers slipped across my skin, my muscles tried desperately to clutch at them, to draw them within me where I could use them to finish what my own imagination had already started. I could see myself almost as a separate person, wallowing in the intensity of being both ignored, for neither of them spoke to me, and yet also admired.

'Turn her round and bend her over, Graham. Let's have a look at her ass.'

I was pulled up and twisted around, legs spread, to stare down at the seat of the chair, at my hands quivering on the cushion, my arms barely able to continue supporting me, my breasts shivering and swaying beneath me. I could see Graham's legs from the knees down standing beside me. It's silly, but I remember thinking that his shoes looked very old.

'What a wonderful fanny, Graham. You are one hell of a lucky guy and I hope you know it. She's a real dream. Does she like it in her ass?'

A hesitation, and the shoes shuffled a little. 'I, er, I really don't know. We've never done that.'

'You should, you know, you should. I'll bet she would love it. Open up her cheeks for me.'

My legs were pulled even wider apart, and a hand on my shoulders pressed me further down on to the chair. Hands on my buttocks were digging at me again, hard and hurting me. I was left there as the two men talked about me, talked over me, but never talked to me.

'Has she got a vibrator, Graham?'

'No, she hasn't.'

'Pity. What does she use, then? Just fingers?'

'Yes, I suppose so.'

How could I betray myself? Why did I whisper such an incrimination, totally aware of the extra humiliation that it must lead to? Why could I not simply have relished his ignorance and kept the silence?

'What did you say, Sal? Speak up, girl.'

Still barely audible, even to me: 'A candle.'

'A candle! Well, well! Where is it, then?'

Whispered, 'Upstairs.'

'Go and get it, then. You will be needing it.'

I couldn't look at them, sitting casually, fully clothed, as I hurried past naked, head down. Upstairs, retrieving the carefully rounded worn piece of inanimate wax from its nest in my drawer, I was tempted to stay, to lock myself away and finish alone. But I could not, I was pulled back down.

'Let me have a look, Sal. Ah, quite a special one, this

is. You've had this a long time, haven't you? Good. Now then, you lie down here on the rug, and show us what you use this candle for. Off you go!'

I lay down, first flat out and then I brought my legs up a little. I felt down there, slowly running my fingertips in the groove, pinching my clitoris between them and down far enough to let the heel of my palm press down and push my lips further open. Then I pulled my hands away. I simply could not do what he asked. I tried pinching at my nipples and, although I could manage that, it would not have been enough to satisfy either the two men or me, and I stopped. This time Stewart did repeat the demand, but I couldn't do it. I'm quite uninhibited in most things, but that was too much, I simply could not bring myself to masturbate with other people there. I had never, in my whole life, let someone see me do that, even though Graham, and one other before him, had begged me. Well, in bed with a man, then I had used my own fingers to help my orgasm, but that was different. That was just helping to bring on what my lover was driving. But here, before two men, to penetrate myself with my candle was impossible.

So again Stewart spoke to Graham, and with a slight chuckle said, 'Well, it's down to you again, old son! But I think she would like it best with the candle this time.'

He was reading me again. Of course I wanted the candle, and I wanted Graham to do it to me, but I couldn't say so and could only dare to think it when Stewart spoke the words. His cool, unflustered tone gave substance to the dreams that I was holding back. I was his puppet; anything he dared to say, I would allow myself to think. Yet the puppetmaster has no limits; he can dare anything for his creatures and move them to his whim, but even he cannot give them breath. Without him, they lie lifeless, waiting for him to stir them again. But if he had demanded again? Pressed on?

238

If he had really insisted, would I have had to give in to his will? Would I then have acquiesced in my own humiliation for his pleasure? Yes, I think I would.

Yet who had won? He had. I had petulantly refused his demand, and all that had happened was that I was having to submit to something no less humiliating. That I had not willingly agreed to masturbate for his pleasure meant nothing when I was stretched out in front of him, meek and unprotesting, to suffer an equal degradation. What was even worse, he had reduced my husband from a co-spectator beside him to a mere servant of his will, and that was my fault too. I knew all this, and yet it did not destroy my pleasure. In fact it didn't trouble me at all. It should have undermined me, but instead it served only to heighten my anticipation of pleasure and to intensify the desire.

I even began to wonder whether I was getting the whole thing backwards. After all, what did it mean to masturbate here? It was a very commonplace action; something I did alone several times a week. Something that everybody did; a nothing, in fact. Yet I became aware that if I simply wanted to masturbate for an audience, I could do that anytime; in that light my refusal had been little more than an affected pretence of respectability. So perhaps in honesty it would have taken very little pressure to break down that barrier. But this! To have my own husband forced to do it to me! This was rare. This was special. Stewart had lifted us on from primary to master class and yet we did not even notice the advancement, seeing only the lack of our own familiarity.

Did he recognise all that, this man whom I barely knew? Could he see so much, read me so clearly, understand my sexuality so completely? Did he comprehend me so thoroughly, almost better than I did myself, so much better than did Graham, a man who had known me for so long, who knew every inch of my body intimately, who had made love to me thousands of times?

I raised my head to look at him. Although our eyes met, he barely noticed me; a quick glance and then he returned to his drink, ignoring me, not bothering even to look down at my nakedness. His expression carried no visible acknowledgment of any special understanding. How could he ignore it? Was this all normal for him?

I wanted to scream at him. Look at me! See me! I am lying here before you, naked and unresisting. I will let you do anything you want to me. Do you not recognise that you have brought me to this? How can you be so unmoved? Do you do this to all women you meet? Do you have all of them literally lying naked at your feet? Am I just one in a line?

He raised his eyes again and this time they held me for long seconds. A slight smile, but was it more than erotic pleasure? Was there any triumph? I wanted to see triumph, if only so that he had to recognise that I had not acquiesced in this, but had put up a resistance; that there had been a struggle but he had beaten me. Had there been? No, not really; I had surrendered at every opportunity. I wilted beneath his gaze and let my head drop back to the floor, so ashamed that I covered my face with my hands and tried to hide from view.

Only then did I fully notice Graham's actions. His fingers which had been busy between my lips were just withdrawing, starting to work the slim candle into me. Through the bars of my own fingers I gazed at the ceiling. I could only partially see Graham's movements, but the sensations they sent rippling up my body produced a perfectly clear image of every little movement, an image that played in my eyes like a vignette filmed from above. I was conscious of every touch he made but Graham was not aiming to spin out this pleasure. I was already disgustingly wet and he

240

knew me well enough to see that I was well on the way. Not even when we were alone, not even when we had both been drunk, had anything like this happened; he had never done this to me before. Not pushed an object up inside me, and he was not being very gentle, but then I was not in a mood for gentleness. The waves were building up inside me, growing in power and frequency, and I found myself rhythmically lifting my crotch to meet him push for push. As the pace increased I could hear my own groans and the squelching of Graham's fingers on my clitoris and the candle in my pussy. I looked up once but the two men were concentrating so intently on the tiny area between my legs that they didn't even notice me. That took me up the last distance and over the top as I clutched at the patch of carpet beside me and at my own breasts in the deepest and most drawn-out orgasm I had ever known.

When the pounding, spinning waves subsided, I heard Stewart's voice calling me. 'Come over here, Sal.'

As I started to stand, I realised that the candle was still inside me. I plucked it out and threw it down on the floor. When I reached him, he pulled my head down and then had me kneel on the floor between his legs; he said nothing and knew no words were needed. I ignored my husband standing beside me, reached for Stewart's zip and undid his fly. He fractionally raised his hips and I followed his direction, unfastening his belt and pulling down the trousers and then underpants (huge things, almost like shorts) to free his penis. It was already erect, and though it was not as long as Graham's, it was fatter. He was circumcised (my first) and I took him straight into my mouth (my third), my hands also helping.

He practically ignored me, but took up the envelope he had brought along and had Graham sit on the arm of the chair so that the two of them could look at the photographs together. I didn't dare to look up in case I met Graham's eye. Surely he must have watched me sometimes, or waited for me to raise my eyes. I worked at it hard and I like to think I'm proficient at that particular line of love-making, but Stewart sat unmoving and unmoved through many long noisy minutes. The texture and taste of him were different to Graham. The head seemed huge in my mouth, like a whole egg, and I could barely reach my tongue around him. Once he glanced down at me and said to Graham: 'She's a real enthusiast at this, isn't she?' and Graham agreed. Most of the time they spoke about the pictures, discussing how I looked in different poses. As far as I could remember from the events of a week ago, the photographs seemed to be in sequence. About the time they started talking about my being naked while Graham held open my lips, I felt the sudden stiffening and quiver in my mouth that showed Stewart was about to climax. I pulled back a fraction but immediately his hand was on the back of my head to make sure I had no choice but to take it all into my mouth. He held me there until I had swallowed every drop.

I stayed on the floor, more slumped than kneeling, but Stewart quickly got up, refastened his clothes and gathered up the photographs.

'I'll keep these in the office if you want to see the rest tomorrow, Graham. Goodnight. Goodnight, Sal.' And he left without even letting me see my own photographs. The minute he was gone, Graham slumped down into the same chair, and I had to kneel for him too. When we were in bed later he kissed me harder and hugged me closer than I could believe.

After that night it all steadily gathered momentum and there was really no looking back. About ten days later Graham came home in the evening to say that Stewart had invited us to a special dinner at the weekend. It was to be held at a hotel, one that I did not know, had never been to, and I don't think that Graham had either. It was quite a long way away from where we lived, on the main road out of town. I asked Graham what was happening and what was special about it. However, he wouldn't say much, only that it was a sort of charity function and we'd been invited as special guests. He claimed that he himself knew little beyond that (I didn't altogether believe him) but he said it was to be a surprise.

It was enough to rouse my curiosity and, by the Saturday, I found myself spending the whole time looking for clues, listening closely to every word Graham said, trying to read meanings, and feeling sensitive to his mood. It did little good because he was clearly highly tensed himself and neither subtle nor direct probing elicited any results. In fact, around lunchtime, Stewart rang and seemed to be giving out more instructions, so maybe I'm being unfair on Graham; perhaps he really did know no more than me.

Halfway through the phone call he said, 'Hold on, Stewart, I'll ask her.'

He cupped one hand over the receiver and then looked at me a moment, glanced down and then said, 'I really don't know exactly what Stewart has planned. He says it would ruin the surprise if we knew everything, but he says this is our last chance to pull out. He has arrangements to make and we must decide now whether we will go through. He says he's sure that we will enjoy the evening but he will not say what the programme is, just that if we go on now, we have to agree to follow his instructions completely from here on. Agreed?'

Graham's enthusiasm was shining out of his face, and so I nodded, excited but also nervous and just waited to see what would develop. Graham scribbled some notes on a pad by the telephone. He said, 'yes' several times and once glanced up at me, but his side of the conversation gave no indication of what was being planned. Finally he just said, 'Right, we'll see you, then,' and hung up.

I said, 'Well?'

'Well, he still hasn't said a great deal. It seems that he belongs to a sort of society type of thing. It sounds a bit like an American version of the freemasons really and they have occasional meetings to raise money for charities that they support. There is a meeting tonight which we will go to; other than that he just said he thinks we will enjoy the experience. We have to be there for seven o'clock. It will take about forty-five minutes drive so we should be ready to leave a little after six. All right?'

There was not much I could say. When I asked him what I should wear, he said it didn't matter much, but then he corrected himself and said, 'Something comfortable. Smart, but comfortable.' He also said I would need overnight things as Stewart had said we would probably stay the night. That too disquieted me, and I think it was meant to.

I started to get ready at four o'clock, partly I hoped that a long hot bath would ease away some of the tension, but it didn't help much. In fact, from the time I started to prepare for the evening, the tension only increased. Taking off my clothes, I wondered whether I would have to undress again that evening, possibly in front of Stewart; possibly more than Stewart. He had not said in any way that this was to be anything but a perfectly proper social occasion, yet as I lay back in the bath and looked down at my body, I somehow felt sure that other people would be looking at me that evening and that they would require that I go further than I ever had before. Whatever happened, other people would be there, so I washed carefully, shaved my legs, and then went higher and carefully trimmed my pubic hair; trimmed it close because I wanted to look my best for whoever was to be my audience and I wanted Graham to be proud of me. When I suddenly remembered that it was only in my imagination that there was any suggestion of this being anything more than a formal dinner, I was very disappointed.

I wore a knitted dress that I have always liked, and stockings, suspenders and new underclothes that I had bought during the week; white and lacy enough to show a little. I did not put on too much make-up, I seldom do, but I was pleased with the result.

The car journey passed in silence for the most part until we arrived at the hotel. We found a modern building, low and long on two sides around the car-park and, although it called itself an hotel, it was really more of a motel of the type that specialises in business conferences, exhibitions and that kind of thing: a place for people to stop only if they have to, and to leave once their business is done. We drove into the car-park and round to the back where a couple of cars were parked. A radio was playing as we passed the open kitchen window, but I saw no other people, either staff or guests, as we made our way through to the reception desk. The emptiness was intimidating. The receptionist came out of a secure back office and was courteous and helpful, but it was a pleasantness born of an effective training programme, not a genuinely friendly personality. A booking had been made in our name although it was clear from Graham's manner and uncertain tone of voice that he hadn't made it himself. Presumably that was Stewart's work. The whole place felt tense; Graham was obviously unsure what was happening and, although he seemed to know where we were to go, I got the impression that he had been given directions, almost a script, but was not entirely certain how the drama was to be played out.

We had barely settled into the room before he was suggesting that we should go down to the bar for a drink and then have dinner; he's not normally much of a drinker, and for him to suggest this was completely out of character.

The bar was quiet; taped music played softly but dust-covered boxes on a small cluttered stage in the corner suggested occasional live music. A young couple were sitting uncomfortably at a table by the door and two men talked together towards one end of the bar. Otherwise, the place was empty. Everyone looked over at us as we came in and there was some whispering, which was not surprising in view of the limited number of people, but I did not like it.

We sat on stools up at the bar and when the barman reappeared, Graham ordered drinks. I wanted to talk, to try to forget the surroundings.

'Are you sure we shouldn't wait for Stewart? What time will he get here?'

'He didn't say exactly; sometime this evening.'

'Didn't he say when? I mean, presumably in time to join us for dinner?'

'Not exactly.'

'Come on, Graham, stop being so difficult. What is "not exactly" meant to mean?'

'Well, the plan is that you have dinner here but then I will be eating later with Graham and the other members of his club.'

'So I have to eat alone? That sounds great. What was the point of my coming at all?'

'You will join us after dinner, and I will stay with you while you eat.'

'Thanks very much. But isn't this rather a reversal of the usual order? Normally the women are at least allowed to eat with the gentlemen, provided we watch our table manners of course, but we are not usually thrown out until afterwards. This seems to be the other way round.'

'Yes, I know, but that's the way it is. Honestly, Sal, I don't know much more than you, only what Stewart has told me. He asked me to trust him and said it would be better for all of us if he kept the surprise.'

The dining room was completely empty. It was still early, and I couldn't face eating there all on my own, so we returned to the bar and I had a toasted sandwich. It was quite awful, and I was beginning to wish we had not agreed to come at all. All the time, Graham was glancing nervously around the room and I again asked him specifically if Stewart would be joining us there but he said not. I couldn't see what he was worried about, or maybe whom he was looking for, either to see or, as it almost seemed, to avoid. I tried to disregard it but could not do so easily.

As soon as I had finished eating, we returned to the room. While we had been away, someone had been in and had left a huge bunch of orchids on the dressing table. They had also turned down the bed covers on both sides and it was only then that I realised how big the bed was – at least six feet wide. Three pillows were lined across the top.

Arranged in the centre of the bed was a large box, tied about with a ribbon. Then Graham looked even more nervous. He came up and kissed me clumsily, when I could really have done with some comfort. It was a quick kiss and he pulled away the instant he felt me reaching for him.

'There are a whole lot of new clothes in there; kind of a costume. You have to take off all your clothes and put these on. You should find all you need in there; underclothes, shoes and everything. I have to go back down now but someone will come to collect you at nine o'clock and bring you down, so you've got plenty of time.'

Before I even had time to ask what it was all about, he'd gone. I stared at the notice, In Case of Fire, where it was still swinging slowly on the back of the door, and listened to the footsteps rapidly dwindling down the carpeted corridor. I felt more frightened at what I might find in the box than I had at anything so far.

I would have liked a drink, but the room didn't run to a mini bar, and I didn't fancy the prospect of either venturing out again or ringing down for room service to bring me one. One drink to a woman alone in a double room requires too much explanation.

I settled for water, and washed my face in the tepid trickle before returning and facing up to whatever was lurking in wait.

In the end, it was all an anticlimax. No PVC catsuit or topless leather basque. Instead, there was just a complete set of new clothes, as described. There was a pale, almost lime-coloured, silk blouse and a patterned silk skirt in a sort of brick red, a white bra and matching knickers, stockings and garter belt and a pair of shoes. At first glance, while they were not the sort of clothes that one would wear in normal circumstances, they looked to be my size and were of a good quality, and well chosen; clearly someone had gone to a good deal of trouble.

It was then only just half past seven, and getting dressed was not going to take long.

The view from the window offered only a roof and the car-park, which was now very much more full than when we had arrived; I wondered where all the people were. A sign on the television told me that the management deeply regretted that it was temporarily out of order but it would be repaired as soon as possible and they hoped it would not impair my enjoyment during my stay. The radio by the bed worked although the choice of music was limited, and there were even some magazines, uninteresting when they had been new, and now out of date, but I read them all the same. When I had finished, I decided I might as well start getting ready. The underclothes they had provided were not very good quality, made of a cheap artificial lace that felt scratchy. I did wonder whether I should keep my own, which were some of my best and much nicer, but

I decided against it. I had been told to put on the new clothes, so I obeyed. By a quarter to nine, I was dressed, had refreshed my make-up, and could find nothing more to do. The car-park was now completely full; more lights were on in the bar and a few more customers were visible in the window alcoves.

At nine o'clock I sat on the bed and waited, but still nothing. I began to wonder if I were meant to have gone down, but Graham had definitely told me I would be collected. Then I started to wonder if this were part of it, the waiting. Perhaps I was being watched. Perhaps they had only wanted to watch me changing. Perhaps they thought I would masturbate if left on my own. Perhaps it was that they wanted to see. I glanced at the mirror, but it looked like any other. I could find no sign of any hidden camera, and I suddenly felt foolish. I sat and waited some more.

I heard no footsteps outside so when the knock came, it made me jump. A middle-aged man – no, older – was standing neatly in the corridor. He smiled politely.

'Ready, honey?' He had an American accent, but softer than Stewart's.

I looked around and followed him out and, although he gallantly stood aside to let me pass in the corridor, I could feel his eyes trying to penetrate through the dress as he walked slowly behind me. We made our way down one floor and along the quiet carpeted corridor to the furthest end of the hotel. The last door had a sign in front of it which said simply: Private Function.

We paused and the man said, 'I'm sorry,' but could I trouble you to put this on?' and he held out a strip of black velvet. Unrecognisable: a tie? A garter? The man smiled again. 'Here, let me help you,' and he held it up to my face; it was a blindfold.

I stepped back. 'No, I don't want that.'

He took a step up to me. 'I'm sorry but it's customary for guests to our meetings. Only Brothers and their

249

Honorary guests may witness the proceedings. It's probably silly, just a tradition that we have built up over the years, but please don't worry. I assure you that you have no cause to be concerned.'

I still hesitated, but then what would be the point in objecting? I had either to go ahead with the whole event and trust Stewart, or else I should withdraw entirely. Playing around with half measures was simply childish. The man carefully positioned the blindfold over my eyes and tied it securely behind my head; it was very effective and I found I could see absolutely nothing but I listened hard.

The man knocked on the door, a gesture that seemed little more than symbolic, an announcement of an entrance more than a request for permission, because I heard no answer during the brief moment he waited before opening the door and pushing me in ahead of him.

From the sound of the voices, the room must have been large – a function room or even a small ballroom – but as soon as I was through the door there was a welcoming cheer, some laughter and a light applause. Yet I felt a warmth and a cheerfulness in the sound that was reassuring. It was as if we were all playing blind-man's buff and I felt no threat or menace in the tone.

As a hand in the small of my back – I assume this was my guide – pushed me further into the room and shut the door behind us, a man spoke from somewhere down at the other end and, although I turned my head towards him, it was really very difficult to tell exactly where it was coming from.

'Right, gentlemen, our Brother Stewart has done very well this evening. Now I must explain that the charming lady herself is not, I am sorry to say, available in the auction. However, she has kindly offered to sell us her clothes. Each item will be offered in turn and the buyer will be asked to remove his purchase.'

I felt the sting of a blush under my blindfold as I

250

listened to a low buzz running round the room and some laughter. A few glasses clinked and a knife scraped across a plate.

'To make sure you all know what you are buying, perhaps I should ask our charity secretary to escort our model once around the table for you all to see. Samuel?'

A man's hand, it may have been the same man, took mine and led me, too fast it seemed for I could barely keep up, on a tour around and several times we turned corners. At the end I was turned once around, slowly, by which time I was totally lost. When the announcer's voice came again, it made me jump, he was so close beside me.

'Now then, where should I start with this delightful package? The shoes? No, to hell with that, let's make it interesting. The blouse! For those who like to know these things, it is silk. Am I offered fifty pounds? Come on, people, fifty pounds, you know the cause we're contributing to, fifty pounds is not much. All right, forty pounds if you like. Thank you, Stewart, forty pounds, and now fifty? Fifty, thank you, then sixty pounds? Come on, sixty? Thank you, and seventy? No? Well if no more bids, Brother Alan will have it for sixty pounds. Sixty it is – once, twice, sold!'

Applause broke out and someone called, 'Go and get it, then!' A chair creaked and then a man arrived close to me, in a sudden gust of wine and brandy. He unfastened the buttons down the front of my blouse, a little nervously, and I could feel his fingers quivering against me. Several calls of encouragement flowed up from the room and much laughter; once I even thought I heard a woman's laugh, but I don't think it could have been. The man in front of me turned his attention to the cuffs, and then pulled the blouse out of my waistband and slipped it off me. I suddenly felt alone standing in front of them all, even though they applauded. Were they applauding the man or me?

'Excellent, Alan, most proficiently done. Anyone would have thought you had been undressing girls all your life. Now then, what next? To maintain a proper order I should offer the skirt, I suppose, but I'm impatient tonight so we will do the bra instead.'

A burst of enthusiastic laughter and some cheers greeted this.

'Where can I start, a delightful white lacy bra? Not much of a bra really, hardly big enough for its job and it does not seem to be keeping the lady very warm from what we can see, and we can all see very nicely, thank you. Still, perhaps it's not the bra itself, but where it is that we appreciate so much. So, fifty pounds for this? Good, fifty I have, fifty-five, yes, sixty, seventy! Very good.'

I was listening to the man next to me but, from the sounds that I could pick out among the general clatter of plates, the clink of glasses and the chatter and laughter, I was also trying to pick up clues to what else was happening in the room. I realised that the sale had finished. I had a vague recollection of a hundred and twenty pounds having been mentioned, and the announcer was inviting someone else up on to the stage to take away my bra. When he came up, he moved behind me and took ages fumbling with the hooks, his cold hands brushing frequently against my skin. Even when he was done, he still held on to the straps to hold the flimsy bit of lace up in front of me. He lowered it slowly and I suppose I held my arms forward to let the straps slip down more easily. As the material slid across my nipples, the clapping and calls came again, louder and more impatient, but I still could not say how many people were in the room looking at me; it could have been as few as fifteen, or as many as thirty. From what my original guide had said, I would never be allowed to see. Another burst of laughter suddenly erupted at the far end of the room; I guessed it was some antic of the man with my bra, assumed the joke was at my expense, and felt myself blushing even more. That brought another thought to mind; was Graham here? With everything else, I'd forgotten him. I had assumed he would be, but then he was not, as far as I knew, a member of this society to which Stewart belonged, and that would seem to rule out his being present. Additionally, I felt sure he would have spoken loudly to let me know. I started listening more closely to try to pick out his voice but couldn't hear him and so had to assume he was not.

'Next item, one dark-red skirt, complete with belt. This too is silk, I'm informed, and there's a good deal more material in this than in the last item. I was also told, but let me just check.' I felt movement behind me against the back of my skirt and another gale of laughter from in front of me; I realised that my hem was being lifted up at the back, lifted quite high. 'Yes, I'm right; sadly, Brothers, I'm afraid there is no slip to offer you. After this we're down to the stockings and suspenders. So that must increase the value of this item. I will start with my own bid of fifty pounds; fifty-five? Sixty, and sixty-five? Somebody offer sixty-five. Come on, Alan, you'll look lovely in this with the blouse.'

There was more laughter, more calls, but I couldn't hear what was said, and so the sale went on. I do not now remember the sequence or the prices of the various items; I was still listening out to see if I could hear Graham at all but did not. It's hard to describe the intensity of being slowly, garment by garment, stripped naked in front of an audience that I couldn't see. Each buyer came up and removed his trophy, to the jeers and jokes of the remainder, and the different levels of confidence with which each one tackled my clothes was itself unsettling and yet arousing. The announcer had asked me to keep my hands to my sides, and I really did try to comply but the urge to cover myself was sometimes too much and I had to give in. It might almost have been easier for me if they had tied my hands behind me. The skirt was sold. Nobody was interested in buying my shoes so the auctioneer offered one shoe together with one stocking as each lot, and then people started bidding. The first buyer took far too long fumbling with the clips and for a moment I wondered whether to help, but he seemed to be enjoying the work, and his hands pressed themselves firmly into the flesh of my thighs, so I left him to manage on his own. The man who bought my suspender belt stood behind me to unbuckle it where, presumably hidden from the rest of the audience, he took advantage of the situation to slip his hand down inside my knickers and squeeze the cheeks of my bottom. It would have been petty to object.

When they had taken everything except my knickers, there was a pause, and a stillness began to fall over the diners. Through the quietness I heard the announcer next to me taking a drink. I could have done with one myself.

'Now then, only one item, the best item, is left. Before the sale, perhaps we would all enjoy a closer look at the item, yes?'

There was plenty of appreciation for this suggestion and I was again led round the room. I tried to get some idea of the size of the audience from the path we followed round the room, but I lost track of my thoughts in this from hearing the comments being made about me as I passed.

We stopped, presumably having got back to the front of the room, and the announcer started again from beside me.

'Now then, you have all seen what is for sale: one rather immodest pair of ladies' drawers. Or should I say, one pair of a rather immodest lady's drawers? As you can see, they seem to have become extraordinarily wet and sticky in one patch; I really cannot think where that can have come from, but I'm sure it will not reduce their desirability.' I do not know whether the laughter that followed this was for the joke or the flood of scarlet that I felt washing across my entire body.

I felt so ashamed that I hung my head and paid no attention to the bids being made. I tried to take my mind away from the surroundings, because I realised that the anticipation of what would happen in the next few minutes was making me even wetter, and even the fact that the announcer had drawn attention to my wetness made it worse. I knew that people were out there, an unknown number of people whom I could not see, and that they were staring directly at the spreading darkness between my legs.

My mind was suddenly brought back to the room by the announcer's voice. 'A bid from Stewart's guest! Thank you, sir, one hundred and forty pounds.'

Who could be Stewart's guest if not Graham? He must be there, having kept quiet but now bidding. Why? Was it really Graham? It must be! If he won the auction, what would he do? Presumably he would let me keep them on, but did I really want that? I was not entirely sure. The price had gone up to two hundred and ten pounds, but there was no further indication who the bidders were, or whether Graham was still offering or not.

'Is that all, then? Two hundred and ten pounds, once, twice and gone! Please come up and claim your prize, sir.'

In the applause and cheers that immediately followed this, I again thought I caught a woman's voice, but still I wasn't sure. Then I became aware of a man moving up close to me. I could smell him, a smell of alcohol that could have been anybody, but he did not speak to me, so then I knew it couldn't be Graham. The man moved to one side and reached across me, I felt his fingers hooking into the waistband on each side, a slight pause and then he slowly pulled down, and I could feel the last covering sliding away and leaving me completely on display.

More laughter and cheers and applause and I grabbed hold of the man's arm, a coarse suit, could have been anyone, to steady myself and to hold me up as I raised one leg and then the other as the man took the item right off. He took my hand and raised it like a winning boxer, but he wanted me to pirouette, slowly, so I was seen on all sides. He paused halfway round, when they could all see my bottom, and then finished the circle. Only then did I hear a voice in my ear, Graham's voice. 'I love you, Sal, you are so bloody beautiful, I have never been so proud of you as now.'

I twisted my head towards him, but he had pulled back a little and moved round behind me. I tried to grab him but his big fists were clamped firmly on my hips holding me straight and face on to my audience. His hands slowly slid down to my thighs and he pulled at them so I had to shuffle my feet apart. His fingers dug in further between my lips and peeled them apart too, then he ran a finger gently down the length of my crease and slowly, pressing firmly, back.

I did not try to fight him, just lay back against his chest as he whispered his love into my ear and pulled at my lips to show me off as completely as he could to the unseen lines of cheering, clapping strangers in front of us. In spite of the smoke and the smells of food and brandy in that unseen room, the scent of my dripping arousal rose up to my nostrils over everything else. When his fingers were running with my juice, he raised them up for the audience to cheer, and they cheered again, even louder, when he offered his soiled hand to me and I lapped eagerly at my own honey.

As the applause began to die away, I was led on a final tour round the table. It was slow, frequently interrupted by people stopping us and one or two hands reached out to run smoothly over my breasts, or my bottom and more than once up between my legs. One stop was at the request of a female voice, as sincere in her appreciation as any of the men, and even more delicate but even more audacious in her caress. It was just after her, it could even have been her own companion, who wanted me turned round again and bent far over so that he could inspect right between my buttocks, and test the pressure of my resistance to that entry.

After that Graham wrapped me in a dressing gown and we left the room, stopping just outside so he could finally remove the blindfold. He wrapped his arms around me and kissed me, holding me so hard it almost hurt.

'You were brilliant, Sal, bloody amazing. I'm so proud.' Then he led me back to my room, passing only two other hotel guests on the way, a young couple who stopped in the corridor and stared. The girl was wide-eyed and clung tighter to the young man's arm as I was led by, for although the short dressing gown was only loosely tied, and although they could probably not see much, they can have been in no doubt that I was completely naked underneath it as I was led through the hotel. I faltered, wondering if Graham would stop and unfasten the dressing gown entirely, but he misunderstood and hurried me on.

Graham left me in my room, saying he would be back in a few minutes and I crawled straight into the huge bed, not wanting to wash off the caresses and scents that had been laid all over me. Later Graham came and joined me, only Graham, but it was still wonderful. We were both supremely, almost unbearably, aroused before we started. We both knew why and did not need to explain or excuse anything, and we relived the evening again. I described how it had felt, having to stand up in front of everybody and being slowly stripped naked, bit by bit, as they all watched, and I climaxed as I told him. In turn, he described sitting there, watching everything, knowing what was going to happen but not how it would happen. When I was standing up there just in my knickers, he said the wet stain was huge and plainly visible from all over the room and glorious. He had been torn between a longing to let it be someone else who finally took my knickers off me and a fear that no one else would have been sufficiently confident and understanding to display me completely and do me justice. He climaxed as he told me.

As it turned out, that evening was the finale of the whole affair. A couple of weeks later came the big stock-market crash of that year in which Stewart's firm suffered badly. All its plans to take over other concerns were dropped, and I gather from Graham that for a few months it was fighting for its own life. In any case, Stewart was immediately called back to America and, although we received a Christmas card the following year, that was all, and we never saw him again. Occasionally in bed, lying side by side in the darkness, Graham and I have talked of trying to repeat the experience with someone else, but the opportunity has never arisen and, in truth, unless the third party were to be sufficiently forceful to make it happen on his own, we could not really instigate it. In any case, nothing has happened – yet.

NEW BOOKS

Coming up from Nexus and Black Lace

Brat by Penny Birch
May 1999   Price £5.99   ISBN: 0 352 33347 2
Natasha Linnet is single, successful, independent and assertive – the
ideal modern woman. But she has only one wish, and not one that
she could ever admit to her smart friends. She wants to be spanked,
and not just by a girlfriend or any of her male admirers. Instead she
needs proper, strict discipline, and from someone stern enough to see
her not as the aloof young career woman she appears to be, but as
what she is underneath – a spoilt brat.

The Training of an English Gentleman
by Yolanda Celbridge
May 1999   Price £5.99   ISBN: 0 352 33348 0
When Roger Prince enjoys an educational summer idyll in Surrey, he
learns the hard way that the female is indeed deadlier than the male.
His voyeuristic host, his insatiable wife and their perverse step-
daughter Florence conspire to humiliate him by imposing severe cor-
poral punishment entirely at whim. His obedience to them and other
ladies earns their adoring respect, and thus encouraged he chooses
total submission to a Mistress as the true mark of an English gentleman.

Agony Aunt by G.C. Scott
May 1999   Price £5.99   ISBN: 0 352 33353 7
Harriet is unlike any other agony aunt, helping clients to live out
their perverse fantasies of bondage and domination. When her servant Tom finds her tied up one day he decides to reverse roles, leaving
her perplexed about her real desires. When he then goes to the con-
tinent to learn the art of correction, she decides to experiment further
with subservience and humiliation, reaching surprising new extremes
of pleasure. Harriet's friends want her to satisfy her fresh passion for
servility with Tom, but she is still suspicious of her former lover. Will
they ever find contentment in correction together again? This is the
fourth in a series of Nexus Classics.

Taking Pains to Please by Arabella Knight
June 1999   Price £5.99   ISBN: 0 352 33369 3
It can be a punishing experience for willing young women striving to please and obey exacting employers. On the job, they quickly come to learn that giving complete satisfaction demands their strict dedication and devotion to duty. Maid, nanny or nurse – each must submit to the discipline of the daily grind. In their capable hands, the urgent needs and dark desires of their paymasters are always fulfilled: for these working girls find pleasure in taking pains to please.

The Submission Gallery by Lindsay Gordon
June 1999   Price £5.99   ISBN: 0 352 33370 7
For her art, Poppy the sculptress seeks out and recreates the heights of submission and domination. Each sculpture she creates is taken from life – a life of total sensual freedom where she meets a strange cast of brutal lovers. From strangers in restaurants to tattooists, from a baroness to a uniformed society of fetishists, Poppy experiences rigorous obedience and tastes power for the first time. The result is her Submission Gallery.

The Handmaidens by Aran Ashe
June 1999   Price £5.99   ISBN: 0 352 33282 4
Tormunil can be an exceedingly harsh place for pretty young serving girls. Destined for a life of sexual slavery at the hands of merciless overlords, the chosen ones are taken to the Abbey – a place where strength is learned through obedience to those who follow the path of the Twisted Cross. Taken into this strange world, the young and beautiful Sianon and Iroise are allowed few privileges. Tormented to the peaks of pleasure, but punished if they seek release, their only hope of escape lies with the handsome young traveller who has fallen for their charms. This is the fifth in a series of Nexus Classics.

BLACK
lace

Village of Secrets by Mercedes Kelly
May 1999   Price £5.99   ISBN: 0 352 33344 8

A small town hides many secrets, and a contemporary Cornish fishing village is no exception: its twee exterior hides activities such as smuggling, incest and fetishism, and nothing is quite as it seems. Laura, a London journalist, becomes embroiled with the locals – one of whom might be her brother – when she inherits property in the village. Against a backdrop of perverse goings-on she learns to indulge her taste for kinky sex. Nothing is obvious and all is hidden, in this erotic exposé of small-town living.

Insomnia by Zoe le Verdier
May 1999   Price £5.99   ISBN: 0 352 33345 6

A cornucopia of sexual experiences is explored in this collection of short stories by one of the best-liked authors in the series. Zoe le Verdier's work is an ideal reflection of the fresh, upbeat stories now being published under the Black Lace imprint. From group sex, SM and spanking, to dirty talking, voyeurism, virginity and love, there's something for everyone, and all the stories are sexy, hot and imaginative.

The Black Lace Book of Women's Sexual Fantasies ed. Kerri Sharp
May 1999   Price £5.99   ISBN: 0 352 33346 4

This book has taken over one and a half years of in-depth research to put together and has been compiled through correspondence with women from all over the English-speaking world. The result is an amazing collection of detailed sexual fantasies, including shocking and at times bizarre revelations guaranteed to entertain and arouse. This book is a fascinating insight into the diversity of the female sexual imagination as we begin a new millennium.

Taking Liberties by Susie Raymond

June 1999   Price £5.99   ISBN: 0 352 33357 X

When attractive, thirty-something Beth Bradley takes a job as PA to Simon Henderson, a highly successful financier, she is well aware of his philandering reputation and is determined to teach him a lesson. When her initial attempt backfires, she begins to look for a more subtle and kinky form of retribution.

Packing Heat by Karina Moore

June 1999   Price £5.99   ISBN: 0 352 33356 1

Nadine, a young Californian, has her generous allowance cut off by her rich uncle. Desperate to maintain her flamboyant lifestyle, she joins forces with her lover, Mark, and together they conspire to steal from a seductive and successful businessman. But the sexual stakes rise when Nadine and Mark try to put the blame on the target's own girlfriend, and their Las Vegas getaway isn't going entirely to plan either . . .

NEXUS BACKLIST

All books are priced £5.99 unless another price is given. If a date is supplied, the book in question will not be available until that month in 1999.

CONTEMPORARY EROTICA

AMAZON SLAVE	Lisette Ashton		
BAD PENNY	Penny Birch		Feb
THE BLACK GARTER	Lisette Ashton		
THE BLACK WIDOW	Lisette Ashton		Mar
BOUND TO OBEY	Amanda Ware		
BRAT	Penny Birch		May
CHAINS OF SHAME	Brigitte Markham		
DARK DELIGHTS	Maria del Rey		
DARLINE DOMINANT	Tania d'Alanis		
A DEGREE OF DISCIPLINE	Zoe Templeton	£4.99	
DISCIPLES OF SHAME	Stephanie Calvin		Apr
THE DISCIPLINE OF NURSE RIDING	Yolanda Celbridge		
DISPLAYS OF INNOCENTS	Lucy Golden		Apr
EDUCATING ELLA	Stephen Ferris	£4.99	
EMMA'S SECRET DOMINATION	Hilary James	£4.99	
EXPOSING LOUISA	Jean Aveline		Jan
FAIRGROUND ATTRACTIONS	Lisette Ashton		
JULIE AT THE REFORMATORY	Angela Elgar	£4.99	
LINGERING LESSONS	Sarah Veitch		Jan
A MASTER OF DISCIPLINE	Zoe Templeton		
THE MISTRESS OF STERNWOOD GRANGE	Arabella Knight		

SAMPLERS & COLLECTIONS

EROTICON 4	Various		
THE FIESTA LETTERS	ed. Chris Lloyd	£4.99	
NEW EROTICA 4			

NEXUS CLASSICS
A new imprint dedicated to putting the finest works of erotic fiction back in print

THE IMAGE	Jean de Berg	Feb
CHOOSING LOVERS FOR JUSTINE	Aran Ashe	Mar
THE INSTITUTE	Maria del Rey	Apr
AGONY AUNT	G. C. Scott	May
THE HANDMAIDENS	Aran Ashe	Jun

Please send me the books I have ticked above.

Name ....

Address ....

....

....

.... Post code........................

Send to: **Cash Sales, Nexus Books, Thames Wharf Studios, Rainville Road, London W6 9HT**

Please enclose a cheque or postal order, made payable to **Nexus Books**, to the value of the books you have ordered plus postage and packing costs as follows:

UK and BFPO – £1.00 for the first book, 50p for the second book and 30p for each subsequent book to a maximum of £3.00;

Overseas (including Republic of Ireland) – £2.00 for the first book, £1.00 for the second book and 50p for each subsequent book.

If you would prefer to pay by VISA or ACCESS/MASTER-CARD, please write your card number and expiry date here:

....

Please allow up to 28 days for delivery.

Signature ....